LYZA'S STORY

LYZA'S STORY

Book One of The Lane Trilogy

Vicki Andree

Vicki Andree

ISBN: 1-59330-782-9

Printed in the United States of America

Dedication

To my brother, Gary Myers, who challenged me to enter the NaNoWriMo (National Novel Writing Month) competition on a cold October night in 2009.

Acknowledgments

God is so good! He arranged the whole thing. We were sitting around my sister's home in North Platte, Nebraska one evening in early November, 2009. My sister, Ginger; her husband, Terry; my other sister, Cynthia; her husband, Dave; my husband, David and I were burnt out on playing Hand and Foot Canasta. I told them about my first book, *On Our Own in Jerusalem's Old City,* and how eager I was waiting for the first published copy and to finally see it on Amazon.

Then I told them that our brother, Gary had challenged me to write fifty thousand words in November and to enter the NaNoWriMo competition. I had never written fiction, but that night I decided to take him up on the challenge. After all, it would take my mind off waiting for the book at Aventine Press.

I wanted to write about someone who gets converted by a Damascus road experience. In no time I was having more fun with my imagination than in a long time. As I read my first scene aloud, my family offered suggestions and encouragement. Before I knew it, Lyza's Story took off. I want to thank Ginger and Terry Ault, Cynthia and Dave Matzek, and David Andree. I had a story to enter NaNoWriMo. Eventually, it grew to over two hundred forty thousand words and three books!

Many wonderful people helped me out in different ways. Thanks to the ACFW His Writers group that encouraged me as a newbie to fiction. I had the time of my life writing fiction and making new friends. Thank you, Donna Schlachter, for introducing me to Tuesday morning write-ins and leading me to the Word Crafters critique group which helped teach me how to mold the stories to the rules of the craft. Thanks also to the Christian Writer's Guild critique group, Word Weavers.

Several individuals helped me by listening to me whine from time to time. Scott Lockhart and Craig Lockhart gave me valuable technical advice. Ginger Ault took time out of her busy schedule to read each book, to tell me 'the truth' and make suggestions. Diane King read rough drafts and provided prayer support. Barb Lem also provided much needed prayer support. Preston Wolfram was the Australia expert, having just returned from a summer of work there. And editor Misti Wolanski made the book much better. Thanks so much to each and every one of you.

Finally, I thank my husband, David. The Lane Trilogy would have never made it to print without David. He has been at my side through the peaks and valleys. He talked me out of it when I wanted to throw it all away. He edited every page several times. He's my first editor, earning the title of my "hatchet man". His constant encouragement kept me plugging away though the years of rewrites.

Table of Contents

Chapter One

Lyza shook her fist at the darkening afternoon sky as a fat raindrop smacked her between the eyes. Muttering, she shook it off and trudged down a street littered with rubbish. Wearing a dirty black coat, she pushed a grocery cart filled with trash bags. Her filthy face and cracked hands yearned for soap and warm water. A gust of wind blew a ragged scarf off her itching head. As raindrops splashed on the pavement, people hurried past, not seeing her. She seemed invisible. Heaven and Earth ignored her. The air reeked like the dress she wore, and her stomach grumbled. A volunteer nodded a familiar hello as he opened the door to the rescue mission.

Lyza Lane jolted awake, gasping as if the nightmare threatened to drown her. The dream always stopped there. Horror choked her. She looked frantically around her elegant bedroom, assuring herself of reality. *No! I'll never be a bag lady.* She caught her breath. *This is ridiculous. We have more money than some countries.* Even so, the nightmare reminded Lyza she had no control over the future. As hard as she worked and as successful as she was, there were no guarantees. Fear gripped her core.

Throwing back the silk comforter that covered thick Egyptian cotton sheets, Lyza Lane slipped into her Claire Haddad peignoir, stumbled to the master bath, and glanced back at the clock on the bedside table. Bright red numbers spelled 3:16 a.m. Polished marble floors, walls, and countertops, designed to her specifications, reminded her how removed she was from the poverty of her nightmare. She turned the gold knob, and water flowed from the mouth of a golden dragon. She chose a crystal decanter filled with lavender bath salts and poured a measure of bubble bath into the tub. She focused on the vase of fresh-cut flowers at the far end of the Jacuzzi; the white orchids were her and her mother's favorites. With a deep sigh, she sank into the tub. As she relaxed in the warm water, her mind wandered, eventually landing where it always did—business.

She hadn't chosen the business. She'd succumbed to the unquestioned expectation that she and her twin sister, Leesa, would carry on the family enterprise.

Why couldn't we have had a brother? Father would've loved having a son amongst the good old boys I have to work with every day. On the other hand, she enjoyed the perks, like the mansion she shared with Leesa. Her mind flashed back to the nightmare. No bag lady would live in the estate she and her sister had designed. Their six-bedroom, eight-bath estate nestled in the foothills of Southern California near the sea afforded special considerations for comfort, privacy, and security.

The main floor consisted of a spacious foyer with a library to one side. The other side opened to a formal dining room, formal sitting room, and kitchen with an enormous marble bar dividing the work area from the informal family room. Staff quarters positioned across a generous courtyard offered privacy for the twins and their employees.

Lyza smiled and shook her head at the ridiculous thought of the bag lady in her dream, picturing herself walking up the wide teak staircase dividing the two wings that mirrored each other. They consisted of large entryways with sitting room, smaller kitchens that were never used, and two large bedrooms with enormous walk-in closets. Lyza and Leesa cared deeply for each other, but they treasured their personal space and maintained separate living quarters, visiting each other when they so chose. Besides the main house, two guest houses and an Olympic-sized pool completed the fifty-acre estate.

Lyza turned on the jets and added more hot water. Trying to collect her thoughts, she prioritized the half-dozen real estate projects. *I should look over the paperwork on the Nuremberg deal. I'll work on it tonight. Too bad Leesa's in Vegas.* Not that Lyza would have confided her personal fears or the recurring nightmare to her sister anyway.

I'm not alone. Cook is sleeping in her quarters. Lyza's mind switched gears again. *The Nuremberg deal will net a hefty profit. A half-billion dollar transaction might impress Father! Wonder how Leesa's deal is going in Vegas?*

Lyza stepped out of the tub and dried with a bath sheet from the towel warmer. She slipped on her designer robe and padded to the ornate cherrywood desk to open her laptop and scrutinize the listings. An island property jumped out at her. A casino consortium came to mind. Representatives from both had communicated with her earlier that month. She considered some creative negotiations. *When I get back from Germany, I want another iron in the fire.* Switching to her online calendar, Lyza confirmed that morning's meeting with her father for a working breakfast before her meeting with all the agents. Normally her sister led the weekly status briefings, but Lyza had agreed to fill in while Leesa was in Vegas.

What were my parents thinking when they named us — Leesa and Lyza, Lyza and Leesa? It makes me crazy. When we were little girls, it was cute, but now… not so much. Years ago they considered changing their names, but once they understood L. L. Lane Unlimited was named after them, they knew it would never happen.

Lyza looked at the inviting bed, considered the time, and lay back down. *If only I could catch a couple more hours of sleep.*

***

At four o'clock in the morning, Cook rested her head on the table in the dimly lighted dining room of her friend.

She felt a hand on her shoulder. "Beverly, wake up."

Dazed, she looked into Doris's concerned eyes, noticing the gray strands of hair slipping out of a tight bun at the back of her friend's head. "I can't believe I fell asleep."

"It's no wonder, as hard as you work for those people. The others left hours ago."

Cook rubbed her eyes. "I've got to get back. Lyza will soon be up."

Doris nodded. "You are amazing. In more than thirty years, you've never missed a day."

Cook took a small note pad and pen from the table in front of her and placed them in the purse on her lap. "You know as well as I do that when God calls you to serve, it can be difficult, but I've never thought of giving up."

Doris sat down in the chair next to her. "Didn't you tell us you started working for the Lanes before those girls were born? Honestly,

I was surprised they let you go to work for the twins when they moved into their ivory tower. I guess they knew the girls needed you. No one else could run their estate as efficiently as you do."

Cook paused before answering. The remark about the ivory tower made her want to defend the twins. Instead, she said what she considered truth. "No one is indispensable."

"Do they ever ask you to spy on the twins?"

Cook wondered why Doris always tried to extract more information than necessary. Cook glossed over the details. "Oh, once in a while, Mrs. Lane asks how they're doing. But, Doris, they're all so busy, so caught up in their projects, that they have little time for one another."

Doris voiced Cook's own thoughts. "Ah, yes. All the more reason for your mission."

Cook's heart lifted at the thought of why she had stayed with the Lanes for so many years. She blinked away a tear of sadness and compassion, then smiled. "Exactly. I believe with all my heart these years of service will pay off one day."

***

Leesa thought about the previous day's consultation as she rode the early-morning shuttle to the Las Vegas airport. *A naïve young couple like them shouldn't get into the casino business unless they have unlimited funds. I couldn't let them get caught up in an investment that would eventually wipe them out.*

She pulled out their file and thumbed through it. Leesa had been surprised by how young they'd looked as they sat around the conference table waiting for the attorneys. The tattooed young woman had looked even younger than Leesa, perhaps twenty-five. While they sat around the conference table, she'd noted their finances and spoken to them directly about their proposed venture before the attorneys arrived.

"This is an impressive undertaking for an independent couple. I take it you looked at the projections for the year."

"Oh, yes." The young man, flush with excitement, pointed at Leesa's file. "This casino's going to make a lot of money. I'm looking forward to working with the other casinos here in Las Vegas. We'll be one of the smallest, but we'll be in the game."

The young woman smiled brightly and proudly announced, "This money is from my inheritance, so it's free and clear. We haven't borrowed anything."

Leesa couldn't count on both hands the number of times that casino had been bought and sold in the past decade. "And what about employees and maintenance? Do you have a director or manager in place?"

"We don't need all that. We plan to do all of it ourselves. We're young and energetic. We can handle it until maybe next year when we have all that money that's going to come in."

Leesa mentally slapped her forehead. "You understand what I said about this property being sold several times in the past, don't you?"

"I saw that. It looked like such a good deal that we couldn't afford to pass it up. I mean, that's probably why they dropped the price."

"I don't mean to dash your hopes, but I see here that your entire income will come from the casino."

The young woman straightened defensively. "That's right."

Leesa shook her head. "That's not how it works."

The young man pointed at the numbers on the page in front of him. "The figures show a profit."

"Projections aren't guarantees. Not that you can't trust the seller I represent—but you can't count on those figures. No one knows the future. What will you do if they don't come to fruition?"

The young man confidently leaned back in his chair. "They will; I know they will."

Leesa sighed. "I could sell this to you today and walk out with your money. I refuse to do it because I have your best interests at heart. This property has been sold more than a dozen times in the last ten years."

The young man slapped his hand on the table. "Did you say you refuse to sell it to us? Can you do that?"

"Save your inheritance. Las Vegas is famous for cashing in on people with money burning holes in their pockets. It's not a good investment for you now. You may be upset today. Trust me, one day you will thank me."

Father will be furious with me, but I don't need to tell him. I simply couldn't take advantage of that sweet couple.

***

It seemed as though only a moment passed before sunlight poured into the room and awoke Lyza. She quickly dressed and ran down to the kitchen where Cook had Lyza's cup of hot coffee waiting.

Lyza took a seat at the long bar in front of her cup. "Good morning, Cook. Those muffins look good."

Cook brought her a plate of fresh-baked muffins. "Blueberry, your favorite."

Lyza chose one and took two bites. "Yum! These are hard to resist, but I'm meeting Father for breakfast. I need coffee."

She took another sip before putting the half-full cup back down on the bar.

Cook smiled. "You have a good day, girl."

"Oh, I intend to."

Lyza, ready to face the day, picked up her attaché case and sauntered to the garage. She climbed into her gray Mercedes-Benz and drove thirty minutes to the Lane office building downtown. She met her father across the street at Cecconi's restaurant.

She gave him her best smile. "Good morning."

"Lyza, you look especially beautiful this morning."

She laughed at the thought of her father looking beautiful and filled her cup from the carafe. "Thanks, Father, so do you."

Not amused, he opened his day planner. "Let's begin."

Leesa appeared at their table. She gasped, "Hi there," likely winded from dashing to the restaurant.

Lyza jumped up to give her a hug. "I thought you were out of town until tomorrow." She hugged her again. "I'm so glad to see you."

Leesa grinned. "I know you are." She laughed. "And I also know how you hate to lead these meetings. That's why I hurried back."

Their father plunged straight into business. "Leesa, how did the Vegas deal go?"

"Oh, it didn't. They didn't understand what they were getting into." Leesa shrugged. "That's the way it goes sometimes. Anyway, I rushed back in time for the staff meeting. You can catch me up."

She sat and turned toward Lyza with a big grin. "I thought you were going to Germany."

Lyza suppressed a jubilant smile. *Thank God I don't have to stay another minute in a boring office. Thank you, Las Vegas! And thank you, Leesa, for liking this part of the job!* "Always glad to hold down the fort for you." She gathered her papers and stood. "But now that you're here, I do have a flight to catch. I'll keep you posted."

Leesa's tone changed slightly. "Oh, I know you will."

As Lyza turned to leave, she caught an uncertain expression on Leesa's face that vanished when their eyes met. *Curious. What are you up to, Miss Goody Two-Shoes?*

Chapter Two

As Lyza's jet descended into Nuremberg, she recalled enduring endless stories of how the grandparents she'd never known had died in a death camp in that godforsaken country. Now she planned to take advantage of some Germans. She rested in the thought that her deeds that day might result in a sweet surprise for Father. Her spirits lifted with the thought that neither her family nor the German government might ever discover her part in the deception that was about to take place. And if they learned about it later, after it was too late, it would be even sweeter.

She had four hours before her meeting. Her limo arrived to take her to the Sheraton Carlton. As they passed through the streets of Nuremberg, she pondered the significance of this city. The Nuremberg Trials and other war crimes trials had taken place in the Palace of Justice after World War II.

Nuremberg had symbolically provided the setting for the trials, and Lyza expected to get a little of her own justice today. Perhaps a little late, she would do her part to add to the collapse of the economy of the country that had allowed death camps.

In addition, the deal promised to be a one of her biggest. *See Leesa top that!* She pulled her mink coat around her. *Father will be delighted.* Her three-carat diamond ring caught a ray of sunshine and spread light across the limousine ceiling. *Life is good.* Her favorite ruby earrings matched her red designer miniskirt and black Dior blazer. They pulled up to the front of the hotel and the chauffeur jumped out to open her door. Lyza hurried past the doorman to the registration desk.

The uniformed man behind the desk greeted her. "Welcome to the Sheraton Carlton Hotel, Miss Lane. Your bags are in your room. My assistant, Max, will escort you to the penthouse. Have a nice visit in Germany. Please let us know if there is anything we can do for you."

She turned toward the elevator. "Thank you. I will."

Max punched the penthouse floor. "Did you have a good flight?"

She smiled. "Uneventful, and that's always good."

The elevator stopped outside the penthouse suite. Max held the door as she exited, then stepped in front of her to unlock the penthouse door. After he showed her around the suite, she handed him a tip and watched his eyes enlarge. Then she closed the door behind him, glad to be alone. After a short nap, a relaxing bath, and a light lunch, she changed for the meeting. The earrings with the fifteen-carat ruby pendant worked with the other red miniskirt she brought. The black Dior blazer would do. Her black stilettos with sparkling diamond chips finished the outfit. She opted for the shorter blond mink to show off her shapely legs. She was ready for battle. *Bring it on!*

***

Father patted Leesa's shoulder. "I think the weekly meeting went well."

She nodded. "Me, too."

He flipped through several pages of notes, then looked up at her. "You did a great presentation. No one resisted the proposed reorganization. Let's celebrate at the club."

Leesa stood to leave, then sat back down. "I'd love to, but can we talk about the Norton deal?"

He tucked reports into his attaché case. "Is there a problem?"

Leesa avoided meeting his eyes. "Oh, no, nothing like that. I'm not sure how much the market will bear on this deal. With all the negative press on real estate these days, I'm afraid the asking price on this commercial property may be a deal-breaker. We meet for final negotiations tomorrow."

He grinned and shook his head. "Leesa, Leesa, Leesa. I thought I taught you better. Don't worry."

"What do you mean?"

"You know as well as I do that price has little to do with this deal. Norton wants this property so bad he can taste it. Downtown ground is expensive, but he can afford it. Don't let him sing you a sad song about the real-estate collapse. Prime real estate demands prime prices." He leaned forward and patted her hand. "There's no way you can mess up this deal, sweetie. Twenty million dollars is chump change to Norton. He needs a building as big as his ego."

"I appreciate your confidence." She smiled. "Since I can't possibly mess it up, I guess I do have time for lunch."

***

Lyza entered the glass-walled conference room. Surrounding the huge mahogany table were young attorneys, gray-haired consultants, and Mr. Klaus Müller of Müller and Sons.

Lyza extended her tiny hand. "Good afternoon, Mr. Müller."

"Miss Lane." Mr. Müller shook her hand. "I trust you had a good flight."

"Oh, yes." She took the chair next to him, placing her attaché case on the conference table in front of her. "Shall we begin?"

Mr. Müller introduced the others. "I'd like you to meet my attorney, Benjamin Schmidt. And this is Gretchen Marx, my personal secretary, and her assistant, Carol." He pointed across the table. "Martin is the architect who will eventually head up the renovation of the property. This is his assistant, Jill, and her secretary, Jeff."

Lyza nodded to the familiar figure entering the room. Elizabeth's thick brown hair matched her dark leather briefcase.

"This is the attorney for the Lane European headquarters, Elizabeth James." Elizabeth took her place in the empty chair next to Lyza.

Lyza glanced at Mr. Müller. "I believe everyone is present."

He nodded.

Lyza stood. "Let me open the meeting by making sure each of you has a copy of the drawings and statistics." She reported to the group that the property consisted of one hundred acres with seven buildings on the Pegnitz River near the Rhine-Main-Danube canal. Concrete parking lots and loading docks surrounded the three four-story buildings. Four smaller buildings sat on a tarmac allowing air transport of goods and materials.

She wound up her initial presentation by stating the obvious. "The beauty of the property is that it will accommodate both local and international distribution."

"Excuse me, Miss Lane." Mr. Müller pointed to a memo in his hand. "Is there any reason for us to confer with governmental authorities regarding international air traffic control?"

"Herr Müller, I believe it would be prudent to do so. I have not looked into it because I'm not sure I know your purpose for the property." Her heart raced at her outright untruth; she knew why they wanted it. "I'm speaking of the potential of the property."

"Of course, Miss Lane."

"Now, if I can continue." Klaus Müller would use the property to manufacture veterinarian drugs. The property included buildings on the Pegnitz River near the Rhine-Main-Danube Canal. She knew Mr. Müller would divert some chemical waste to the waters surrounding the property as the former occupants, pharmaceutical manufacturers, had done. Part of her plan was to alert governmental agencies after the sale—but reporting Mr. Müller's indiscretions was for the future. Right now she had to concentrate on the subject at hand and close the deal.

"The mantra of real estate is location, location, location. In addition to river access for barges, you can see this property sits north of connecting roadways, allowing easy access for trucks. Each building contains the utilities needed for manufacturing. The layout, the offices, and the open floor spacing offer many choices."

Lyza continued for the next forty-five minutes with details of the property. Everyone at the table leaned forward in rapt attention.

Finally, she closed. "That concludes my presentation regarding the property. Does anyone have any questions?"

Silence.

"Is there anything anyone here would like to discuss further?"

All eyes were on Klaus Müller.

"*Ja, ja, ja,* it is all exactly as you say." Mr. Müller tapped his papers. "I have done some research through my friends here." He motioned to those around the table. "As you say, a property with much potential. We must close the deal."

"As you say."

Lyza smiled. *Cash or charge?*

***

Leesa readied herself for the meeting with Norton. *Father is right. This deal is personal, totally emotional. The man wants the property and Frank gets what he wants.* She chose the bright yellow spaghetti-strapped Vera Wang sundress with black Burberry Ottoman coat and black five-inch platform pumps. A champagne diamond ring with matching earrings and pendant completed her apparel for the meeting. She collected the keys to her yellow BMW.

A beautiful California day greeted her. Light traffic gave her time to reflect on the lovely weather and on Norton. The man was old enough to be her father—actually, grandfather. His son was older than Leesa. Still one of the good ol' boys, Frank was usually good-tempered and ready to party. He and Father often went golfing or fishing, so she was used to running into him now and then.

Leesa looked forward to the meeting, expecting to celebrate the day's deal. *What could be better? He wants the property. I want the sale. Simple.* She parked the car beneath the Lane building and walked to the elevator where she ran into her Father's old friend.

She smiled up at his gray mustache. "Oh, hello, Frank."

He removed his Stetson, his gaze frozen on her mouth. "Well, there you are, little missy. This is my attorney, Joyce Lander."

She pushed the button, and they entered the elevator. "It's nice to meet you, Joyce."

Joyce smiled and nodded.

Leesa turned back to Frank. "Our meeting is in the fourteenth floor conference room."

"Well, how nice. Perhaps we could get started here." He moved uncomfortably close, towering over her.

Leesa glanced at Joyce. The tiny young woman shrunk in the corner, looking at the floor of the elevator. Leesa tensed, but kept her tone lighthearted. "Now, Frank, let's not get ahead of ourselves."

He chuckled and backed off.

Men. Will they ever get over themselves? I wonder how Father would react to having one of his daughters hit on by his old golfing buddy. Then she recognized it as one of her own favorite ploys. *Nice try, Frank, trying to rattle me before the negotiations.*

Even aware of his intention, she felt uncomfortable leading him down the long hallway to the conference room.

Once settled, with the title company personnel in the room, Leesa relaxed. "Mr. Norton, I'll get right to the point. Our price is nonnegotiable. The price of the property you asked us to investigate is twenty million dollars."

Frank Norton triumphantly slammed his hand on the table. "I never intended to pay less than that for the property. Let's get this deal done. Where are your lawyers?"

"Coming right up, Mr. Norton."

As she leaned over to push the call button, Norton slapped her on the derrière and boomed, "Good job, Leesa."

How dare he! She spun around to face him. "Who do you think you are?" She held up her hand. "Stop right now. As far as I'm concerned, this deal is over." She stormed out of the room.

***

Back home after salvaging Frank Norton's deal, Leesa could hardly wait for Lyza's return. She texted Lyza to learn whether the Nuremberg deal closed and got a "+" reply.

She lingered in the library near the front entrance reading her ebook and bounced to the door when she heard it open.

"You're home!" Leesa hugged her sister.

"I am." Lyza sank into a nearby chair. "As real estate goes, it was a fabulous deal. You wouldn't believe how stupid they were. We made a huge profit on this one."

Leesa sat on the sofa across from her. "You must be exhausted."

She sighed. "I am. They call them first-class seats, but I can never sleep on those long flights." Then Lyza brightened. "But we need to celebrate. I'll grab a nap and we can go out."

"My thoughts exactly." Leesa jumped up and grabbed her sister's bag, and they headed for the staircase. "My deal went through with flying colors, but we can talk about all that later."

Lyza yawned. "What time do you want to go?"

"Take at least three hours. Let's leave about eight o'clock."

After helping carry Lyza's luggage upstairs, Leesa returned to her afternoon of reading, checking e-mails, and shopping on the Internet. She sought an unusual piece of jewelry to indulge in, her usual celebration after closing an important deal, but she couldn't find anything captivating. Perhaps her usual jeweler could help her find something new. After all, something glitzy seemed an appropriate reward, particularly after putting up with Norton.

Leesa preferred diamonds. *Yes, those sparkly, bright stones are a girl's best friend.* She pulled up the jeweler's website. Immediately she disregarded the small grouped-type settings and browsed the jewelry with larger stones. Humming the tune to "Diamonds Are a Girl's Best Friend," she moved to rubies, then emeralds.

She looked at the tanzanite stones, and then jewelry with sapphires. Looking for more "fire," she turned to opals. The red ones in particular especially reminded her of herself—soft, rare, precious, and beautiful. Before she knew it, it was time to get ready for an evening of fun and celebration. *Already? Time flies when you're shopping.*

She strolled into her spacious closet, enjoying the luxury of leisurely preparation for a fun night out on the town. Dresses arranged by length and color lined one wall of the closet. Another wall displayed blazers, jackets, and business clothing. Jeans, casual tops, and sports attire occupied the third wall. In one corner, a stand held every kind of belt and boa imaginable. The island, completely covered with shoes, made matching outfits easy. Choosing a purple miniskirt with a sequined crop-top and matching heels, she entered the small room at the side.

Leesa changed and studied her outfit in the vaulted room's floor-to-ceiling mirrors. *Not perfect yet.* She turned to the island of thick glass drawers that contained her collection of fine jewelry—even better than Lyza's, in her opinion. Finding the perfect earrings, pendant, watch, ankle bracelet, arm bracelets, and rings would take some time.

***

In her own room, Lyza woke refreshed, and she glanced at the nightstand clock. She'd slept deeply for the past two hours and felt ready to party. Lyza quickly showered, then whipped through her closet, choosing the pink shift, matching shoes, and jewelry. Feeling festive, she added a light pink boa for fun.

At eight o'clock, Lyza watched her sister descend the stairs looking like something out of a fashion magazine. Lyza teased her sister by imitating Frank Norton. "You look fantastic, Miss Lane."

"*Ja, ja*, so do you, my little missy," Leesa echoed, imitating Klaus Müller.

Lyza giggled. "Oh, yes, Klaus Müller sounds exactly like that. And the 'little missy' stuff was so hilarious, trying to sound like an American from Texas."

Through the laughter, Leesa gasped for air. "You should have been at my closing with Norton. You wouldn't believe it. Let's talk about it at dinner. Is the Willow River Grille in the Roosevelt Hotel all right?"

Lyza licked her lips. "I love their fish. Let's do it."

They hopped in their shared red Mercedes convertible, top down. Leesa drove while Lyza picked a CD, and they cruised into LA, music blaring as the twins sang along like teenage girls out after curfew.

At the restaurant, the valet took the car, and the women strolled into a packed house. The host seated them immediately. Lyza looked around to see familiar faces. These were her people. Not that she knew everybody in the room, but she recognized faces of people frequenting this and her other haunts. Most patrons were friends of her parents. Edith Hudson, host of the *The Talk of the Town* talk show, looked as if she'd come in off the beach, her blonde hair wind-tossed. Film producer Ted McKee and his family sat directly across the room. The distinguished mayor of Los Angeles sat at a round table on the patio with seven other men dressed in business suits; it looked like a working dinner.

Lyza ordered the best champagne on the menu. After the wine steward poured, she lifted her glass to toast her sister. "To success."

Their glassed clinked and Leesa returned to the conversation of her closing with Norton. "You wouldn't believe what that good ol' boy did after we closed our deal. Norton had the nerve to…" She laughed. "It's not funny, but now that I look back on it, maybe the guy has a sense of humor. More likely he's just an old letch. Lyza, he slapped me on the rear! Can you believe it?"

"You have to be kidding." Lyza couldn't help grinning. "I mean, does the guy not know that cavemen are out of style?"

Leesa grimaced. "Evidently he didn't care."

Lyza set her drink on the napkin in front of her. "Well, what are you going to do about it?"

"I reprimanded him in front of his attorney, then our attorneys came in. I made them wait ten minutes before I went back into the room. He apologized right there in front of his attorney, our attorneys, and the secretary. His face was bright red, and he actually stammered his apology."

Lyza's eyebrows shot up. "Old man Norton stammering? That must have been a sight to see."

Leesa wiped at a drop of champagne on her chin. "Then he said it wouldn't happen again. I had to wonder what his woman attorney puts up with."

"He has a woman attorney?"

Leesa nodded and looked around for their waiter. "Oh, yes. I e-mailed her this afternoon. I told her she didn't have to work for a letch like Norton; after all, she's an attorney, for heaven's sake. Turns out, he's her uncle. She told me she had to work for him for three more years because he paid for her schooling and that was part of their agreement. One day he's going to mess up and she'll get the courage to leave. Anyway, I think she enjoyed watching him grovel as much as I did. I let him stew a few minutes before I told him it had better never happen again."

Lyza frowned. "You forgave him? You are such a softie."

Leesa held her hands up. "You should have seen him. He held up both his hands, like it was a stick up, and begged me. He kept saying, 'It won't, it won't—I promise. It will never happen again.' I finally accepted his apology, signed off on the deal, and left."

"So you completed the contract, that's good." Their waiter appeared, and Lyza stopped talking. She chose the fish of the day with house salad, and Leesa duplicated the order.

Leesa leaned forward. "Your turn. What happened in Nuremberg?"

As the waiter served them, Lyza down played the drama of the negotiations in Germany. "Smooth sailing. In fact, it turned out easier than I thought it would. The attorneys had already worked everything out, and it was a matter of the presentation and signing the papers."

Leesa picked up her salad fork. "You mean you had no objections, no walls thrown up at the last minute?"

Lyza winked. "Not at all. Piece of cake. In fact, I enjoyed it. We are lucky, just incredibly lucky, aren't we?"

Lyza put up her hand for a high five.

Leesa grinned. "We are the luckiest people in the world."

Their hands slapped together over their salads.

Lyza sipped her champagne as her eyes stared into the space between them. "I'd love to do about a hundred more deals like that one in Germany."

Leesa tilted her head. "What do you mean by that?"

Lyza took a bite of her fish. "Oh, never mind. Let's talk about your deal."

Their conversation went on all evening. They talked about their deals, the office, and shopping. Finally, the restaurant emptied, and the twins prepared to leave. After their two bottles of champagne, Lyza decided they should take a taxi back. Cook could send the butler to pick up the car in the morning. Once in the taxi, they leaned back on the seat and closed their eyes.

"We should do a shopping trip," Leesa suggested sleepily. "Let's take the week off and go to Paris or New York and find something to wear to the benefit. I'll cancel the Monday morning meeting. What do you think?"

Lyza looked over at Leesa. "What a great idea. I'm all for it."

Then Lyza watched Leesa's eyes reluctantly close again. Her rhythmic breathing deepened.

"Okay, then—Paris," Lyza whispered to herself.

Chapter Three

Chuck O'Malley dreamed of retiring early. It had become an obsession. *My entire life revolves around this job. There's got to be more to life. I'm sick of the meaningless everyday grind. I need a change. God, let me find something to be passionate about. I'm not a religious man, but I know you could help me if you wanted to.* Everyone in the office had left, but Chuck worked late again. Exasperated, he threw his pen at the wall and shouted into the empty office, "I want a life!"

The past two years, he had thought up scheme after scheme to get out of IBM and into the world. *If I had the money, I would be gone in less than an instant.* They were dreams. He never acted on any of them.

His father had teased him when he was in high school. "You and your buddies don't do anything but hang out at the computer lab. Don't you know your classmates call you guys nerds? How are you going to meet girls? You should go out for football or track or something physical."

Chuck didn't care about names. "Guess what, Dad? I *like* being a nerd. Those other kids waste time hanging out at the mall. Bits and bytes are far more interesting than giggly girls and airheaded cheerleaders."

His father scoffed. "Oh, yeah, bits and bytes. What on Earth does that mean?"

Chuck tried to explain. "Computers speak bits and bytes. To get them to do something new and different, I have to speak bits and bytes, too. Think of it this way, Dad. You don't have to be an electrician to enjoy toast from a toaster, but you have to know electronics to design a better toaster. Computers are going to do more and more over time. Do you remember when an office full of noisy typewriters meant they were doing a lot of business? I've seen it in old movies."

His father put down the newspaper he'd been reading. "I remember the IBM Selectric. I loved it because when you hit backspace, it would lift the error right off the page."

Chuck went on to prove his point. "Now no one hears typing in an office. If you did, you would know they were obsolete, and you wouldn't want to do business with them. My teacher told me about that IBM Selectric. What used to be done mechanically is now done digitally. We all laughed when my teacher said that the IBM Selectric, like the pony express, enjoyed a short history."

Chuck's father shrugged. "Okay, you may know the future like all teenagers, but life is more than bits and bytes."

When he got out of graduate school with a 4.0 average, Chuck landed a good job at IBM and ended up in Poughkeepsie, New York.

His proud dad often bragged. "My son works for IBM. He's really smart and I taught him everything he knows."

One day, a buck slip with a memo attached arrived at Chuck's desk with an interesting message:

> IBM is opening a branch in Australia and is looking for fast track career-oriented men and women to jump-start IBM Australia. We need customer engineers, salesmen, managers, and system programmers. Contact Human Resources for more information.

IBM needed people to train new programmers for the Australian offices. The pay was much more than he currently made, so Chuck filled out the necessary paperwork.

Within the week, his manager called him to his office. "Chuck, you requested a transfer last week and I received the notice this morning. Pack your bags. You're going to Australia."

Chuck was speechless. "I—I don't know what to say."

His manager gave him a brilliant smile. "You don't need to say anything. This is a great opportunity for you, and I know you'll do an excellent job."

Still stunned, Chuck managed to choke out a few words. "I didn't think it would go through."

His boss stuck out his hand. "Well, your application has been accepted, and you've got two weeks to check in with your new supervisor. Congratulations. We're going to miss you."

Chuck regained his composure, straightened, and shook his hand. "Thank you, sir. I've enjoyed working for you."

He sold everything he couldn't take on the plane and left for Sydney, Australia exactly ten days from that meeting.

Flying into Sydney, Chuck found himself strongly attracted by the aerial view of the famous opera house. He found an apartment near the office and immersed himself in his work. In a few short years, he had trained enough eager programmers to ensure proper service for IBM accounts in Sydney and transferred to Brisbane.

"O'Malley?" coworkers would say. "You can depend on him. He's a dedicated and loyal IBMer. In fact, he borders on genius and uses his creativity to better the company. You can tell he loves it here."

Chuck loved his work, but little did they know that he longed to break out of the corporate world. He dreamed and schemed between projects. *If I could find a way out of here, I would leave in a New York minute. It boils down to money. I can't leave and still enjoy this income.* He reconciled himself to the fact that he probably would stay right where he was and never get out of IBM.

He decided to take night classes at the local university for a diversion. Desiring something foreign to programming and computers, he chose geology. He thought studying rocks would get him out into the countryside and force him to see more of Australia than the cities and tourist traps. He was right. He found himself out in the Australian bush… and he loved it. Then he met George.

***

The Malibu Club events coordinator followed Lana Lane around the newest facility on Malibu Beach.

"Mrs. Lane, you have exquisite taste. This is the most exclusive venue in the area."

Lana Lane's nose went up. "Even so, it will be necessary to make a few small changes in the décor for the Save the Orchids benefit. The drapes need to be changed out from these royal blue linens to forest-green silks with imprints of palm trees and hanging vines. See my assistant for details."

The events coordinator made a note on her clipboard. "Yes, Mrs. Lane, we'll get right on it." Then she tried to make a point. "The blue linen was just installed."

Lana ignored the remark. "The royal blue carpet will never do and must be replaced with the hunter green speckled with tiny orchids that I chose last week. Now take me to the kitchen. I want to speak to the staff."

"Please, follow me through this door." They walked into a sparkling commercial stainless kitchen. The coordinator raised her voice so the workers in the room could hear. "Please gather around. This is Mrs. Lawrence Lane from Lane Unlimited. She would like to have a word with you about the upcoming Save the Orchids benefit."

Lana looked into the confused faces of the kitchen staff as they gathered around her little group. She fairly bristled as she spoke. "I chose this facility as the venue for the annual Save the Orchids banquet. I intend to make the evening a spectacular event, even by Hollywood standards. I know each one of you wants to make it a success, too."

The coordinator spoke up. "You know we have a reputation above all other venues."

Lana stepped in front of her and continued speaking to the kitchen staff. "I want everyone to know my desires for this benefit. These are my assistants. If you have any questions after my directions, please speak to them. First, every dish on the buffet tables must be decorated with an orchid, and there must be many varieties visible throughout the rooms."

Everyone nodded in agreement while the events coordinator furiously scribbled notes, trying to keep up with Lana's instructions.

Lana continued. "The main buffet table centerpiece consists of a giant ice sculpture of the rarest orchid to date, the centennial orchid. Scholars believe this orchid last bloomed in 1910. I'm excited at the prospect of seeing this beautiful plant portrayed in ice. The width of the bloom exceeds three feet; it is the brightest pink ever seen in a flowering plant. The ice sculpture will be done by the winner of the ice sculpture competition held in Aspen, Colorado, last year; I want all of you to be extremely cautious as you work around it."

"Yes, yes." The event coordinator nodded. "Every precaution will be taken to protect the ice sculptures and other plants your people bring."

Lana looked down at the coordinator. "Work with both of my assistants." She motioned to the women standing behind her. "I'm confident the Malibu Club staff can pull together and make this the best event of the year."

Both assistants stood behind Lana, nodding and smiling. So much planning and detail went into this charity event that Lana needed two assistants. Each assistant had an assistant of their own. The immense pressure on the primary assistants showed in their eyes. Lana never said it, but all of them knew if anything went wrong on the night of the benefit, it very well could mean death to their careers.

Lana turned to her assistants. "Make sure the staff and servers all understand the level of perfection I expect."

Lana ignored one of the kitchen staff whispering to her colleague with a thick Hispanic accent, "Lana Lane has no problem blackballing an employee who doesn't perform as expected. I feel sorry for her assistants. What she expects takes superhero power."

"I know," the coworker answered. "The good side to working for Lana Lane is that the project promises a big, creative, and exciting experience with no limit to expense. L. L. Lane Unlimited pays exorbitant salaries, and with success comes the praises of the Lane family; then you're set for life."

Lana left the kitchen and walked back into the oversized foyer to sit in a red overstuffed chair. "Over here." She motioned to her assistants. "Let me give you a picture of my expectations."

The coordinator and assistants joined Lana in the small conversation grouping near the fireplace. Each of them pulled out their notepads.

"The evening begins with the arrival of celebrities, stepping on a wide red carpet from their limousines. After entering, checking coats, bags, and whatever, the guests drift into the foyer bar. Champagne, wine, mixed drinks, and hors d'oeuvres, served by waiters in specially designed jungle print tuxedos, will give guests time to mingle before dinner."

"Excuse me, Mrs. Lane," one of the assistants interrupted. "I wonder about the jungle print tuxes. Have those been ordered?"

Lana snapped tersely, "Well, that's what you're supposed to know. There had better be jungle print tuxes. Understand?"

"Yes, Mrs. Lane."

Lana's voice changed to one of instruction. "Allow me to continue. At precisely nine o'clock, those huge carved wooden doors to the dining room should slowly open, revealing a spectacular array of buffet tables laden with hor d'oeuvres and a dinner buffet with a chef ready to handle any special requests because of food allergies. I'm allergic to white pepper, so I'm very aware of the needs of others in that area, and I want you to be especially accommodating to those who need extra attention. "

Lana turned to the coordinator. "Each round table must have a vase of orchids in the center, then I want them sprinkled over the tables, leaving space for guest's plates and drinks."

Then Lana put her finger to her lips. "Now to share my secret only among us, in utmost confidence. If this leaks to the press, every one of you will be fired, and I'm not exaggerating. My secret concerns the entertainment for the night. The performing artist commands respect around the world. Every guest attending should find their expectations more than fulfilled. My favorite artist consented to make this benefit a priority."

The coordinator brightened at getting insider information. "Oh, Mrs. Lane, that's very exciting."

"Well, other entertainers also agreed to perform. Therefore every moment offers interesting entertainment, with no boring breaks. This event is my baby. I gave birth to this benefit, and it better come off with no hitches!" Lana's eyes narrowed slightly.

The coordinator nodded. "Yes, Mrs. Lane. Everything done to your specifications can only result in success."

Lana spoke to her assistants. "I expect daily reports until the last week. Then hourly." She stood, turned around, and walked through glass doors to the parking lot.

Once in her car, with the air conditioning turned on, Lana Lane called her husband. In a mock-secretive voice, she whispered, "Lawrence, the chicken's in the pot."

She started laughing, and Lawrence chuckled, "I love your sense of humor. I guess that means this benefit is beginning to cook."

Lana leaned back in the seat. "Oh, indeed. It's getting positively steamy. I want to thank you for your support."

Lawrence reminded her of a promise made years before. "A long time ago, you told me all I had to do was pay for it and attend. Your gift to me means I simply enjoy. I look forward to both escorting you to the ball and paying for it."

"Yes, dear, and I know you love it. Maybe not as much as I do, but you enjoy all the fun of these nights whether you admit it or not."

"I'm glad the chicken's in the pot, dear. I look forward to spending an evening with a thousand or so of our closest friends."

"You should, because this campaign has blossomed for me like the lovely flowers the charity represents. Of course, we must remember orchids attempt to resemble the creatures they need to pollinate them. Right, my sweet?"

"Are you speaking of the blossom that so resembles a butterfly that butterflies actually land on it in an attempt to mate?"

Lana gleefully answered, "Darling, you are so right. Before they discover the trick, the butterflies have already pollinated the plant. When you think about it, it could be a little like this benefit. A little flower here and there may charm the money right out of their bank accounts."

***

Paris did not disappoint. The women awoke to pleasant temperatures mixed with sunshine.

Leesa sang the lyrics to "I Love Paris," slightly off-key, as they rode the elevator down to the hotel coffee shop. They ordered espresso and French pastries. After breakfast, they ventured onto the streets of Paris.

Leesa spread her arms wide to embrace the day. "Just breathe in deep that fashion air."

Leesa and Lyza strolled down the streets of the fashion district. They ogled the latest fashions by designers Versace, Yves Saint Laurent, and Hermes.

Leesa stopped to look up and down the street. "I love this place."

Lyza looked at the dress in the window and her task-oriented personality kicked in. "Leesa, you are such a funny one. Anyone can tell I'm older, even if it is just by eight minutes. Let's get down to shopping business. Did you see that Versace creation? Too much! I'm getting it."

Leesa grabbed Lyza's arm. "No, no, no, not yet. It's much too early to buy. Slow down. Stop and smell the roses, as they say. We have all day."

"We may have all day. But time goes fast in Paris. Let's move on to Chanel and Dior shopping over on Avenue Montaigne and Avenue des Champs-Elysees. There's a Zara's there, too."

Leesa stopped and looked across the street. "It's not a race. Can't we stop at Ladurée for one of their legendary macaroons? Designer shopping can wear you out."

Lyza wrinkled her nose. "We just ate breakfast."

"I don't care. We're in Paris. Besides, it can be lunch. Humor me."

After devouring designer coffee with exquisite macaroons for an early lunch, they leisurely wandered through familiar streets taking in the sights, sounds, and smells of Paris. Both Lyza and Leesa lost track of time, and as predicted, the women were still in the thick of shopping, picking, and choosing when shadows grew long and evening fell. Still they ventured on.

The Louis Vuitton shop manager invited the young women to sit down. "Please sit here. Let me get wine or coffee or whatever you would like to enjoy while watching our fashion show."

The twins sank into the white leather sofas, slipped off their shoes, and curled up for their private show. Three models showed off several new fashions.

Leesa pointed at the long black gown. "I like that one. The way the fabric moves looks so elegant."

"I liked the miniskirt with the blazer; red polka dots remind me of Red Hots. Remember that candy we used to chew on in school?"

On the way back to the hotel, the driver passed a dock. "Look, Lyza—there's our yacht. Remember when we were little and all of us spent time cruising the Seine?"

"Those were fun days. I remember how you had to take that stupid teddy bear everywhere you went. You were such a baby. I can't remember what you used to call him."

Leesa got a faraway look in her eyes. "Oh, how I loved that teddy bear. Mr. Ted went everywhere with me. He made me feel safe at night. I still remember how good it felt to hug him as I fell asleep—until he mysteriously disappeared. After he was gone, it took me weeks to get to sleep. Cook sat with me for hours before I would fall into a fitful sleep."

Lyza burst out laughing. "Can I help it if he decided to take a swim?"

Leesa felt her face get hot. "Is that what happened? You wouldn't… Did you…?

Lyza couldn't control her laughter. "You should have seen Cook. She almost fell in trying to save him."

"Really?" Leesa's back clenched. "You and Cook shared this little secret for a long time. I can't believe you did that. And you never told me before tonight." Innocence and shock turned to accusation. "You always were such a little sneak." *Some things never change. You're still a little sneak, Lyza Lane. It's a good thing I'm not vindictive. I loved Mr. Ted, and you drowned him.*

They watched the Eiffel Tower in the distance, lights illuminating its sleek, tall form against the black night.

Their limo passed a young couple on the sidewalk holding hands. Further down the street, a young man held his lover close in a long, passionate kiss. Paris was romantic, but romance was one area of ther lives that lay completely barren.

Leesa nudged Lyza. "That guy could use a hair cut."

Lyza shook her head and snickered. "Love is blind."

Chapter Four

Chuck O'Malley signed up for the geological hiking group, fulfilling a vow not to spend every Saturday in his IBM cubicle in Brisbane, Australia. *I am not Dilbert.* Now sweating with a small group of college students in the outback, he remembered collecting rocks as a kid. *I had a good time then. Collecting rocks kept me active and enjoying nature. I still love being outdoors and getting my hands dirty. I haven't done it for a long time.* The group stood around the trailhead at dawn, waiting for the man getting out of the dark green pickup.

Walking up to the group, the lanky Aussie with unruly sun-bleached hair used his forefinger to push up the brim of his straw hat. "G'day, how ya goin'? Let me introduce myself. I'm your group leader." He put his hands on his hips and stood with his feet planted about shoulder width apart. "You can call me George, because that's my name."

The group chuckled while George continued, "And because I'm your leader, we're going to have a lot of fun today learning about various rock formations and minerals that abound here in the Australian bush. Here's my sidekick, Sam."

George smiled and nodded toward a black lab jumping from the back of the pickup. "Be nice to him. He's a good dog, and he likes bushwalkin' just as much as the rest of us."

Sam slowly walked to George's side, stopped wagging his powerful tail, and meekly sat.

George studied the list of participants on his clipboard. Most of the group were from the United States; no locals attended. The group, mostly college-aged young men, with the exception of Chuck O'Malley, gathered around to ask questions.

A short young man with a crew cut spoke up. "What's bushwalkin'?"

George pulled off his hat and wiped his already sweating forehead. "That would be hiking to you foreigners."

Yet another of the young students piped up. "Will we find any precious stones out here?"

"You might. Anything's possible. Opals are mined, but we aren't going below ground today. The major mines are at Coober Pedy, Lightning Ridge, and White Cliffs. We're nowhere near any of those."

Still another student gestured with one hand at the vista of grassland, hummocks, and mountains in their view. "The outback is huge."

George looked in the direction of the student's gesture. "Now that depends on your terminology, son. People often use the term 'outback' in reference to any lands outside urban areas. With that in mind, we could say that we are in the outback, though we are only a couple hours outside the city."

Chuck surveyed his surroundings. A thin canopy of eucalyptus shaded the wooded area with a few woody shrubs and bushes. He turned back to George. "Would you say we're in the 'bush' now?"

"Yes, that's the term I would use for where we are. The 'bush' is not usually as remote as what we call the 'outback.'"

The crew-cut young man commented. "George, you know quite a bit more than any of my instructors. Most of them ignore my questions or say they'll get back to me and never do."

George's modesty was matched only by his tact. "As important as it is, son, academia can never match experience."

The first young student pressed for more information about the outback. "How do we get to the real outback?"

George pointed away from the city. "If you really want to experience the outback, you need to fly to the center of the country, then rent a four-by-four. Then after all that trouble, all you're gonna find is desert. We're not doing that today."

They started bushwalking. Chuck found the two-hour trek through the national park invigorating. George took great care to identify rocks, land formations, and even plants throughout the hike. The more Chuck learned, the more he wanted to know.

Chuck continued asking question after question long after the others left. George patiently answered every one of them in detail. The hike rejuvenated Chuck, and he wanted to know more. The two men wound up eating dinner in the local pub.

Just after midnight, George pushed his beer glass away from him and stood. "Listen, Chuck, I'm ready to call it a night. I'm going bushwalking in a couple of weeks, and you're welcome to join me."

Chuck nodded as he laid out a few bills for a tip. "I look forward to it. Today was amazing. You're an encyclopedia."

His companion laughed. "Sometimes I feel that old."

Chuck stood, grimacing at his stiffness. "Like my sore muscles after today's hike."

"Every year it gets more difficult. No matter. I couldn't give it up for the world. I'm pushing fifty and still going strong. Anyway, they say fifty is the new forty." George looked young for his age.

"That's what *they* say, but I never trusted *them*." Chuck added, "I'm forty-four and I'm sure I'll feel like a hundred in the morning."

They agreed to meet two weeks later for another hike.

George recommended several books and websites for Chuck to use to prepare for it.

Thirteen days later, on a Friday, Chuck's office phone buzzed. "Chuck, this is George, your geologist bushwalking coach."

Chuck perked up. "Oh, yeah, is the hike planned?"

"I was thinking about making the next outing an overnighter."

Chuck's heart beat faster. "You mean like camping?"

George surprised Chuck with the change in plans. "Just overnight. I think it would be fun to take you deep into the Aussie outback, the Never-Never. It's incredible the things you can find out there. It'll be the experience of a lifetime. You're gonna love it."

Chuck's mind filled with thoughts of adventure and excitement camping in the Ausse outback. "Can't wait. What do I need to bring?"

"You'll need the usual—sun screen, bug repellent, matches, snacks, and toothbrush. Oh, and you'll need a sleeping bag."

"What else?"

"It's not going to be the Holiday Inn. We'll be sleeping under the stars. I have everything we need for the campsite packed. We sleep in our clothes. Bring an extra canteen, and like I said, some snacks and your sleeping bag."

Early Saturday morning, Chuck boarded George's small rickety Cessna at a tiny airstrip on the outskirts of Brisbane.

George placed their bags in the small space behind the back seats in the tail. Then he walked around the plane, making a cursory inspection of the fuselage, wings, and tail.

George got in next to Chuck and began checking the instrument panel. "I believe all is in order. Prepare for takeoff."

Chuck shouted over the noise of the engine as they broke the bonds of gravity and barely sailed over a nearby copse of trees. "You are full of surprises. Where are we going?"

George checked the instrument panel. "A few weeks ago I saw a landing strip up around Peera Peera Poolanna Lake between two deserts. It looked pretty desolate, but I think it will be a good place to put down. From there we can explore the wonders of the Australian outback deserts. Buckle up, mate. We have a couple of hours before we get there. You're going to see a lot on the way."

Chuck watched the airstrip below slowly shrink as the plane gained altitude.

"You're about to see more of Oz than most folks ever do. So relax, hang on, and enjoy the ride."

Chuck swallowed hard. His mouth felt dry. "You sure you know how to fly this thing?"

"Oh, yeah, I've been at this a few years. It's really the only way to get around in Oz. Everything's so spread out. You could drive, but it would take us at least all of daylight and add a couple of days to the trip. This is much better. Don't worry. She's an old plane, but I keep her up."

"I didn't want to ask, but since you mentioned it, how old is this plane?"

"Hang on, there; she's older than I am and still runs like a clock. She's a Cessna 170 four-seater. They don't make them like they used to. She's a classic."

Oh, great. Chuck sat back in his seat and tried to relax. A sense of dread pervaded his thoughts as he listened to the loud buzz of the engine, and he tried to keep his overactive imagination at bay. *What have I gotten myself into? I hope George knows what he's doing. I might find an early grave in the Aussie outback. Heaven forbid.* The plane shuddered, as if responding to Chuck's mental battle. For the next two hours, the ride intermittently went from smooth to bumpy. Chuck never relaxed.

Almost two hours into the trip, the plane began to pitch and the engine coughed. George fumbled with dials and levers cursing under his breath. He barked at Chuck, "Secure your seat belt and brace yourself!"

Terrified, Chuck pulled his seatbelt tighter and looked out his side window. The silence created by the stalled engine filled his ears as the ground rushed to greet them.

George suddenly became eerily calm, his tone professional. "Look for any smooth place. Any smooth place without shrubs, boulders, or craters where we can land."

Chuck looked to his right. In the distance, he noticed a clear piece of terrain that looked like a dirt road set on a strip of elevated ground, above a dry landscape with a scattering of brush and stones here and there. *A landing strip? I don't believe it!* He punched George on the shoulder and pointed. "Do you mean something like that?"

When George saw the landing strip, the tense lines in his face disappeared. His mouth curved into a smile. "That's exactly what I mean, mate."

The plane banked right, lining up with the newfound airstrip. The smooth landing surprised Chuck. Even so, he gratefully anticipated the feeling of his feet touching ground safely. The Cessna 170 rolled down the airstrip kicking up dust behind it, finally coming to a stop.

George sighed deeply and leaned back in his seat. "That engine timing mechanism goes out sometimes. Really, mate, it's not a serious problem. I can fix it in a jiffy. Let me get back there behind the back seats. I have a bag of tools."

Chuck opened his door to step down upon the dusty land. His weakened knees gained strength once his feet touched the ground. He seriously considered getting down on his shakey knees and kissing *terra firma*, dirt and all. Meanwhile, George began whistling as he rummaged through the tool bag and inspected the engine.

A few moments later, George came around where Chuck leaned on the shady side of the aircraft. "It's all good. Just as I thought—it's the timing belt, and I readjusted it. We'll be fine. It happened a couple of weeks ago, so I was pretty sure that was the problem.

"Let's look around. I should let the owners know why we landed and give them my information." George nodded toward the other end of the landing strip. "This place looks desolate. Let's go see who we can find."

The thin trail of red dust following their footsteps reminded Chuck of his childhood in Oklahoma. They reached the dilapidated building perched at the other end of the airstrip. There they ventured through the empty hangar and out the other side, passing over a small rise. Below them spread a huge house that, in its prime, would have impressed a Texan. A wooden door flanked by eight columns dominated a large porch that reminded Chuck of the movie *Giant*. On the second floor, sagging gables stared at them. The large windows near the door were dark and caked with years of dirt. The place had been magnificent decades ago.

About a football field south of the big house stood a large building that had probably once housed ranchhands. Fifty yards across the way stood another smaller building that might have served as a guest house. Remnants of a road wound for half a mile to outbuildings and corrals. The chicken coop and pump house barely stood, their roofs sagging. A hay barn leaned to one side, and faded wooden fences with broken boards cried out for restoration.

No apparent signs of occupation confirmed George's first observation. It certainly looked barren. Furthermore, it was creepy, out in the middle of nowhere with no one around. Now only the wind blew through this ghost ranch.

George pointed to the barn and corral behind the house. "Looks like a cattle station—cattle ranch, to you Americans. From all the housing and barns, this place looks like it rocked with activity at one time. People moved out here with lofty dreams. Sadly, it only takes one or two years of dry weather to clean them out. I'll bet that's what happened here."

Chuck looked around for a source of water. "It's huge. I wonder how much the total acreage is. With all this homestead, there had to be one heck of a lot of livestock grazing."

George put his hands on his hips. "Well, there's no one here now. I'm guessing that we're around a hundred miles from the edge of the

Sturt Stony Desert. There had to be more vegetation when this was a working ranch."

Chuck looked at the landscape of red dirt, with a smattering of brush here and there. Large and small rocks jutted from the ground. "There's not enough food here for cattle, that's for sure."

"Look over there." George pointed to some tall rock formations far in the distance. "This is new territory for me. It's not what I planned, but as long as we're here, let's do some exploring. Let's hike over to those rocks and see what we can find."

They strode back to the aircraft and retrieved their gear. George strapped a canister of water on his back in addition to his pack. He pulled another one out of the back seat. "Each of us should have five liters of water per day to hike in the outback. Here, let me strap it on."

Chuck felt the weight on his back increase. "How much is this? I guess I can't complain. It looks like your pack is twice the size I'm carrying."

"You've got about ten liters there. Can ya handle it, mate?"

Chuck swallowed. "I'm good."

Turning toward the rock formations in the distance, they stepped off the airstrip into the outback desert. Carefully picking their way, they made slow progress, drinking often.

After an hour, George stopped and dug through his backpack, then offered Chuck a piece of beef jerky. The midday sun bore down on them. "We need to eat something on the go if we're going to get over there before dark."

They hiked and chewed on beef jerky, taking drinks often while making slow progress. Because of uneven ground and rocks, they watched each step, lest one of them twist an ankle or worse. In addition to the different rock formations, the sparse plants, and sandy stretches, the land itself proved interesting.

Chuck struggled to keep up with George, but he wasn't about to ask him to slow down. The rock formation loomed far ahead for what seemed forever. He sorely misjudged the distance from the airstrip, but he guessed that George knew exactly how far they needed to hike. Finally, they stopped under the shade of a bluff near the formations.

The sun was beginning to set. A small herd of camels sauntered past.

Chuck leaned with his back against the rock face. "When I first came to Australia, I was shocked when people told me there were camels. I can't believe I'm finally seeing them."

George loosened his pack. "Oh, yeah, the government started importing them to use for pack animals back in the eighteen forties. They had a big part in the development of the railroads. I think they stopped bringing the animals in somewhere around the turn of the century."

Chuck took a deep drink from his water pack. "Camels are beautiful animals with ugly knees and stubborn personalities. I always say I love to see them outside spitting distance."

George let his pack fall to the ground. "Once they were all domesticated, but now they're wild. There's probably a million of them here now, and their population can double every nine years."

"That's scary."

George shrugged. "Yeah, the government brought them in from India. Now they've gone wild to fend for themselves."

Chuck gulped another swig of water and sopped his forehead with his handkerchief. He found a stool-like rock to sit on. "This adventure is beyond what I could have imagined."

Out of the corner of his eye, George spotted a dingo in the brush. "Don't move."

Chuck froze, and then slowly turned to face the direction George looked. He whispered. "What is it?"

George relaxed and turned around to face Chuck. "No worries. It's a dingo."

The animal turned away from them and continued his way, sniffing at the ground.

Still a little rattled, Chuck asked, "Are they dangerous?"

"On their own, they're harmless. A pack of them is dangerous. This one's alone, but I wasn't sure when I first spotted him."

A strange-looking little lizard ran across in front of them. George pointed down at the little critter. "This little guy looks like he's from the horned toad family. They look like lizards, but they're really toads."

The lizard, about the size of a gecko, suddenly stopped between the two men and raised his head. He stood perfectly still, sensing he was in danger. George made a quick swipe at him to catch him. At the last second, the little guy took off, leaving a puff of dust.

Chuck thought he recognized the little critter. "We have something like them in the southwestern US. Those little toads shoot blood from their eyes when startled."

George shook his head. "No way."

"I used to keep them as pets in a cardboard box when I was a kid. When I discovered blood on the sides of the box, I did some research."

George attempted to grab another of the little reptiles, but missed again. "They're quick little buggers. Blood from their eyes, eh? I'll have to remember that one."

The sun sunk to the horizon, and George finally made the announcement Chuck was waiting for. "We should probably make camp here. It's going to get dark fast."

Relieved, Chuck surveyed his digs for the night. His legs ached. "This has been a most eventful day."

George began picking up sticks to start a fire. "Oh, brother, you ain't seen nothin' yet."

Chuck wondered what else could happen that day and assumed George spoke of the coming day.

They built a roaring campfire, and the two of them enjoyed the heat and beauty of the flames.

After a chuckwagon-type dinner, George pulled two bottles of slightly warm beer from the soft cooler he had carried all day. The two of them told camping and hunting stories until the huge fire burned down to glowing embers in the fire pit.

"Over here, Chuck. Here's a good place for your sleeping bag. You'll need to clear out a few stones. I'm sleeping on the other side of the fire. That way we'll both get the benefit of those dying embers."

Chuck kicked a couple of rocks off his dirt mattress. "Sure, thanks."

Soon he lay in his sleeping bag, looking up at a magnificent star-studded sky.

George softly spoke. "This is what I was talking about. Anyone who doesn't believe in God needs to experience an outback night sky."

That night, Chuck decided he could never leave Australia. "Amen."

***

Gary Wagner sat in the plush downtown office of Axum Oil, holding the invitation. He shook his head as he reread the expensive, but tastefully printed summons. He picked up his phone and speed-dialed his friend.

"Hey, Tim. Gary here."

"What's up?"

Gary cut to the chase. "Did you get your invitation to the Lane benefit?"

"No. If I got it, it hasn't made it to my office. I certainly expect one. Nothing's changed, has it?"

Gary sighed drily. "Oh, no, nothing's changed. It's party as usual and we'll be expected to escort the twins."

Tim laughed. "It's not bad. I know a hundred guys who would be ecstatic to escort either one of those two. Are you bailing out on us this year?"

"Of course not, we always have a good time. It seems so... pointless."

"Last year was such a hoot. Whose big idea was it to sneak out? Oh, yeah, it was yours. That was nothing less than brilliant."

"Actually, I was checking to see whether you were still in the game."

Tim's voice increased at least a decibel. "I'm in the game for sure. It's become a tradition. You and Lyza, me and Leesa, at the Save the Orchids benefit so the world can see we are all one big happy family up here in corporate America."

Gary's voice went flat. "Yeah, then something happened; I fell for Lyza, and she's all business. I haven't seen her—you know, been out with her—since last year. That's ridiculous."

"Listen, we are there for show. Neither one of those girls has time for anything but business. Take the friendship, and enjoy the time you spend with her."

"And if someone else swoops in and steals her?"

"Yoo-hoo, Earth to Gary. Every gossip columnist and reporter in LA is waiting to catch one of these gals with a guy. Trust me. Tell her how you feel or move on."

"That advice rolls off your tongue when you know very well this isn't your everyday ordinary situation. If I told her I was nuts about her, she would tell me she didn't want to see me again."

"Listen to yourself. Why are you pining over someone who doesn't give a flea's eyelash how you feel?"

"It's a bit difficult when we always go double. I don't get a minute alone with her."

"There's a reason for that. She doesn't want to take a chance on you doing something stupid."

"Fine." Gary heard his voice take on a wicked twinge as he pictured Lyza partying in Paris that week with some good-looking Frenchman. "You can order the limo. Make it white this year. In the meantime, I'll be thinking of something stupid to do."

Chapter Five

Chuck sat on a short rock stool eating a rasher of bacon and eggs. "George, this grub is the best breakfast I've had since I came to Australia. You're going to make some little gal a great wife."

George filled their mugs with coffee. "You're just trying to get on my good side."

Chuck loved the feel of the crisp morning and cooking outdoors. "Pass me one of those tough biscuits."

George tossed a biscuit to Chuck. "No more insults."

Chuck caught the biscuit and smeared butter on it. "You know I'm just having a little fun with you."

"I learned to cook in the army, and if you don't stop teasing me, next time I'll fix what I cooked back then."

Chuck feared he had insulted his friend. "Now I know you're serious. Sorry."

George laughed. "That's more like it. Give me the respect I deserve."

Chuck held out his empty cup. "Pour me another cup of joe. It's just the way I like it."

George couldn't resist. "Oh, it's the way you like your women, right? Hot and strong."

Chuck leaned back. "How could you tell? But now I'm curious. Why is a good-looking guy who knows how to cook outdoors still single?"

George's face turned sad. "I never met the right woman." His faced reddened, revealing an obvious lie. "Well, I did meet the right woman, but she turned me down. She married a rich fellow and moved to England. I haven't heard from her since. I guess it's been more than fifteen years. Hard to believe how fast time goes. How 'bout you?"

Wanting to lighten the mood, Chuck grinned. "I thought you knew. I've been married for over twenty years to the same demanding, but generous, woman."

George looked confused. "You didn't tell me."

Chuck drained the last of his coffee. "Oh, yes I have—repeatedly. I'm married to IBM and you know it. The only reason I got to come this weekend is that I found someone else to take my place on emergency call. It's not a particularly happy marriage at this point."

George shook his head and chuckled. "She's quite a taskmaster, eh?"

Chuck took on the Australian accent. "Right, she is that indeed, mate. I'm about ready for a divorce."

"Oh, yeah? What's keeping you there?"

Chuck considered the remark for a minute. Then he admitted the truth. "She'd cut me off without a penny."

George rolled up his sleeping bag and began gathering gear. "I get it."

Chuck repacked his backpack. Remembering how they'd eaten lunch on the hike yesterday, he placed the snacks where they would be easiest to reach.

George started to break camp and prepare for their hike back. After packing up, he took his sweatshirt off. A chilly morning would soon give way to hot sun, though now the sun barely peeked over the horizon.

George stood and surveyed their position. They walked for a few hundred yards and stopped. "Well, I have to admit I'm on unfamiliar ground here."

A slight chill went through Chuck. "Are we lost?"

Chuck shook his head and looked at his compass. "No, I know how to get back. I just haven't been out this far before."

A native leaped from the brush next to them and bounded away.

Chuck jumped, too. "Oh, that was creepy. I didn't even see him."

"Me either. Those kangaroos can be fast little buggers."

Chuck took a deep breath to recompose himself. "The outback is full of surprises."

***

After their first campout, they explored the area around the ghost ranch on several camping trips. What George said was true: Chuck loved it.

Chuck met George at the local pub regularly.

Chuck took a swig of his beer. "George, I did some research and found out the ghost ranch has been vacant more than ten years. And you were right; the previous owners got starved out by the drought."

George remembered the drought some years back. "About twelve years ago, there was a horrible drought out here. No doubt they held on as long as they could. Too bad, because they might've been able to do something else with the land."

Chuck found that hard to believe. "With that piece of dried-up space? Whatever could they do with it?"

"For one thing, they could have tried to drill for oil."

Chuck straightened up. "Are you kidding me? There's oil out there?"

George matter-of-factly remarked, "Well, it's outside the normal drilling areas, but it's a possibility."

Chuck noticed a young couple come in and take the booth behind him.

George lowered his voice, leaned forward in the booth, and started drawing on the napkin. "It's kind of exciting. I believe there is a good possibility that oil reserves could be in that region. If there is oil, I bet I could find it."

Chuck's voice cracked with excitement. "Oil? Are you kidding me?"

A defensive looked crossed George's face. Chuck had attacked his professional knowledge. "No, I am not kidding. I'm sure if I could get a core sample, I'd find hydrocarbons in layers of rock beneath the surface."

Chuck frowned. "I'm no oilman, so that doesn't mean anything to me. Is that good?"

"Oh, it's very good." George chuckled and then got serious. "I'd need to check porosity. That's a measure of the openings in a rock in which petroleum can exist. They're tiny openings in the rocks called pores. Reservoir rock must also be permeable, meaning the pores must be connected somehow so hydrocarbons can move and flow from one pore to another."

Chuck wanted to know more. "You say you need to get a core sample. How does that happen?"

George's chewed-up pencil made little circles on the napkin. "When you think there's oil, you get a core sample. That's how you find out whether or not the oil is worth drilling for."

Chuck thought he understood. "So now you're talking about the grade of oil, right? How you can tell if it's good."

George leaned back and clenched his hands behind his head, stretching. "I don't know if I told you before, but I did that kind of work for years with Scandinavian Oil. Then they laid me off, and I was out of work for so long I retired. That's why I sit in this bar almost every night. I have nothing better to do." The tempo in George's voice picked up from excitement. "But if the samples are good, the next step is the actual drilling. Then I could test 'cuttings' for the presence of oil."

The waitress slapped their tab on the table, and Chuck got out his wallet.

"Hey, George, I believe you know what you're doing. You might have something."

George grinned and smoothed out his napkin. "You've got to have mineral rights before you can drill for oil."

Chuck laughed a little more loudly than he intended. "I sure wouldn't want to buy it and find out there's no oil. As much as I love to camp out there, I really don't want acres of worthless, waterless cattle range. The only reason anyone would buy it is because of oil on the property. If only…"

George nodded. "Yeah I know, I know. That's the big risk in the oil business. You buy the mineral rights before you know whether there is any oil. There is one other thing."

Chuck looked George directly in the eye. "Only one?"

"You never know about the quality of an oil find until you drill. I mean, you actually have to drill before you can know whether it's any good or not. See this?" He turned the napkin toward Chuck. "This is what you have to do."

Chuck's mind raced. *No one else wants this property in the middle of nowhere.*

But is the property even for sale? Who could I talk to about it? Chuck felt a sense of urgency. *Is this the chance I've been waiting for? Has my luck finally turned?* He had heard of gold fever. *Is there such a thing as oil fever?*

If so, Chuck had a terminal case of oil fever.

***

After an enjoyable week of shopping in Paris, Lyza had returned home. She rode with Leesa to the Lane building in downtown Los Angeles. The flight home failed to provide the needed sleep Lyza craved. *Paris was fun, but now it's time to get back to work. I've reviewed my notes since five o'clock this morning. This time I can honestly say I'm ready for the briefing. I hate Leesa's Monday morning meetings. Father made a point of telling us he was taking over this one; I can only guess what he is up to. Just look at her, she loves these meetings. Oh, what am I thinking? She loves everything.*

The meeting began sharply at seven o'clock with coffee and pastries available. Fifteen commercial real estate agents filled the room, mostly men. Leesa and Lyza sat at the end of the long conference table, furthest from their father. Lyza studied her father to see if he was in a good mood. A serious-looking man with more black than gray hair, Lawrence Lane's five foot ten stocky frame commanded attention when he stood to open the meeting.

"Good morning, everyone. I hope you're not too disappointed to see me standing here instead of Leesa. I usurped her usual Monday morning meeting so I could have a personal word with you and to make some announcements."

Having grabbed everyone's attention, Lawrence sat down. Opening a thick file folder, he pulled out a small stack of about twenty sheets. "As you know, L. L. Lane Unlimited is an unusual business. It's a family-owned conglomerate involved in many aspects of the business world, and real estate comprises only a piece of the pie. I will grant it's been one of the most fun and rewarding pieces, and Lyza and Leesa both seem to love real estate. However, my goal continues in seeing all aspects of the business succeed. I'll be getting more involved in those other aspects. So I'll start by talking globally and narrow it to our office."

Several agents leaned forward and began taking notes.

"Recent changes in international banking laws have created interesting opportunities. Just as the Rothschild family took advantage of opportunities that presented themselves in the past, we intend to take advantage of the current situation. Therefore, I will continue focusing on international banking and financial markets, only now more than ever. Lyza, Leesa, and Bill can work out the details and inform you as to upcoming changes in policy that will affect your quotas and bonuses."

One of the agents raised his hand. "Mr. Lane, does that mean you are leaving the real estate side of L. L. Lane Unlimited?"

Lyza knew her father wouldn't.

Lawrence pointed at the chart on the wall. "You know better than that. I'll always be part of the real estate side. Now let's take a look at a rundown of the current commercial listings. Several billion dollars in revenue are hanging out there just waiting for you guys to bring it in. The financial side needs cash to invest."

One of the agents pointed at the chart. "But, sir, sometimes deals like these take years to bring to fruition. No disrespect, sir, but this looks like an unrealistic goal."

Lyza cringed and looked over at Leesa. Father never took criticism well.

Before Lawrence could respond, another agent interjected, "Achieving unrealistic goals is what made L. L. Lane Unlimited the conglomerate it is today."

Lawrence nodded toward the chart on the wall. "Now let's talk about how we can get these numbers up. It's all about the bottom line, and every one of you knows it. Leesa closed a local deal that bumped up the number on the bottom line this quarter. Lyza closed a terrific deal in Germany, making us a seventy-five million dollar profit. Let's give her a hand."

He started clapping his hands, and slowly, obediently, all the agents in the room followed. Leesa's face flushed as she joined the applause.

Lyza beamed. *Hey, when Bill handed out the leads, Leesa turned that one down. It's not my fault Leesa didn't get it. I grabbed it as soon as I saw she rejected it.*

"If my daughters can work deals like this, I expect you guys can do as well. I want you to show me. Prove it to me. Now, get out there and show me some action."

Lyza agreed. *Right, Father, I'd like to see any one of these guys sell as well as I do.*

Lawrence left the room.

Lyza headed over to Bill just as he made it to the door. "You got anything you think I might be interested in? Get me something like that last one. Seriously, I'm interested in getting started on something ASAP."

Leesa looked up. "Well, I'm sure you would." She stood up. "By the way, Bill, I work here, too." She turned on her heel and nearly sprinted toward her office.

Lyza left Bill standing alone in the conference room and trailed Leesa down the hall. "Leesa, wait a minute."

Leesa stopped abruptly, put her hands on her hips, and turned around. "Sure, what do you need?"

"What do I need?" Lyza repeated. "Leesa, I can't help what Father says. You know that as well as I do. Anyway, you had the same option I had on the Nuremberg property. You didn't want it. Remember?"

Leesa folded her arms. "So?"

Lyza walked toward her. "So why are you angry at me for a deal you turned down that I picked up and made work? No one in this world has any control over what comes out of Father's mouth. You know I can't stand it when you're mad."

A grin played at the corners of Leesa's mouth, and her shoulders relaxed. "How can I be mad when you put it like that? It hurt. You know I did my job, too, Lyza." Leesa swallowed hard. "Why does he always manage to make me feel like I'm not as good at anything as you are? I thought he was retiring."

"He will, eventually." Lyza put her arm around Leesa. "Until then, we have to put up with him."

Bill walked toward them with a sheaf of papers in his hand. "Look, it's not much, but here are a few leads. There's nothing like Nuremberg right now; perhaps next week. I'll keep both of you posted." *Lord help me. It's bad enough trying to balance Lawrence and the twins. Now I guess I'm going to learn to juggle.*

Glad to get the Monday morning meeting over, Lyza tried to adjust her attitude about being back at work and helped Leesa divide the sheaf of paper Bill had handed them. Lyza and Leesa walked down the hall together, then split at the elevator to enter their separate offices.

***

As Leesa stepped into her office, she flipped through the listings to see whether anything looked like something she could sell quickly. The abandoned mining operation in Utah didn't impress her. Five thousand acres in Wyoming might as well have been in Antarctica, as far as she was concerned. A five-story apartment building in lower downtown Chicago—no way would she work that one. Nothing looked good to her. Then she remembered what Lyza said, the part about her turning down the Nuremberg deal. That hadn't looked good to Leesa, either, but Lyza had done so well with it. *Maybe I should hold on to these for a while. I need to think about all of them. I don't have to do better than Lyza. I'd like to do as well. If I could just find something I could be passionate about.*

***

In her office just across the hall, Lyza slapped the sheaf of papers down on her desk. *What a bunch of garbage this is! I refuse to even look at these until I've had another cup of coffee.* She padded down the hall to the break room and ran into Bill.

He poured his cup of coffee and moved out of her way. "What did you think of those leads I gave you?"

Lyza didn't want to chat. Still irritated at having to apologize to Leesa for something she did right, and nursing a bit of a hangover, she snapped, "Really, Bill, give me a break. I just got back from Germany, turned around, and went to Paris for the week. They're sitting on my desk. They haven't gone anywhere. We've been out of our meeting for five miutes. Can I wait until I clear my head before going through them? Will that work for you?"

He shrugged and filled his cup. "Okay—just making conversation."

Lyza added extra sugar to her cup before filling it. "I'm not up for chatting. Coffee I need; conversation, not so much."

Bill paused as he exited the doorway. "You had a good day today, Lyza. There's no reason to shoot yourself in the foot."

Lyza frowned. "I'm going to pretend you didn't say that, Bill. I don't care if you were here from the beginning; you don't talk that way to me."

Bill stood just outside the door, held his cup, and stirred. "Exactly. I was here from day one. I worked beside your mother and father from the first day this business started, and I can tell you this: There's no room for ego. We're all working for the same goal here."

She stepped past him into the hall and turned to go to her office, spilling a few drops from her cup. "I am, for sure; sometimes I wonder about you."

***

Chuck O'Malley was on a mission. The midday sun glared down on the hood of the rented four-by-four. He ran his hand through his salt and pepper gray strands and replaced his weathered straw hat as he bounced along the rutted country road of the Australian bush. Neither the heat nor the three hundred miles of bad or no road deterred him.

If I hadn't found a place to rent a four-by-four this morning, I never would have made it before dark. George isn't the only bush pilot around. Who could have known I would find a pilot from Moomba? Talk about remote. The guy knew right where to land for someone to rent a vehicle. I needed to come alone this time. It's just over that rise, and then I can get a full view of the property.

He took a swig from his water bottle and glanced back at the containers of extra fuel in the back. He had also packed extra rations and water. *I've got a decision to make.*

This is going to take every bit of my 401K, inheritance, and whatever else I can come up with, but if my hunch is right, it'll be worth it. The Land Rover chugged over the short summit and came to a full stop. O'Malley surveyed the shallow valley below with his field glasses. He scrutinized the abandoned ranch. Thick silence surrounded him. A hay barn leaned to one side. A few trees nearly blocked the view of familiar buildings. He felt like a trespasser, infringing on someone else's property. The description fit.

GPS coordinates confirmed he was in the right place. The long view across to the horizon was breathtaking, and the dried-up grazing property accompanying those old buildings afforded a view of the inland of the continent to die for. Suddenly his mission became urgent. *Has someone else already seen this place and decided that they want it? That's just crazy.*

This could be my chance to get out before I die in my cubicle at IBM systems in Brisbane. This property might be my last chance.

Chuck O'Malley wouldn't admit that he owned as much greed as the next man, and yes, he did love the property with the stupendous view. Spending time there the few nights with George were the best times he remembered having since leaving the U.S. The property had been a cattle station. Chuck had no interest in ranching, much too labor-intensive. His true interests lay below the surface.

His mind raced. *I might be able to get enough money to buy the place as-is. Then they could drill. But then there's the nagging question: What if I buy the land, and they drill and find no oil? What then? Then I'll be stuck with a worthless wasteland far from civilization.*

He continued arguing with himself. *I mean, there's nothing else to do with this place. It failed as a cattle station because of the lack of water. I will have sunk every dime into an insignificant blot on a map of the Australian bush. I will have lost everything I've worked a lifetime to save.*

What if I drilled first? The nearest neighbor is more than a day's drive. Who would know? I wonder if George would go along with it. Do I dare bring up the idea of drilling to find out if there is oil? No way. I know George. He would never go along with a plan like that. George is way too honest and law-abiding to get into something like that. However…

An idea flashed out of nowhere, the answer emblazoned in his mind: *What if George thought I owned the place? He's content with his life as it is, and he really has no stake in this. Besides,* Chuck rationalized, *the less he knows, the better it will be for him. I don't like the idea of lying to him, but it's in his own best interest that I do. If I tell him I bought the place, he'll help me get the drilling done. That way I'll get what I want, and he won't feel like he's doing anything wrong.*

Bright golden rays crossed the sky from a flaming horizon as the sun began to set. Feeling peaceful and at home with familiar surroundings, Chuck built a fire at the place where he and George had last camped. He spread out a tarp and laid his sleeping bag on it. Alone, lying on the ground, looking at a crisp, clear Milky Way, Chuck felt a sense of peace and resolve. *I can do this. I can drill for oil, and George will go along with me. He's the only one I trust to do this with. All I have to do is lie.*

Chapter Six

Edith Hudson strutted onto the set for *The Talk of the Town* as though she'd received the nomination for the Best Daytime Talk Show Award.

She stretched her hand toward Lana Lane. "Lana, how good of you to join us today." *How good of you to join us underlings that have to survive in the real world. Today's sure to challenge me. You always do exactly what you want, whether or not it's on my agenda.*

Lana shook Edith's hand and smiled sincerely. "It's always fun to interview with you."

I'll bet it is. Edith masked her dread of the coming interview by flashing her finest welcome smile. "I've been looking forward to it," Edith lied, hoping Lana would actually follow interview protocol this time.

Edith pointed to the cream-colored overstuffed chair next to the one she eased into. "Please sit here. We have five minutes before air time. This is a half-hour program, so you will actually be talking for about twenty minutes at five-minute intervals, which gives us plenty of time to talk about your Save the Orchids benefit and perhaps get into other activities you're involved in."

Lana smiled as she dug through her purse for a breath mint. "That's why I'm here. I want to educate the public on the importance of orchids to the planet. As far as other activities, orchids are my passion."

Edith nodded, feeling her interview already beginning its fall into a rut. "Of course. You will get as much time as we have. So it will go like this: We talk for five minutes, then there is a commercial break. During that break I'll fill you in on what I believe our viewers would like us to talk about. You'll have a minute or two to think about that topic before we go live again. Then we do it all over, three more times."

Edith glanced in the direction of the cameras. "Oh, looks like we're ready."

The director began the countdown. "In five and four…" He held up three fingers, two, one, then pointed to Edith.

Edith turned on her best Hollywood smile and faced the camera. "Good morning, Los Angeles. Welcome to *The Talk of the Town*. Lana Lane, one of the founders of L. L. Lane Unlimited, joins us today to tell us about her Save the Orchids campaign."

Edith turned to face Lana. "Good morning, Lana. Let's begin by stating the obvious. You love orchids, don't you?"

Lana leaned forward. "I've loved orchids ever since I can remember. Once I saw them growing in the wild, I knew I had to do whatever I could to save them from destruction. The Save the Orchids campaign grew out of that love. I have orchids in nearly every room of our home. They're the largest group of flowering plants on Earth, and they're among the most fascinating of all the flowers. Did you know there are twenty-five to thirty-five thousand different species of orchids growing in the wild?"

Genuinely surprised at the number, Edith repeated, "Twenty-five to thirty-five thousand? I had no idea. That's amazing. What first got you interested in orchids?"

Lana took a deep breath. "I'm glad you asked. It started about ten years ago after I had a meeting with Al Gore, and he opened my eyes about this global warming situation. You know the destruction of rain forests throughout the world is destroying the orchids."

Edith remember covering the event when she worked for the morning news show. "That's right. I remember you hosted an event for Al Gore a few years ago. If I'm remembering correctly, it was a Democratic Party event."

Lana nodded. "Yes, it was a political event. Even so, I left there unconvinced that politicians would save the world or the rain forests. And what a sad world this would be without orchids. Within a week, I had set the wheels in motion to save the orchids. You know they grow in the most beautiful areas of our planet—South America, Africa, and Asia."

Lana turned and looked directly into the camera as though she was hosting the show. "With the added species and hybrids developed by man, there are about a hundred thousand more varieties. Many varieties can grow easily in your home, office, or apartment."

Come on, Lana. The viewers want to hear about you. Edith made an attempt to divert the interview from orchids to Lana. "So you grow them yourself?"

Lana looked at Edith. "Most definitely. It's quite an adventure. As an orchid grower, I can always find something new and fascinating. Some small varieties fit on the end of your fingernail, and some grow to the size of dinner platters. You can find all types, patterns, shapes, and sizes."

"Interesting." The director was giving Edith the 'break' sign. "More about these amazing flowers and the founder of the Save the Orchids campaign when we come back." Both women continued smiling into the camera.

Immediately after the red light on the camera went out, Edith turned to her guest. "Lana, you sure know your orchids. When we get back on the air, I want you to talk about how your family gets involved."

Lana looked perturbed. "Well, obviously they support the campaign both emotionally and financially."

Edith held up her hand to stop Lana because she had less than two minutes to make herself clear. "Yes, Lana, you know that and I know that, but our viewers want you to tell them about your family and your shared interests."

Lana shrugged as if to say, 'What's the big deal?' "My family loves orchids, too."

Edith pursed her lips. "Of course they do, but our audience would like to know more about the way the family works together to pull off this enormous benefit. Take a minute to think about how you could share that with our television audience."

In less than a minute, the director began the countdown. "Three, two… and—" He mouthed the *one* and pointed at Edith.

Edith smiled big at the camera. "Welcome back. We're here today with Lana Lane, talking about the upcoming Save the Orchids benefit." She turned to Lana. "Lana, your family is known throughout the country as being powerful and astute in business affairs. How do they support you in your campaign to save the orchids?"

Lana turned on her bright smile and took the floor. "They are very supportive. But I want everyone to know orchids actually grow on all the continents except Antarctica. I don't think I made that clear earlier. My greenhouse has exactly the correct temperature and lighting for many species that grow around the Equator. If truth be told, the orchids in my greenhouse are to die for!"

Edith adjusted her mic, and it made a soft crackle. *Did you not hear what I said during the break, Lana?*

Lana glanced at the mic on Edith's lapel and continued. "But wild orchids also grow all along the coast and inland in the rain forests. And this will surprise you, Edith. Most orchids don't grow in soil; they'll grow up the side of a tree with their roots hanging down in the air. Roots can hang three or four feet, absorbing water from the humidity in the air."

Edith managed a smile for the camera. "Well, I have to admit I didn't know that. We're learning a lot about orchids today." *More than I ever wanted to know.*

Lana was on a roll. "People often think orchids are parasites, but they're not parasites. They just happen to grow alongside trees. They're epiphytes. Have you heard that word before?"

No, and I'm sure I'm about to get a detailed explanation as my audience switches channels. "No, I don't believe that in all my years interviewing people I have ever heard that particular word. What does it mean?"

"It means orchids don't care whether the tree is dead or alive; it's just the proper place for them to hang their roots to grow." Lana reached over and touched Edith's arm. "Orchids are addictive. I must confess that I'm addicted to them—there are so many varieties. And they make me feel good."

Edith desperately wanted to get a human element. *When are we going to get to the gossip about the Lane family that everyone wants to hear?* The interview wasn't going in that direction, but she was not giving up. "Do they make the rest of the family feel good, too?"

Lana waved the question aside and scolded, "I truly want to focus on the orchids, Edith."

Lana turned to face the camera and glanced at the countdown clock behind the camera. She sped up her words and her voice raised a few decibels.

Then she held up her thumb and pointed at her thumbnail with the other forefinger. "One of my favorite species is the Phalaenopsis, and it's a common species. Its only purpose is to get pollinated so it can reproduce. Once pollinated, it can take six to twelve months for the flower to produce a seed pod. The seed pod is the size of the end of my thumb and contains a large number of seeds."

Edith's face burned. *I don't care if they're the size of your foot. We're going to have a serious talk during the next break.*

"In the wild, only a few of those seeds will reproduce plants, while most of them will die off. Commercial seed pods usually produce plants in a five to seven years and almost all of the seeds germinate. They place the seeds in flasks. I tried some, and nearly every seed is rooting. In five to seven years, I hope to have my own flowers and then seed pods."

An idea struck Edith for how to change the topic. "Excuse me, Lana, but didn't you say most of these exquisite orchids grow in the jungles around the world? Isn't the jungle dangerous?"

Lana snapped back at the interruption. "Of course the jungle can be dangerous. People die every year from injuries sustained in the jungle. But you can't let the fear of dying keep you from your passion. People get on airplanes everyday. There's plenty of risk doing that, just ask the TSA."

With extreme difficulty, Edith kept the sarcasm out of her voice. "You made your point. We need to take a break here, but when we come back, I'm sure our viewers want to hear how Lyza, Leesa, and Lawrence are helping with the family event." The red light on the camera went out.

The director called for make-up to powder Lana's face. Edith peered into her compact, powdering her nose while she spoke. "Lana, the viewers want you to talk about the benefit. They like to hear about how your family and the Save the Orchids organization is helping put the evening's events together. It's a tremendous undertaking, and people want to know how you pull it off. Don't you want to share all the excitement of preparing for this great event?" Edith hoped she could build Lana up to where she would start talking about herself instead of orchids.

Lana found her own compact in her purse and checked her mascara. "My efforts are nothing compared to the people out there finding orchids every day."

"What? Explain that to me. I don't understand what you just said."

The director's voice interrupted. "Ready in five, four." *Three*, he mouthed. He mouthed and held up two fingers, then one, and pointed to Edith.

Edith opened the segment. "We're back. If you just tuned in, we are visiting with Lana Lane, one of the founders of L. L. Lane Unlimited. She's talking about her upcoming Save the Orchids benefit. Lana, what can you tell us about the preparation that goes into an event like this?"

Lana leaned back in her chair. "Not much. In actuality, most of that goes on in the background. I just let it be known to the staff that it's time to do this benefit again. You know this is the tenth year. Then I tell them what I want and *voilà!* it happens." Her hands shot into the air as though she had released a white dove from a magic hat.

Edith glanced at the blue note card in her hand, notes that had long since been made irrelevant. "I think you're being modest. But my hat's off to whomever 'them' is."

Lana's shoulders relaxed, and her voice slowed. "Let me tell you about an experience I had last year on one of my expeditions."

Finally, something personal. Edith gratefully relaxed. *I'm going to get my interview. Hallelujah! The botany lesson is over… I hope.*

Lana took a deep breath. "Edith, now this is especially interesting. You said your viewers wanted to hear something personal, so let me tell you about one of my adventures. You see, in the wild, pollinators are attracted by the various smells, colors, sizes, and shapes. I'm thinking of one orchid plant in particular. We were on an orchid safari deep in the South American jungle, near the Amazon. I spotted the orchid while we were still a good ten feet away. I knew what was about to happen, so we stopped talking and stood very still. It wasn't long before a butterfly landed on it."

Edith smiled, but inside she cringed. *You think you can do anything you want on my show. I guess you're right. Lord, give me strength.*

Lana's voice dropped to just above a whisper. "This orchid had a four-foot stem with a single flower. The flower bobbed and wove in the wind just like the butterfly. Its entire purpose was to attract that butterfly that was seeking a mate. The butterfly didn't get to mate, but it did pollinate the orchid."

Lana's hands flew up and her voice increased two full decibels. "What a thrill to see nature in action. That particular flower will last only three or four weeks, then dry up and drop off, but another will flower right below it. That very stem will keep producing flowers and tricking butterflies up to five or six years."

Edith caught Lana looking at the director, who was holding his hand over his mouth, laughing behind the camera. A frown flashed across Lana's face, then she took a deep breath and began speaking faster. "Did you know that commercial flowers don't have the fragrance of those that grow in the wild? In the wild, you can smell them before you see them. An impressive example is the Catteya. The Cattleya grow in south Florida and Mexico, the tropical areas of our continent. They have a clove fragrance, spicy or sweet, that is strong enough to fill the room. Many times, one plant will flower several times. I love them. They are to die for; right now there are some in the foyer of the studio. Edith, did you notice them when you came in? How could you miss them with that wonderful fragrance? I brought them especially for you."

Edith seethed inside, but she cheerfully answered Lana out of politeness and for the viewing audience. "Thank you, I will take them home."

"I just want to fill you in on a few more varieties." Lana faced the camera. "This might be of interest for some of you orchid fans out there. Phalaenopsis orchids are the most common orchids and can last six months. Not to brag, but I've been able to keep some of mine alive for as long as seven months. They grow in the tropical areas of the South Pacific islands, like the Philippines, under the protection of the large leaves of the rain forest and don't require direct sunlight. Dendrobium is a huge group of plants that grow throughout the tropical Asian area, from high in the Himalayas all the way down to Australia and throughout the Pacific islands. As you may have guessed, they grow in a wide range of temperatures."

Edith began to panic. The director signaled time for a station break. She had to interrupt Lana Lane's flood of words. She stood and the camera focused back on her. Lana took a quick breath. Edith had time to say, "We'll be right back."

The camera's red light went off, and Edith sat back down. "Lana, people want to know about your family and the benefit. They want to know who's going to be featured at the benefit. They want to connect with you. When we go back on the air, let's talk about people." *Not plants, please no more plants.*

The director called out, "Last segment in three, two." He mouthed, "And... one," and pointed at Edith.

Lana jumped right in. "Some of my favorite orchids are Oncidium orchids, which include intergenerics. They're bright yellow from the tropical Americas and flower all year round. When crossed with other plants, they produce flowers that look vastly different, but grow the same as the Oncidium. They got me started with orchids. Their fragrance is like vanilla and chocolate, like chocolate cookies baking in the oven. I love the smell."

Edith held up her hand to get Lana to stop talking for a second so she could get another question in. "Lana, the chocolate cookie orchids remind me. Who are your caterers this year? Rumor has it that you fired the ones from last year."

Lana bristled. "Rumors? Really, Edith, have we been reduced to that? I demand only the very best for this event. So think about the very best caterers in the country, and you'll have your answer."

Edith felt tension rising, so she took a different approach. "There's no doubt the food will be most excellent. Who are you featuring as musical guests at the Save the Orchids benefit? I know in the past you've recruited many famous names to help with the benefit."

Lana's face brightened. "Famous people grace us with their talents. Everyone would recognize their names, were I to disclose the surprise, but it would take away from the event. That's part of the fun of it. No one knows who they are until the curtain opens. And speaking of names, orchids have some of the most beautiful names. The Paphiopedilum varieties hide buds under the bloom at the top of the stem. Usually three other buds hide under that top flower. They're so amazing. These plants don't get huge like some others. They sometimes have spots and strips in white, brown, or purple coloring. Flower life for these is maybe three to four months." Lana's voice picked up speed again.

Edith's panic gave way to resignation. She settled back in her chair. She felt helpless.

Lana was speed-talking now, not stopping to breathe. "Vandas grow in tropical Asia. They take five to seven years to get a good bloom and like a warm, moist environment. Their roots can get quite long, three to four feet. These roots keep moving higher and higher on the plant. They like to flower in the spring and summer months. Some get very tall, but some also are very small. I love to go see the Angraecum that grow in the wild in Madagascar and East Africa."

Edith, smiling for the camera, mumbled, "I'm sure you do."

The voice in her ear bud from the sound booth reminded her, "Be nice, Edith; remember, her husband owns the station."

Lana shot Edith a *look* for the interruption. "Even the famous evolutionist, Darwin, noted that Angraecum have a flower spur coming out of the back of the flower to pollinate it. They're fragrant, but only after dark, which I just find incredible. It's amazing to experience, but I can tell you the jungle is completely different, noisy, and frightening after dark. Now, Angraecum flowers have an unusual leaf structure. They can grow in stream beds, but they mostly grow as the others do, on trees. Then there's the Miltoniopsis that grow in the tropical Americas. They like more moisture than most orchids. They have a teardrop in the center of the flower. I find that so touching. These usually have several blooms on one plant, sometimes as many as a dozen."

Edith leaned forward. "Lana, our time is up."

"No, no—wait a moment." A look of panic crossed Lana's face, and she frantically continued, "You have to hear about the terrestrials. They're the octopus and spider orchids. Other terrestrials have large leaves with grasses all around them and can produce over one hundred flowers. And the turtle shell orchids are green with bright purple speckles. And mosquito orchids are so cute. They're a very small flower decorated with brown stripes and little antennae. They resemble the color and shape of the insect they want to use for pollination. Did you know that vanilla comes from an orchid plant?"

Edith tried to interrupt. "Lana, we need to go."

"Well, I want the viewers to know that you could study orchids for a lifetime and find something different every day. My favorite vacations are hunting trips to explore new and different species and their exotic locations."

Wow, we finally got some human interest. Edith stood and the camera zoomed in on her. "Thank you, Lana Lane, for an unforgettable interview. Tune in tomorrow to see another *Talk of the Town.* Our guest will be Chef Shelly with some great new recipes. Until then, this is Edith Hudson bringing you *The Talk of The Town.* See you tomorrow." *I don't care if her husband owns the network. This is my show.*

Chapter Seven

Chuck remembered the first day he'd met George three months before. They ended that day by going to supper after Chuck's first geological hike with a group of college students. Tonight they sat in the same corner booth as they had that night, only now Chuck suffered from a debilitating case of oil fever, and he had a scheme. They ordered beers and burgers with fries.

Chuck hoped his exuberant tone of voice and excited face would convince George he had actually bought the property. "I have big news. I didn't want to tell you until everything got settled. So be glad you're sitting."

George munched on his French fries. "Well, I'm sitting. Hit me with it. You look like the cat that swallowed the canary. Hand me the catsup."

Chuck leaned forward and handed George the bottle of catsup, whispering, "I bought the ranch."

George's brow drew into a straight line. "Say what? You bought a ranch? What ranch?"

Chuck nodded and salted his fries.

Understanding crossed George's face. He slapped his hand on the table. "You *bought* that dismal place?"

"I did."

George dropped his French fry back onto the plate. "I'm in shock. I thought you had no interest in that old cattle station. Surely you're not going to live out there. What are you going to do with it? "

Chuck picked up his burger. "I don't know yet. I like the fact that it's so remote. I guess I fell in love with the place over time while camping out."

"Yeah, but you can't raise livestock there. You can't farm. I guess you could make it a tourist attraction."

Chuck's grabbed the suggestion, anything to get George on his side. "I thought I could offer backpack tours and wilderness tours from there. It would make an impressive hotel and headquarters for meetings to entertain tourists that want to learn about the outback."

George shook his head and resumed eating his meal. "Sounds like you've put a lot of thought into this, mate. You never mentioned anything like that before. I hope you have a ton of money."

His brain could hardly keep up with his mouth. "We've had such great trips out there that I went back to experience it by myself. The experience rocked my world. While I was there I had an epiphany. Being out there surrounded by silence and the thought of being able to share all that inspired me. Everybody should experience the Australian bush. I love that place. The more I thought about it, the more I thought I'd like to own it."

"I… I don't know what to say. Wow. If you don't mind my asking, how much did it set you back?"

Chuck shrugged. "Let's just say it took nearly everything I had, including my 401k."

George backpedaled. "Hey, mate, if you left your 401k in the stock market, you could lose it all. At least you have something to show for it. I suppose congratulations are in order."

Chuck drank his beer out of the frosted mug. "I don't know about that. There's a lot of work to do out there."

"Well, congratulations anyway, I think."

"Thanks. No matter what I end up doing eventually, I had an idea about what we talked about last time."

George tilted his head. "Last time?" Then he slapped his fist on the table. "Oh, no. You did not purchase that land because we talked about the *possibility* of oil on the property."

"I've thought about it."

George pushed the plate of fries away and frowned. "Chuck, I never said anything for sure. I only said there was a possibility. You can't hold me to that conversation."

Chuck looked around to see the place empty except for the two men sitting at the bar. He lowered his voice. "I'm not holding you to anything. However, the fact remains that I own the land, and now I'm interested in exploring the possibility of finding oil." Chuck's voice dropped just above a whisper. "George, do you know anyone who could get a drilling crew together on the QT?"

George asked the question Chuck didn't want to hear. "Why don't you want anyone to know about it?"

What can I say to divert his suspicions? Chuck sounded confident when he said, "If everybody knows about the drilling and we don't find oil, I'll be the laughingstock of Brisbane."

George shook his head. "I can't get over the fact that you actually bought that worthless piece of land. Now you're suggesting drilling for oil, based on information gleaned from our past conversations."

Chuck motioned to the waitress for another round of beers. "Think about it. At least think about it."

George shook his head. "Well… I might know a crew that would, but I wouldn't trust them to keep a secret. Interesting… It is remote. I'll get back to you. I'm not the only one out of work these days."

***

Lyza studied the listings Bill had given her the day before. *I should pick a low-profile project. Honest to Pete, I can't do everything for her, but I can give Leesa a chance to shine. I should give her a turn in the spotlight. I can't give her success, but I can get out of the way. At least I'll give her a chance.*

She flipped through the stack of papers. *A lumber mill operation in upper Washington state? That doesn't look very interesting.*

How about an island off the coast of Alaska? Hmm. Who would buy property like that? A polar bear with a hermit complex? An abandoned cattle station in Australia? That looks boring. Wait a minute. This might be the perfect deal. This might be the deal that no one would be impressed with if it did—by some miracle—close. I think I'll explore this possibility, after all.

Lyza had last been to Australia when her father took them to Australia for a month when they were eighteen. *We had so much fun walking the shore near the Gold Coast.* The subtropical climate with beaches, canal systems, surfers, and tourist attractions ran through her mind. She especially remembered visiting the rain forest.

That time Father stayed the whole time, and we all had fun together. Mother went nuts about all the orchids. Yes, she wanted to go back. *I'll take this project on; I don't care what they say. I'm sure the other agents will make fun of it, but I'm doing it. Sure, it looks like a loser, but everyone will wonder if I have inside information.* She let out a chuckle. She would do it.

Lyza phoned Bill. "I've chosen my project. I'll be working on that Australian ranch property. I'll need travel arrangements to Brisbane."

"What, ah, Australian cattle station property? I guess I don't remember that one. Let me pull it up here on my computer. Hmm, this can't be right. Give me a minute. I'm checking to see whether I have the right property. Listing 084473?"

Her voice turned to acid. "0-8-4-4-7-3. Yes, Bill, that's the ID number. Is it all right with you if I choose this deal?"

"How could it not be all right with me? I'm not the boss. I'm just the office manager."

"That's right. Let me know when my itinerary is ready." She was intentionally curt. *What right does Bill have to question my decisions? I'll show him.*

No, wait a minute. I'm not going to show anybody. I'm flying under the radar for a while. I'm giving Leesa a chance to shine. I'll go and inspect the property and get out of here so she can go do her thing. In the meantime, I'll find out why it was abandoned and why it hasn't sold in ten years, like I would any other property. It might be fun.

She laughed to herself. *It'll be like the good old days when the other agents got first pick, and I was always left with some piece of trash no one could sell. I learned a lot from those days. No one took me seriously at first, but that soon changed. It didn't take long for clients to start requesting me to do their deals. It's not easy being the brilliant one.* Lyza's phone buzzed.

"Lyza, this is Bill. I wanted to clear the timing with you. The orchids benefit is Friday night. I assume you want to fly out after the benefit?"

Lyza never missed the benefit. As far as Mother was concerned, it was the highlight of the year. "You know I won't leave until after the event. Make my flight on Monday."

Lyza closed her eyes and leaned back into the soft leather office chair. She would use the weekend for recovery and planning. After a night of drinking and glad-handing, she'd need it.

Her intercom buzzed. "Lyza?"

She pressed the button. "Yes, Bill. What is it?"

"The best flight goes out at eleven twenty-three p.m. on Sunday, arriving at six ten local time on Tuesday morning. Should I reserve it?"

Lyza flipped open her calendar. A blank page stared back at her. "Sure."

***

Bill nodded through the glass wall to the young man who made travel arrangements for the Lanes and confirmed Lyza's flight to Austrialia. The young man gave him a thumbs-up and turned back to his computer. Bill liked the office space he'd designed with Lawrence's approval years ago. From the main hall, it looked like any other office in the building.

However, Bill's office was the center of a world of activity. His office had three glass walls connecting to the travel department and accounting. Each wall included a glass door, giving him immediate access. He wanted his finger on the pulse of the Lane enterprises, and the office accomplished a portion of that goal, only one of several tactics. From this vantage point, Bill could see everything going on in those departments. His plain walnut desk sat in the center of the room, facing the glass wall opposite the entrance to his office from the main hall. Three split-screen computers monitered the commercial real estate enterprises, along with various other holdings across the hall.

The first time Lawrence saw the finished space, he had congratulated Bill on a job well done. They stood in the middle of Bill's new office. "Amazing job, but why didn't you have one-way mirrors installed and maintain your privacy?"

Bill motioned toward the glass wall. "This way they can see when I'm in and when I'm available in case anyone needs me."

Lawrence slapped him on the back. "There's no one in the business more dedicated than you. It doesn't have to be like this. My offer for Chief Executive Officer is still open. That's where you deserve to be. You stood with me in this enterprise from the first day, and I couldn't have done it without you. I have no intention of putting you out to pasture. You're part of the inner circle."

"Office manager is enough for me. I do best in the trenches. Besides that, you need someone here that you can count on."

Lawrence shook his head and put his hands in his pants pockets as he viewed the cubicles through the glass. "We've had this discussion many times and I respect you enough to give in. You're my right-hand man. What about General Manager?"

Bill rocked back and forth on his feet. "Let me support you here. You can play ball with the big boys and come to me whenever you want to bounce some idea off me. You know I'll always be here. I don't need a title."

Lawrence shrugged. "It's not what I want, but you've made your point, and we didn't get into this to argue about semantics."

Bill grinned. "And yet here we are discussing something we agreed to months ago." Bill motioned to the glass walls in front of them. "Hence, this brilliant setup. I'm only steps away from the executive offices and I expect you to call me in now and then."

Lawrence folded his arms. "You've been here from the first day. You worked side by side with me and Lana like it was your own from the time this baby was an embryo. For that reason, and only that reason, I'm backing off. I'm accepting your mandate, but I want it on record that I accept reluctantly. And I'm going to take you up on your offer. I'll be calling you in more than once in a while."

Bill chuckled. "I'll bet you will."

"You're the only person I know that can make me do something I don't want to do. Be forewarned. I'll want you present for major meetings, and I'll want you ready to travel when need be. I'm going to need you on the front lines from time to time. You've been devoted to this enterprise from the first, and I trust you implicitly."

Bill tore his gaze from the glass wall and looked into Lawrence's eyes. "Except for the two years."

Lawrence frowned and looked at the carpet. "Two years in the Israeli Defense Forces… I don't think Lyza ever forgave you. It was the timing, that's all."

"She was two. Lana would have eventually come back to work anyway. I had to go; it's my duty to defend my Israeli home. You told me to go, and Lana couldn't get back to work soon enough. She told me herself that she wanted to work with you again, like it was before the girls came."

"Yes, and she threw herself into it like she does everything. We do work well together. But I know Lyza still blames you. One day she will understand. In the meantime, I have to apologize for the way she acts around you."

Bill walked over to his desk and sat in the leather chair behind it. "It's all right. I really don't blame her. Lana loved the business. She became as driven as you still are today. That had to have an effect on Lyza."

Lawrence sat in the chair across from Bill. "It's water under the bridge, Bill. A lot has happened since then. Lana's back home, all involved in charities and social events. She doesn't give a fig about business anymore. She's into orchids."

That conversation stuck in Bill's mind even though it had taken place over ten years ago. He chuckled as he remembered Lawrence saying that Lana was into orchids. He leaned back in his chair and folded his hands behind his head.

He watched the day shift filter out of the office and the evening shift arrive. Keeping tabs on L. L. Lane Unlimited's international concerns throughout the world demanded twenty-four-hour coverage.

Bill relaxed. *Maybe Lawrence was right. One day, Lyza might understand. In the meantime, she's doing a great job.*

Chapter Eight

Leesa sat at her desk. *I have time to look these over. I should at least pick one to focus on.*

She thumbed through the sheaf of papers Bill had given her. *Out of more than twenty prospects, not one jumps out at me. Borrring.*

She stared out the window at the buildings below. *I need to concentrate.*

Leesa pulled up her e-mail on the computer. Lyza's message reminded her of Mother's upcoming benefit, as if Leesa needed the reminder. *Thanks, Lyza, how could I forget the biggest social event of the year?*

She switched back to the listings. *I need to get back to these leads and concentrate!* The page blurred in front of her. *Too much! Oh, well. I can't get involved in anything until after the benefit. Still, I would love to find something where I could start the groundwork.*

One page caught her eye. *A canning factory in Washington state? Who wants a canning factory? Anybody out there dying to get their hands on a canning factory?* She laughed to herself, then got a flash of insipiration. *If I could make something out of nothing, I know Father would be impressed. Maybe a canning factory in Washington state would be the ideal project. It's no chemical factory in Germany, but maybe, just maybe, I could turn it into something magnificent. Seattle would be fun.*

She pulled up the listing on the computer.

Kramer's Kanning Factory

Located four miles off the coast of Seattle, Washington state

This property consists of an island approximately two miles by three miles off the coast of Seattle. The operational cannery contains all equipment. Commercial loading docks with lifts and warehouse make this a unique operation. Little effort is required to bring the buildings up to code.

The island includes several buildings and a few vacant residences.

Leesa did some research and found the previous owners. The Kramer family had canned salmon to support their family. That business had been successful, but three bad years had drained the bank account, and they were forced to close. The spec said the cannery was operational. With all mechanics in place, someone could buy it and start producing almost immediately.

She grinned. *Someone might buy a canning factory, but having your own island off the coast of Seattle would be fun. Maybe I should buy it. I could make it a tourist attraction by giving tours, perhaps including a small café that would offer Seattle's famous Starbucks Coffee.* Leesa began to dream up a fantasy around the canning factory. That was Leesa's expertise: making lemonade out of lemons.

She worked herself up to an excitement about the old, abandoned canning factory. *Really, all it takes is money. Yes, I might be interested in a project like that myself.* She remembered visiting Seattle; a good friend of her mother lived there. They had played with her sons and called them cousins. Leesa and Lyza had spent a couple of weeks with their 'cousins' on Bainbridge Island each summer. They liked to hike, walk the beach, or take the yacht out and go fishing. Her first time out, she'd caught a big fish, and Lyza didn't catch anything.

The Eisner boys hunted mushrooms, sailed, fished, hunted, climbed trees, and did all the things that boys do all over the world. It didn't matter. Whatever they were doing, the girls had idolized their pretend cousins.

I wonder if Todd still lives in or near Seattle. No doubt John moved away. All he ever talked about was what he was going to do when he could leave home. Her curiosity got the better of her and she decided to check the Internet for information about John and Todd Eisner. She had barely started when Bill's voice came over her office intercom.

"Leesa, just wanted to remind you about your mother's benefit coming up."

Her interest in her 'cousins' vanished as she changed her focus to the benefit. "The weather should be perfect. Am I going to see you in a tuxedo again this year?"

Bill chuckled. "The benefit is the only time I get gussied up. You know me well."

"Well, I'll be looking for you. I'm out of here for the day."

She shut down her computer, picked up her purse, and headed out the door. She needed accessories for the fundraiser and suitable Seattle clothes. Shopping was in order.

***

After work that day, Lyza walked into the kitchen to find Leesa rifling through the refrigerator. "What are you looking for?"

Leesa poked her head around the refrigerator door. "Cook made fried chicken. Want a piece?"

"No, thanks."

Leesa stuck a drumstick in Lyza's face. "I thought you'd never get home. I got your e-mail about Mom's benefit. Have you talked to Gary?"

Lyza backed away. "Oh no, get that thing out of my face. I'll call him now." Lyza pulled her cell phone out of her purse. "Have you called Tim?" She dialed Gary's number.

Leesa took a bite of the drumstick and answered with her mouth full. "No, I haven't. I haven't thought about it since the invitations went out." Leesa swallowed her mouthful and grinned at Lyza. "Remember the year we attended without escorts?'

Lyza sat at the kitchen bar. "That will always be remembered as the year of the social faux pas. Did you feel mobbed like I did?"

Leesa finished off her drumstick and took an apple from the bowl of fruit on the bar. "Of course I did. Every dance, three or four guys clamored over to see who could get to me first. I only danced with them because it was Mother's benefit."

Lyza held the cell phone to her ear. "I didn't get a chance to eat. Those knuckleheads didn't let me sit out one dance, not one. I was so tired and hungry."

Leesa nodded. "That mistake will never happen again."

Someone picked up; Lyza spoke first. "Hello, Gary? This is Lyza."

"Yes, Lyza," Gary replied in his deepest voice. "Is it already that time of year?"

"You know it is."

He pretended to moan. "I read all about it in this morning's paper. She's outdone herself this time. The Malibu Club. Why doesn't she just give all the money she spends throwing this shindig to the charity itself? That way she wouldn't need to have the ball."

Lyza knew how to get to him. "Gary, what a fabulous idea! Let me tell Mother your ingenious plan."

"Don't you dare!" Gary knew Lyza's mother well enough to know her reaction.

Lyza played along. "Seven it is. And don't forget a corsage for my dress. Make it a white orchid."

***

Tim checked the caller ID and saw Leesa's name. He waited for the third ring before answering. "This is Tim."

"Hi. It's Leesa."

"Hey, girl. I'm looking forward to this year's extravaganza. I know you'll be the belle of the ball once again. What time should I pick you up?" A sharp beep indicated another call coming in on Tim's line.

"Seven o'clock, sharp!" she quickly answered.

"See you then. Sorry, I hate call waiting, but I need to take this call." Their connection broke as Tim switched to his other call. "This is Tim."

"Tim, Conner here. I just got the *Candy Cane* out of dry dock. Are you up for a sailing day Friday? I can't wait to take her out again!"

Tim chuckled. "Friday? No can do, buddy. I got a better offer. Gotta 'Save the Orchids' on Friday. You know, the annual Lane charity ball. It should be fun; want to come?"

"Of course I want to come, but isn't it by invitation only?"

"I can get you in on my invitation. I'll call and tell them to add you to the guest list. Everyone you ever needed to know in business will be there."

"You just made me an offer I can't refuse. I'll call Sandy. Let me get back to you. No, on second thought, just get me on the list. We'll be there. Thanks, bud."

Tim hung up before Conner could thank him again for the opportunity to mingle with the richer and more famous.

Chapter Nine

Glad she'd left fried chicken for the Lane girls, Cook parked outside the one-story brick building. Light from behind closed blinds revealed shadows of people moving about. Cook knocked.

Within seconds, Doris opened the door, her gray hair pulled back into a tight bun. "Come on in, we've been waiting for you."

Cook stepped inside and saw everyone around the table in the middle of the room. "Hello, Doris. I suppose I'm the last to arrive."

Doris hugged Cook. "Always last to arrive and last to leave. We're glad you're here."

Doris locked the door and joined everyone at the table a few steps away. "You didn't miss much. We barely got started. Jack was telling us about his nephew in rehab."

Cook found a seat and took off her jacket. She settled in as Jack continued, "Just pray for the boy. I've done all I can do for him. It seems the more I do, the less he cares, so I'm wrestling with how to handle the situation. Pray for me, too."

Doris looked at Cook. "Now I know that you have prayer requests. We are a small but mighty group of prayer warriors." She motioned to the other two women at the table. "There's nothing the five of us can't accomplish through Christ, Who strengthens us."

The group replied, "Amen."

Doris nodded toward Cook. "Go ahead, Beverly. How can we pray for you?"

Cook looked at Jack. He had to be in his mid-seventies, his shoulders rounded, elbows propping his head over the table. He blinked moisture from his eyes.

Cook placed her hand on his arm. "Never give up. Here I am, more than fifty years old, and I feel like my biggest job is still ahead of me. I've worked for the Lanes since before the twins came into the world. At first, I felt like a piece of property, like a piece of furniture, and wondered when God would give me something meaningful to do. For thirty-three years, I have been asking Jesus to protect this family and draw them into the Kingdom. God honored the persistent widow's request, and I know He will honor ours. We just need to remain patient and faithful. Now I see that God had a long-term mission for me."

Jane, the younger woman sitting to Cook's other side, commented. "I don't know if the Lane family will ever be able to see past their wealth and privilege. Money can blind one to the reality of the gift of life. They have no need of a savior because they simply don't believe there's anything money can't buy."

Cook nodded. "What you say is true. However, God did arrange it so that I'm working at the twins' estate now. I must say I was surprised and grateful when Lana and Lawrence placed me there. Hard as it was to leave them, I knew it was such a God thing."

Doris folded her arms and sat back in her chair. "Those girls needed someone to oversee that monstrosity they call home."

"I do less work there than I did at the Lane estate. Now I just see that everyone else does their job. The twins treat the other employees like they don't exist. I'm the only one they really talk to."

Jack leaned forward. "Is it true their father never allowed them to play with other children?"

Cook dug through her purse for her tissues. She felt a sneeze coming on, found the tissue, turned away from the table, and sneezed. "Oh, sorry. I think it's allergies. Pollen. But yes, the girls had an interesting childhood. Lawrence taught them that their family can do anything and they don't need anyone else. In spite of that, the girls and I have formed a special relationship."

Doris bristled. "Well, I would hope so. You practically raised them."

Cook held up her hand to stop Doris's comments. "Doris, don't say such a thing."

Doris faced the group. "Well, it's true. They've been around her more than they have their own mother. Every time they went on vacation, she had to go. Lana always had something more important to do than take care of her children."

Cook took on a defensive edge. "Lana was no spring chicken when they arrived, and twins take a ton of energy. Anyway, that's water under the bridge. The parents are older and wiser now."

Jack's forehead wrinkled. "Are the girls identical twins?"

"They're identical as far as the eye can tell, but their personalities are unique. Lyza is assertive, but can be protective of her younger sister. Leesa has a soft heart and a sunny attitude most of the time. Lyza creates her own stress, while Leesa hums along no matter the situation. Sadly, both of them long for the attention of their parents even though they are grown women."

Jane spoke up. "The old man still watches over his conglomerate like it's the only one on Earth. I think Lana got bored with it when it got so big. In the beginning, they both worked all the time, then everything took off and she quit. I don't know, but I'm guessing she felt she wasn't needed on the business side any longer, so she found something else to do."

"That gets me to the point of tonight. Lana's passion is her 'Save the Orchids' crusade. It seems something always comes before the girls. When they were tiny, it was the business. And now for Lana, it's those temperamental parasites." Cook nearly spit out the last few words.

"Oh, yes," Jane said. "I saw an interview today. Lana was telling all about orchids. And Beverly, they are not parasites. They are efficites, or errifites, or something. I don't remember, but they aren't parasites."

"What they are is a diversion. She doesn't have to face the pressures of the business or bother with the girls. As soon as they graduated from Stanford, they immediately interned at Lane. I felt so sad for them. They've had no social life. Those girls—I should say young women—would rather watch the stock ticker than socialize with anyone outside the family."

Evelyn had not spoken since Cook had come in. "Exactly what shall we pray for tonight?"

Cook filled her in. "We always pray for the Lane family to come to know Jesus as Lord and Savior. Our little group has met for many years and seen no progress. We trust the Lord for His perfect timing, but we still need to pray for the family's salvation. Tonight, I'd also like to pray about the future of these two young women. Pray that they find godly men who will point them in the right direction. Pray that the Lord will prepare these men to find these young women. Pray that the Lord will prepare the Lane twins for the men He chooses to bring into their lives. Pray that they will find more to life than dollars and cents."

***

The morning of their mother's Save the Orchids benefit, Lyza and Leesa arrived at the Ritz Carlton Huntington Spa at ten a.m. They were immediately led to the mud room for a treatment with mud from the Dead Sea in Israel.

The young Oriental attendant held up a spatula of black goo. "This 'magic mud' contains natural minerals guaranteed to heal, restore, and repair your body."

As the little woman rubbed a thick coat of the slimy black mud over Lyza's back, Lyza sighed. "This feels so good. I may fall asleep."

"Ugh," Leesa remarked. "It's so heavy. I think it's added about twenty-five pounds to my weight."

"Oh, yes," the little woman answered. "It adds about twenty-five."

"Twenty-five pounds?" Lyza laughed. "That's going to be a lot of mud."

The attendant smiled. "Not so much." She finished applying the mud and left, telling the women she would return in thirty minutes.

Thirty minutes later, the attendant returned and pulled back a curtain, revealing a room of shower spigots.

Leesa squirmed. "How much longer?"

"You can shower now." The attendant held back the curtain.

Lyza stepped into the shower first. "Finally!"

When Lyza finally got washed off, she felt light enough to lift off and float to the ceiling.

The attendant gave a professional smile. "Now time for facial. You follow me."

Lyza rolled her eyes and followed the woman to a small room with a massage table.

Lyza waved as Leesa went with another attendant to a room down the hall.

After their mud baths, body wraps, and facials, the first woman led each of them to their pedicures and manicures.

Leesa examined her nails. "Lyza, did you choose your next big project?"

"You know we don't talk business at the spa. I made that rule a long time ago, and I'm not about to break it."

"You always pick something so extravagant. I couldn't find anything very exciting in the listings Bill gave me. Do you want to trade?"

"No, Leesa, I don't want to trade. And I'm not going to talk about it. All I'm going to tell you is that I've chosen something, nothing newsworthy. The choices I had were no better than yours. If you'd like to have my leftovers, I will gladly give them to you."

Leesa looked uncertain. "That's not why I was asking. There wasn't much in my selections, but I did choose something, sort of."

Lyza laughed and shrugged. "Well then. Why are we discussing it? I think we're done."

"Okay, I'm through with it. The subject is closed. What are you wearing tonight?"

"I want to surprise you, and I know you want to shock me." Lyza began to feel light and fun. "Tonight is going to be good for me. Gary is just the ticket tonight. No pressure, just some good fun while supporting Mother at the same time."

"I wonder what surprise Mother will unveil this year. Every year, she raises the bar and pulls off some unexpected surprise. Remember when she brought in a section of rain forest from along the banks of the Amazon in South America?"

Lyza started laughing at the memory. "I'll never forget that. The Sierra Club had a cow. The local tree huggers went ballistic. They had to cut a hole in the top of the outdoor deck where she displayed her twenty by thirty piece of rain forest, with tons of orchids dripping from the branches of tall trees."

"Mother has an impressive imagination. Sometimes it's scary, but so far all participants have survived."

"Except for the caterer that used South American bananas at last year's African-themed event." Lyza shivered thinking about it.

About three o'clock, the twins finished at the spa and entered the waiting limo.

Lyza wasn't ready to go home yet. "Let's stop at Gina's for a latte. We have enough time. More to the point, we can try our new look out on Carlos." Carlos, Gina's barista, constantly joked with the twins, and they enjoyed him.

Leesa agreed with the idea. They pulled up in front of Gina's and took the few steps up to the patio.

"Good afternoon." Carlos met them at the door sporting a warm smile. "Inside or patio?"

After they were seated on the patio, Carlos took their order of the usual coffee frappés. "What are you lovely young women up to this afternoon?"

"Why, Carlos, can't you tell?" Lyza teased. "We've come from the spa."

Leesa jumped in. "Tonight is the orchids benefit. You didn't know?"

Carlos raised his hands to the sky. "Mercy! How could I forget? Oh, that's right, I didn't get an invitation."

Lyza laughed. "I'm sure it was an oversight."

He turned to ring up their order. "I'm sorry. I must go home right now and search for my invitation."

In a few moments, he returned with their frappés. "I found my invitation. Unfortunately, I have to work tonight." He winked at Leesa.

Leesa lifted her cup. "Okay. I'll give Mother your regrets."

The shaded patio afforded front seats to a sunny California afternoon. A warm breeze made a pleasant respite before the activities that would come that night.

Lyza sipped her iced frappé, leaned back, and sighed. "I'm looking forward to tonight."

Leesa eyed the floral display across the patio. "Me, too. I haven't seen Tim since last year. We should do something nice for them. They've always been willing to take us and we have lots of fun together."

Lyza brushed Leesa's shoulder with her napkin. "What do you mean? We *are* doing something nice for them. They get to take us to the benefit. Remember when we got bored and left early?"

Leesa smiled. "We were so naughty. Sneaking out and bowling in our designer dresses and high heels made the evening exciting. After three frames, you took off your shoes."

"You must have thought it was a good idea, because you did it after I did. I have to admit that night is one of my favorite memories. Gary can be inventive and spontaneous. I couldn't believe it when he suggested we leave the benefit."

Leesa grinned. "I cracked up when he said, 'Let's blow this pop stand and go bowling.'" They howled with laughter at the memory until tears rolled down their faces. Leesa began dabbing at her newly made-up face. "Oh, no. My makeup's ruined!"

Lyza dabbed her eyes and blew her nose on the napkin. "The bowling was only part of it. It was hanging out in the lounge and watching television with them. We didn't get home until two o'clock the next morning." Lyza returned her sister's grin. "That was fun. Who knows what will happen this time?"

Chapter Ten

From the the heavy gold jungle print envelope, Edith Hudson pulled the embossed green jungle printed card inviting her to the Save the Orchids benefit. She scowled.

Edith called out to her secretary. "How long has this been in my 'IN' basket?"

Her secretary poked her head into Edith's office. "It just arrived by courier this morning before your show."

Edith dismissed her with a nod and snickered. "Uh-huh." Out loud she said to herself, "The benefit is tonight."

She glanced at her watch. *Two o'clock. Really?*

Edith tried to surpress her distaste of the Lane family, Lana in particular. She couldn't help fuming at the late invitation, even though the thought of attending the Save the Orchids benefit had never entered her mind before that moment. *Well, well, well. How nice of you to think of me at the last minute. Or perhaps you have another motive. Oh, of course you do. Lana Lane doesn't do anything without a motive. I'm sure there's more to it than raising money for those poor starvng orchids all around the world.*

Her mind flashed back to the interview. She reached for her bottled water and took a gulp. *Maybe this is her way of apologizing for being such a witch during the interview. Talk about someone who can't take directions.*

Yeah, right, an apology from Lana Lane. Probably not. I can't imagine Lana apologizing for anything.

Then it occurred to her that Lawrence may have insisted Lana invite her so she could interview attendees and report on the happenings at the benefit. *That's more like it. Although, I wonder if she takes instructions from him. If anything, I'll bet it's the other way around. Well, I suppose I should feel honored, because they never invite press to this affair, and there will be some interesting people.*

A desperate feeling draped over her as she dialed the number of her hairdresser.

She felt triumphant when Candy answered the phone. "Candy, I need you."

Edith heard Candy take a deep breath. "Sure, Edith, what can I do for you?"

Edith's voice went into pleading mode. "I need to get my hair done for an affair this evening. I know it's Friday and it's last-minute, but I wouldn't ask if it wasn't important."

Candy sounded harried. "Yikes, Friday is my busy day. I've got one under the dryer, one with a perm waiting to be unrolled, and one with bleach on her head."

Edith pleaded. "Is there anyone there that can do it? I prefer you, but I just now found out that I have to be at the Save the Orchids benefit tonight. I have a few hours to find a dress and get my hair done, and that means going without a facial unless you have someone else?"

"Can't your makeup people do your facial?"

Edith frowned. "Television makeup is not what you want to wear to an affair like this. Believe me, I wouldn't let one of those maniacs touch me for this."

Candy sighed. "I know you won't be happy with anyone but me. One of the other gals might take over for me. I'm about to get five women very ticked off at me, but how soon can you get here?"

Ten minutes later, Edith was sitting at Candy's beauty station enduring the stares of several irate women. "Thank you so much; I didn't know what I was going to do. I owe you, big time."

Candy led her over to the shampooing station and began wetting her hair. "You can say that again. Mrs. Boone probably will never book me again."

Edith felt Candy apply the cool shampoo. "I thought we were going to do facial first."

Candy's fingers massaged the shampoo into Edith's scalp. "Let's mix it up a bit. Someone's in the facial room now. We'll shampoo, then do the facial, and then I can fix your 'do. How does that sound?"

Edith relaxed for the first time since she'd opened the invitation. "This feels so good."

A few moments later, Edith lay on the facial bed, feeling even more relaxed.

Candy applied the first round of oils to Edith's face. "I saw your interview with Lana Lane a few days ago. I had no idea you were so interested in orchids. I didn't catch the whole interview. I love that necklace you had on."

Edith wanted to avoid discussion of the interview. "That necklace was a gift from one of the Holly sisters. You know, the trio from Wisconsin that I interviewed last month? It was made by a man from some Native American tribe in Wisconsin."

Candy wiped cream over the oil. "I never think of Indians in Wisconsin. So you're going to the benefit tonight. Will you be interviewing celebrities?"

"Actually, it's an invitation. Nothing says anything about working tonight." Edith considered that thought for a moment. It really was an invitation and only an invitation. She wasn't commanded to interview anyone or to do anything but attend. "I'm trying to decide what to wear. I would have liked to shop for something, but really, I have plenty of dresses to choose from."

"That's no lie." Candy rubbed the oil down Edith's neck. "The one you wore for the opening of *On The Deck* blew me away. The blue chiffon swayed just like an ocean wave. Perfect for that movie premiere. Didn't your daughter attend that one with you?"

"She came with me, but that was before they moved. She and her new husband like the east coast. They're living in New York. I sure hope they move back before they have children. Hopefully that's years away. I'm too young to be a grandma."

Candy patted her softly on the cheek. "You're right about that. Now just relax for a few moments and let this soak in. I'll be back when it's time to remove it. Let me put some soothing music on." She pressed the button on the remote and soft music filled the room.

Edith closed her eyes and felt almost like sleeping. She anticipated the evening and thought again that it wasn't work, but an evening hobnobbing with people she usually interviewed. It might even be fun. Her mood turned, and soon she looked forward to an evening of smiles and light conversation. Maybe she could get one of the celebs to be on her show. Even if she couldn't do that, there would be enough craziness at the affair to report on. *Everyone always wants to know what's going on with the Lanes.* Yes, *The Talk of the Town* surely would benefit from this benefit.

***

Tim Young and Gary Wagner arrived in a white limo. They came to the door holding identical white orchid corsages in crystal plastic boxes wrapped in gold ribbon to grace the wrists of their dates.

The butler opened the door before they rang the bell. He smiled knowingly, then dutifully rang intercoms to the twins' respective rooms. Leesa confidently sauntered down the curved staircase from the west wing.

Seconds later, Lyza stepped down the curved staircase from the east wing. The men, surveying their prospective dates, simultaneously said a slow, "Wow!"

Lyza's upturned hairdo showed off her diamond necklace. The black Dior 'wrap' ankle-length dress shimmered with reflections from innumerable sequins. Her black diamond-studded heels included those famous red soles. *This is definitely not bowling alley attire,* she thought, a little sadly.

Leesa's Versace gown, scarlet with a diamond cummerbund, showed a front slit to just above her knee. Her scarlet Christian Louboutin shoes with red soles and scarlet diamond-studded clutch bag finished her glamorous look.

Gary held out the clear box containing the corsage. "May I present for you, Lyza, an unworthy flower for your wrist?" He bowed deeply.

Opening his clear box, Tim fished out the flower and took Leesa's wrist. "Let me help with this."

That done, the group turned as if the entire evening had been choreographed and Act One had begun. The butler opened the door for them. They stepped out into the cool evening air.

Gary opened the limo door and Lyza got in. Tim opened the other side door for Leesa.

Leesa smiled. "Thank you, sir."

As the limo pulled away, Tim asked Gary, "Did your father ever convince you to get into the oil business?"

"He's stubborn and sure that it's something I should do. I fought it for years, but in the last few months, I've begun hearing him with changed ears."

Tim's eyebrows shot upward. "You must be kidding. You always said you would never get into the same business as your father. That surprises me."

"I'm not in yet. I have to admit that we *are* talking about it. I've gone on a few sites with him this year and it's been interesting. Especially with all the off-shore drilling."

"I thought off-shore drilling was a no-no these days," Tim ventured.

Gary began sounding defensive. "Well, it is and it isn't. Off-shore drilling typically refers to the discovery and development of oil and gas underwater off the coasts of continents. But it can also mean drilling in lakes and inland seas. And yes, there is opposition to off-shore drilling, especially in the arctic or close to the shores, presenting environmental challenges."

Wow, Gary's worked up about this. Tim egged him on. "I agree with those who fight off-shore drilling. For instance, look at the event we attend this evening. I believe off-shore drilling is dangerous for rain forests where those precious orchids grow."

Lyza whispered to Leesa, "That sounds like a slam."

Leesa whispered back, "Let's give him the benefit of the doubt."

Completely unaware of the twins' exchange, Gary went on. "We use many different types of off-shore drilling platforms. They range from shallow-water steel jackets and jackup barges, to floating semisubmersibles and drillships that operate in deep waters."

Leesa smiled at Lyza, who rolled her eyes out of Gary's line of vision.

Gary continued explaining, "Right now there are off-shore platforms in the Fields Sea, in the Gulf of Mexico; in the Campos; and in Santos Basins off the coasts of Brazil, Newfoundland and Nova Scotia. Not to mention the fields off the coasts of West Africa, Angola, Southeast Asia, and Russia."

Lyza jumped in. "Gary, you sound like an expert. Tell me you aren't serious."

Gary took a deep breath. "You know what, Tim asked me and I'm telling him. This is a serious business. Off-shore oil and gas production is much more challenging than land-based installations because of the remote and harsh environments. Don't kid yourself; we're going to need every bit of oil we can get drilled right here. I don't see you using less gas and oil."

"Hey, no reason to get personal." Tim held up his hands mocking-defending himself against a physical attack.

"I'm guessing you don't know that the trend today is to conduct more of the production subsea. We can separate sand from oil and reinject sand before oil is pumped up to the platform or even pumped onshore. That way there are no installations visible above the sea. Subsea installations help us find oil in deeper waters, locations that were previously inaccessible, and overcome challenges posed by sea ice, such as in the Barents Sea."

Tim grimaced. "You've already told me more than I ever wanted to know about oil exploration and off-shore drilling,"

Lyza lifted an eyebrow and drily remarked, "We get it."

"Before you shut me down, you should know about off-shore staffed facilities. They are fascinating and present some real human resources and logistics challenges, because an off-shore oil platform is a small community in itself. I did a lot of research on this, including spending three days on an off-shore platform. Helicopters transport employees for a two-week shift. Ships bring supplies and remove waste. The cramped quarters and two-week shifts are unpopular."

Tim tried to interrupt. Gary held up his hand and kept talking. "Subsea facilities help move more workers onshore. Subsea facilities are also easier to expand using new separators or separate modules for various oil types. They're not limited by the fixed floor space of an off-shore rig." Gary took a long breath.

Tim still couldn't believe Gary was going to work for his father. "I don't want to shut you down. I'm still in shock about this new interest in your father's business. You were always so against off-shore drilling and drilling at all."

"I'm not ignoring environmental risks. However, history teaches us that wars start when people want land or other resources that are in short supply. And wars decimate the environment." Gary stopped for a second, looked a little embarrassed and took another deep breath. "Tim, I guess I should ask what you've been doing since we last saw each other."

Tim smoothed out his pants. "Not much. Conner called the other day to go sailing."

Lyza chimed in. "Sailing. I haven't been sailing for at least a year. Sounds like fun."

Tim knew Conner would love to have the Lane twins come along. "Well, we didn't go. I had other plans, but I do want to take him up on it soon. Maybe we could all join him sometime."

Gary pressed for more information. "But I mean what are you *doing*, like, for work? What are you working on?"

"Now I have to make a confession regarding the vows we made long ago about never working with our fathers," Tim ventured.

"Oh, no!" Gary placed his hands over his ears. The twins laughed.

"Yes, it's true. Cal Young Architect may become Young & Son." They all laughed, Tim most of all, holding his sides with tears running down his face. "Please, somebody, stop me! Don't let me go on like Gary did."

Gary was unrelenting. "No way, buddy. You put me through it. I want to hear the full confession."

Leesa coaxed him. "Come on now. We want to hear all about what you're up to these days."

Tim started talking like he was reciting an informational manual. "We design spaces that reflect functional, aesthetic, and environmental considerations."

Lyza slapped her forehead, and Tim kept talking. "You know architecture isn't just drawing pretty buildings. It requires the use of materials, technology, textures, light, and shadow. It also includes the pragmatic elements of design, like planning, cost, and construction. I might use a wider definition of architecture by saying that architecture may comprise all design activity from the macro-level, which consists of urban design and landscaping, to the micro-level, which involves construction details and furniture."

Leesa squirmed in her seat, anticipating another boring diatribe. "Hey, Tim, we know that well-designed buildings are easier to resell."

"Right, and architectural works are often perceived as cultural and political symbols and as works of art. Historical civilizations are often identified with their surviving architectural achievements."

Lyza butted in. "So you're going to be an architect? Is that what you're saying?"

"It's looking that way right now. I always liked engineering, but this past year, I learned that architects plan, design, and review the construction of buildings and structures using creative organization of materials and components with consideration to a bunch of factors, including cost, construction limitations, and technology, to achieve an end that is usually functional, economical, practical, and often artistic."

Lyza yawned. "Oops, sorry. Didn't mean to yawn in the middle of your sentence."

Tim took a deep breath and fell back in his seat. "It wasn't in the middle of my sentence. What I'm trying to say is what distinguishes architecture from engineering design, which has as its primary object the creative manipulation of materials and forms using mathematical and scientific principles. Architecture is more artistic, and that's what really appeals to me."

"Of course art appeals to you," Leesa said. "I could have told you that a long time ago. All you had to do was ask." They all chuckled.

Chapter Eleven

Half a mile from the Malibu Club, the two couples spotted bright marquee lights flashing 'Save the Orchids.' The bright flashing lights moved back and forth through the night sky, pointing toward the stars and reflecting off a few low clouds. A string of black and white limos lined the curb in front of the club. Doormen dressed in jungle print tuxedos opened limo doors, helping designer dresses accompanied by impeccable tuxedos emerge onto the red carpet leading into the Malibu Club.

Paparazzi pressed against restraining ropes, vying for pictures of the rich and famous. When Leesa and Lyza moved onto the red carpet, one of the paparazzi called out.

"Leesa, Lyza, are you ready for your mother's surprise twist this evening?"

Lyza paused and yelled back, "If I were ready, would it be a surprise?"

Flashes and camera clicks muffled chuckles from the picture-taking gallery. She turned to walk purposefully toward the entrance.

"Leesa!" the same paparazzi yelled. "Do you have anything to add?" Leesa smiled and waved, hooked her arm around Tim's and followed her sister and Gary.

Tim looked around, trying to get a count. "I'll bet there are a thousand people here."

"At least," Leesa answered.

They crossed the threshold into Lana's arms. "Welcome, girls, and you, too, gentlemen. What a momentous night! So glad to see you."

"You know we wouldn't miss this—ever!" Leesa exclaimed and gave her mother another hug, then turned and kissed her father on his cheek. Lyza duplicated Leesa's actions with an extra hug for Lawrence.

Their escorts hugged Lana with pretend kisses and shook hands with Lawrence.

A pleasant young woman in a jungle print uniform came by with a tray of crystal champagne flutes. She presented the tray of bubbly to the center of the group and each of them helped themselves. Then she floated to another group.

Lawrence turned his back on her and offered a toast as he raised his flute to his family. "Let's drink to a successful evening."

"To success," Lana, the twins, and their escorts echoed and clinked glasses.

Lawrence noticed Edith Hudson strolling through the entrance. He leaned over to Lana. "What's she doing here?"

Lana finished her sip of bubbly and whispered, "I made an executive decision. I'm sure she'll behave herself. She's not working. No doubt the subject of this benefit will come up on *The Talk of the Town* sometime in the future."

He snickered. "Certainly, like Monday."

Lana smiled up to him. "Now let's be happy tonight. Don't worry about Edith."

"Darling, if you invited her, I know there's a reason." He smiled and lifted his glass.

Lyza, Leesa, and their escorts strolled throughout the large foyer filling up with attendees. They stopped near the center of the room and formed a small circle to talk amongst themselves. Every so often they would peek around one or the other to wave at someone or smile and nod. Champagne, hors d'oeuvres, and celebrities did the Hollywood shuffle all around them.

Lyza watched Lana making the rounds, mingling with someone for a minute or two, then moving on to the next guest while Lawrence followed.

Gary followed Lyza's gaze. "Your mother is amazing. I believe she is going to personally speak to everyone here."

Lyza grimaced. "It looks like Father is having a difficult time keeping up. He doesn't know how to have a short conversation."

Leesa turned to look. "He's doing all right. You know Mother has to say a few words to everyone here before the evening really starts."

At exactly nine o'clock, large wooden doors with palm carvings slowly swung open to the dining room. The sight of the room, void of people, filled with orchids, the huge ice carving, and the sound of a full orchestra playing softly welcomed the guests. People began sauntering slowly into the room, looking for suitable seats among the one hundred large round tables.

Twenty minutes later, the principal serving room opened. Chefs dressed in jungle print uniforms proudly displayed fresh lobster, exotic fish dishes, beef, chicken, duck, ostrich, emu, llama, and some other sea creatures Lyza hoped never to "enjoy." The finest salad bar artistically displayed all sorts of fruits and vegetables. Waiters carried dishes, accompanied guests to their tables, and took drink orders.

Dessert tables resembled Japanese flower gardens with cakes in the shapes of various species of orchids. Chocolate orchids of all colors and shapes filled ornate serving platters. Fruit, pastries, and made-to-order crêpes rounded out the choices. With more than two hundred service personnel, each service person pampered five guests throughout the evening.

Lyza smiled as they sat down. The slice of fruit on the frosted plate in front of her must've been the Kuliangle fruit her mother had enjoyed for breakfast with the natives deep in the jungle on her last trip to Costa Rica. She'd wanted to bring some home for them to try, but like Biblical manna, it spoiled after twenty-four hours and had to be enjoyed the same day it was harvested. She'd described it as a fruit with the texture of a fine croissant and the spicy sweet flavor of a bosc pear, with a hint of honeydew.

Exactly one hour after the entrées, doors opened, and Lana took center stage in front of thick, forest green stage curtains. She spoke into the mic. "I want to thank all of you for coming tonight."

The chatter throughout the room stopped as the audience turned their attention toward their hostess.

"I appreciate your presence here tonight and your willingness to help save the orchids." Wild applause broke out.

Lana held up her hand to quiet them. "I wanted to say that I don't think you will leave disappointed. Not only are your donations going to support the Save the Orchids foundation and all the work it does to preserve orchids all over the world, but you also support continuing research for new orchids."

Applause broke out again. "In appreciation of your efforts, we have put together an evening of rare entertainment. So get comfortable, sit back, and enjoy the rest of the evening. Before I introduce our opening act, here is a short documentary about orchids and the history of our organization."

The lights dimmed, and large monitors on either side of the stage displayed a twenty-minute video about the Save the Orchids foundation, with numerous pictures of beautiful orchids in settings around the world. Most of them included footage of Lana standing in a waterfall of orchids as she narrated. After the documentary and some polite applause, Lana took center stage again.

"Now that you've seen the reason for tonight, let me introduce our opening act."

Lana turned stage right and extended her hand. "Please welcome Hollywood's comedian of the year, Miss Mallorie Fields." Wild applause filled the room.

Mallorie hugged Lana, and then took center stage as Lana returned to her front row seat. "Good evening, everyone. Isn't this just crazy? Here we are gathered together to save the orchids. And I guess you know how this all came about."

Mallorie winked at the crowd. "I was shopping on Rodeo Drive and ran into Lana. She had a huge bouquet of white orchids with her, and I said to her, 'Lana, careful now. Don't drop those beautiful flowers.' She started to drop them right then and there. Luckily, I have a long reach. I got to them just before they hit the ground. So I saved the orchids. Then she planned this evening to celebrate."

Someone whistled and started applauding. Mallorie waited for the room to quiet. "No?" She looked back at Lana shaking her head and said, "I was sure tonight was all about me. Oh, it's about saving orchids all over the world. I know a little bit about orchids. They make perfume out of them. Oh, no. Is that like saying what they do to old horses while attending a horse race? What? No applause? Oh well, I've already had too much to drink."

Mallorie's performance picked up, but was cut short when she confessed, "Folks, I think all the caviar I ate before dinner is about to make me sick."

She grabbed her throat and pointed down to the audience table in front of the stage. "Here's Jefferson Grant," she croaked as she exited stage left.

Jefferson Grant ran up to the mic and in less than a minute had the entire room laughing with his antics. He entertained them through dessert for the next thirty minutes. When Jefferson Grant jumped down to return to his table, Lana was back in front of the crowd as their applause died.

"Now here's the moment we've all been waiting for. Let me introduce our main show."

One shrill whistle and a few shouts rang out together with a spate of wildly clapping hands.

Lana smiled an impish smile. "There's nothing I can say about this group except… enjoy!"

The green velvet curtains began to part slowly. Quiet enveloped the crowd, then suddenly percussion loudly kicked in and Bingo and his Amazing Rock Band began playing their hit song "Craziness."

The crowd went wild. Lyza and Leesa shrieked in excitement and grabbed each other's arms. All the young women screamed while their escorts yelled, raising their fists with big grins on their faces. "Yes!"

Lyza knew that Bingo, in addition to being famous for his music, was notorious for his activism concerning starving children in India. Lyza and her father flashed a look between them. She wondered if they were thinking the same thing. *How much money did she contribute to Bingo's benefits in India to get him here?* After their first number, Lana appeared back on the stage.

"You might know him as Bingo and his Amazing Rock Band! That's the best introduction I could come up with this evening. Of course, I don't need to introduce him." She stretched out her hand. "Everyone knows Bingo. But what you might not know about this gentleman is that he won the International Peace Prize two years ago for his work in Indonesia and, in addition to his many trophies, was named Person of the Year by *Worthy Magazine*. He graciously agreed to spend this important night with us to support our Save the Orchids benefit."

Bingo gave a deep bow and Lana continued. "To all of you who chose to attend this evening's benefit—and most of you have been to at least one of our benefits in the past—we do not make pleas for money and support. The desk inside the small room near the entrance is where you make your commitments to this honorable cause. We welcome you and—" she turned toward Bingo, "—Bingo, we are honored to have you and the Amazing Rock Band!" Lana bowed and left the stage.

Wild applause filled the room again as the band played "How Did I Ever Find You." Bingo said a few words about the next song, and then went into their performance of "Why."

Bingo and his Amazing Rock Band presented their talents to an excited and energized crowd for over an hour. As the band began to wind down on one song, the entire west wall of the building slowly lowered. People in the audience gasped as night crept in. Lights were extinguished, and the room turned dark. Only the sound of silver waves rolling onto the shore broke the silence. Suddenly the crowd heard a loud explosion and the sky ripped open, commencing the largest fireworks display since the Paris, France, fireworks at the Eiffel Tower on New Year's Eve.

For more than twenty minutes, lights filled the sky with brilliant colors and shooting stars. The Amazing Rock Band supplied the musical background, frantically matching the fireworks. The final burst revealed a huge red orchid in the sky that also reflected off the ocean below. Golden threads shot out of the center of the orchid and wafted slowly to the sea. Then the music stopped. For a moment, silence reined.

Applause broke out. "Bravo! Bravo!" Cheers continued for a full minute. The overhead lights blinked in response.

Lana remained sitting at her table and beamed. Lawrence winked. He patted her hand. "You did it again, kid."

Conversation filled the room as the wall resumed its normal place and the lights went back on. Couple by couple, the attendees began leaving. People, still dazzled by the evening's events, stopped to say their good-byes to their hostess. Orchids and pieces of orchids lay on tables and chairs and on the hunter green carpet with the tiny orchid print. Wee hours of the morning sucked the energy of the night away. What remained were the spoils of war, the remnants of a party: a mess to clean up.

Everyone else smiled and shook their heads as they left. Lana heard remarks from all around her. "What an incredible evening."

Lana heard Edith Hudson comment to the the woman walking next to her as they approached her. "Absolutely amazing."

The other woman nodded, eyes glistening.

Edith Hudson shook Lana's hand. "I can't believe everything that happened here tonight. You outdid yourself this time."

Lana smiled with great satisfaction. "Gotcha! I knew you wouldn't mind the late invitation."

***

Leesa and Lyza climbed into their white limo. Their escorts sat next to them, still glowing from the presence of Bingo and his Amazing Rock Band.

"I can't believe she did it." Gary sighed.

"How did she get Bingo?" Tim asked. "That's just crazy."

Leesa said, "Well, I was impressed with Mallorie Fields, weren't you? I mean, she looked so young. How does she do it?"

Lyza laughed. "For me, it was the fireworks. Incredible."

The hour demanded sleep, but they tried to stay awake. They didn't want to be rude to one another. However, it took effort to keep their eyes open, and further conversation seemed like too much effort.

The limo stopped in front of the twins' estate.

Leesa turned to Tim. "I'm so tired. Let's say good night, and I'm off to bed." With that, she jumped out of the limo and ran in the front door.

Lyza clutched the door handle. Gary's hand covered hers. "I'll walk you to the door. Looks like Tim's already asleep."

She looked over and grinned. "It took all of two seconds for him to conk out."

Gary pushed the door open and helped her out. She unintentionally leaned against him as they walked up the two steps to the door. They stopped in front of the elegant teak carved doors flanked on either side with leaded stained glass.

He gently took hold of her chin and turned her face toward him slowly, then leaned over and kissed her full on the lips. Dreamily, she sank into the moment, returning his passion. Drinking in the smell of his cologne, she allowed strong arms to enfold her.

Suddenly she realized what she was doing. *What's going on?* Panic set in. That had never happened in the ten years they had known each other. She straightened and stepped back.

He moved with her, still holding her. He felt the tension in her body and released her. "Lyza, I'm sorry."

She couldn't think. "Uh. Uh, I don't know what to say."

He smiled down at her. "Neither do I. Just say good night."

Lyza pushed him away. "Good night." She abruptly turned and went inside, closing the door softly. She leaned against the door for a moment. *What just happened?* She slowly climbed the stairs to her room and fell on the bed, confused. Sleep came quickly, but dreams accompanied her sleep, and she was kissing Gary in front of her door over and over again all night long.

Saturday's morning light broke through Lyza's window, and she slowly opened her eyes. The morning seemed surreal. Why was everything different from any other day she woke up in the morning after a late party? Why did everything seem as though she was living in a dream? Could it be because of a silly kiss?

I am a thirty-one-year-old career woman. What's a little kiss going to do, change my life? I think not. Time to get a grip here and get back to business. You need to prepare for next week. She looked out the window and for the first time noticed the picturesque palm tree outside. Her mind drifted back to the kiss… and to Gary.

He's probably thinking what a little nut I am. I was so shocked and tongue-tied, I didn't know what to say. He must think I'm a complete idiot. Oh, what do I care what he thinks? But she did care what he thought, and that bothered her. She wanted to go back to sleep, but knew it would be impossible now. She showered, dressed, and wandered down to the kitchen for some coffee and breakfast.

Leesa greeted her. "Good morning. I woke up this morning, and all I could think of was Bingo and his Amazing Rock Band." She started humming one of the tunes they played the night before, then she laughed gleefully. "Wasn't last night mind-blowing? I can't wait to tell Mother!"

Lyza gasped. "*What*? What do you mean, 'tell Mother'? Tell Mother what?"

Leesa looked at her as if she was crazy. "Tell her what a great benefit she put on last night. What did you think I meant? Are you all right?"

Lyza wanted to get the focus off what might be wrong with her. "Yes, I'm just tired. It was a long night." But it was the end that she kept remembering: the kiss, and how the Earth had moved beneath her.

Chapter Twelve

The Earth trembled and rumbled beneath Chuck O'Malley's feet. The rig foreman yelled, "Run! Everybody run!"

Chuck, George, and the rig crew ran as fast as they could from the shaking rig. Huge drops of oil fell on them like a tropical monsoon. The noise of the blowout drowned any verbal communication.

Thick drops of oil rained on them. Chuck O'Malley, George, and the rig crew tried to find cover and make as much distance as possible. The rig shook like a rocket about to take off—or worse, fall on them.

The noise of the blowout and the groaning of the ancient machinery drowned out any verbal communication less than full-throttle yelling. The crew foreman gave instructions to his motley crew. "We've got to get a cap on this baby! Shut her down!"

Once Chuck realized they were out of danger, he stared at George in shock and awe. Both of them started to grin. Grinning broke into laughter, and laughter into dancing. "We did it! We did it! We struck oil!" Chuck shouted into the blue sky as they high-fived each other. "George, you were right. You said there was oil here, and you were right!"

George grinned again and wiped his face with an oily hand, smearing more oil all over. "Chuck, you had the guts to go with my suspicion, and it paid off. Don't ever doubt anything I say—ever again."

Like giddy grade school boys, they began smearing the raining oil over their arms and faces.

George yelled above the noise. "It tastes so good; it feels so good. I can tell you right now. This is high grade crude oil. You're gonna be rich!"

"The Ballad of Jed Clampett," sung by Jerry Scoggins, went through his head. He compared himself to old Jed, who became a millionaire overnight because of an unexpected oil find. Pictures of expensive cars and big houses ran through his mind. *What a break from my boring life! It'll change things, but for now I want to drink in every second of this moment.* He looked at all the activity around him. *Now this is exciting!*

He was as far from his real life as he could get. And he was having a difficult time getting his head around it. He wasn't a risk-taker. He didn't knowingly break laws and bring others into outlandish schemes. He did not trespass on other people's property. *Who is this person, and where did the real Charles O'Malley go?* And the other question that lurked in the far reaches of his mind was—would he ever find that old Chuck O'Malley, or was that man gone forever?

"I brought this along just in case." George popped open a bottle of warm champagne. It was in the cooler, the ice long since melted. Warm or no, George produced two plastic glasses, filling them to the top with the warm champagne. They leaned on his oil-splattered pickup, dipped the glasses toward each other, and guzzled it down like cheap beer.

Chuck held out his glass as they watched the crew pack up. "Hit me again."

The well was capped as the foreman had instructed. "I can't wait to get into production, but not until I talk to the right people. You understand, right?"

George looked around. "Sure. It's your business. This is the fun part. The crew will clean up and get out of here shortly."

Chuck still couldn't believe they'd found oil. One of his preposterous ideas had finally come to fruition. "Now I need to find out who to contact in order to start production."

What I need is to find out how to buy this place quickly. I can make a reasonable offer on the property. Earlier he had made a few inquiries and discovered he needed to contact a company with a branch office in Brisbane. *I'm pretty sure this parcel of property is back, way back, on someone's back burner.*

The crew left, but George decided to stay. He and George drank themselves to sleep in their makeshift camp. The well fell silent a few yards away. Stars glowed brightly over them. They talked and laughed and fell asleep. Chuck awoke in the wee hours. He could smell fresh crude oil on the ground nearby. He looked across at a snoring George and realized that over the past few months, George had become his best friend. *No, he's not my best friend; he's my only friend. I hope he never finds out I lied to him.*

***

Lana snuggled up to Lawrence as the early morning sun filtered through their bedroom window. He whispered into her sleeping ear, "No one can pull off a benefit like you do, sweetheart."

Lana opened her eyes and smiled. "We did it. Everyone had a great time and I believe they were surprised at the entertainment."

"Surprised is an understatement. Who wouldn't be? Even I was surprised. You know how to keep a secret."

She smiled again. "I have a few secrets."

Lawrence pushed her away. "I have a secret, too."

She turned and looked suspiciously at him. "What have you got up your sleeve, Mr. Lane?"

He held up a bare arm. "Nothing is up my sleeve as you can see. What a terrible accusation to make to your loving husband."

"Now I'm really suspicious. Tell me."

"It's my secret. I'll tell you when I'm ready."

She grabbed the pillow and held it over his face. "Tell me or you'll be sorry." Lana pulled the pillow back to see if he was ready to talk.

He started laughing. "No, you can't force it out of me."

She got up. "Well, I guess I can get on with my life." She started out of the room.

"Okay, okay, I'll admit that I've been working on something that we talked about a few years ago. Let's breakfast on the patio, and I'll tell you."

She grabbed another pillow out of an overstuffed chair and threw it at him. "You'd better."

Half an hour later, they sat on the patio drinking coffee. Lawrence held the newspaper in front of him while Lana thumbed through her latest orchid magazine.

Lana spoke into her magazine. "Hmm, I think I remember something about a secret you were going to reveal at breakfast. Here we are, and you're ignoring me by reading the paper."

He didn't answer. She pulled his newspaper down to the table to see his amusement.

"You have five seconds to start talking, Mr. Lane."

"Okay, okay, here's my surprise; we're going to Jerusalem."

She was taken aback. She knew that could only mean one thing. "Jerusalem. Are you sure?"

"I'm sure. I think we're ready. We need to do it."

"Just thinking about it brings up so much emotion."

Lawrence insisted, "I know it does. But I think it's something our parents would have wanted us to do. They loved Jerusalem. Remember the Passovers we celebrated with our families?"

Lana's eyes filled with tears. "They always ended by saying, 'Next year in Jerusalem' and promised to take us there someday. Now that they're gone, we could honor them and pay tribute to all the others who died in the Holocaust."

"We'll go to Yad Vashem."

Lana's gaze clouded. "I… I don't know if I can go there. I can go to Israel. I can go to Jerusalem. But Yad Vashem…"

Lawrence took her hand. "There's nothing to fear now. Both our parents knew what was coming and hid us with trusted friends. We need closure for all those nights of feeling alone and defenseless, all the nights we hoped for their safe return, and all the days and nights since."

She blinked away a tear. "We were so fortunate to find people who took us to safety in Britain. I was an infant, but you were old enough to remember."

He took her other hand and clasped them in his. "At least my brother was ten; I was three. Before he left he promised me that Father would come take us from the orphanage, but it never happened. Sweetheart, the people who took us in will always be important to us, but our parents died tragically and innocently. They deserve to be remembered. We need—I need—to go to Yad Vashem."

Lana pursed her lips. "Then we'll go. We can visit the Goldsteins. Remember they made aliyah and moved to Israel. They left New York and moved everything to Jerusalem."

"They're not the only ones; remember the Levys? They pulled up stakes years ago and moved to a little town outside Karmiel. We could drop in on them."

Lana stood and walked to the edge of the pool. "Going to the Holocaust museum will be difficult, but if it's something you feel we must do, I will be by your side. There's such a raw place inside me; I function by blissfully denying that it happened. It's not as bad as it used to be, but even now I have my days. I thank God every day that we ended up in the same orphanage. You've been my rock. It will take all the strength I can muster, but I'll go with you. What about the girls?"

"The girls have been protected by time and distance. They know little of the horrors of that time. I don't think we should tax them with our burden."

Lana turned and faced him. "They've heard stories, but you're right, it's not the same."

"Both of them are quite busy now. I think we can do this without either one of them lifting an eyebrow. Anyway, I have another commitment in Jerusalem. You'll get a day to yourself to sightsee and shop while I'm at an international finance conference. Actually, it's a small group of businessmen. It shouldn't take but the one day, enough time for you to do something interesting. Perhaps you'd like to see the Rockefeller Museum. We'll leave day after tomorrow."

"That's quick. I can be ready."

"I'll alert the pilot. We should leave late, fly to New York, refuel, fly to London, refuel, and then to Tel Aviv."

***

Lyza boarded the fourteen-hour flight to Brisbane, Australia at midnight Sunday night. First class offered seating that converted into sleeping quarters. Although she seldom slept on a flight, that night she was ready for the sleeping part. She hadn't slept well since Friday night, the night she felt drugged by champagne and Gary's kiss.

I should sleep soon. I need to sleep as long as possible to overcome jet lag. These long flights always mess up my body's time clock. I'm glad I wore my gray velvet sweats for ultra comfort. She kicked off her shoes before the flight pulled away from the terminal. *This long flight can do without my fashion statement.* She dug out a pair of bright red house slippers from her carry-on.

The flight attendant picked up the mic. "Welcome to Qantas Airways flight number QF16, to Brisbane, Australia. If you are not going to Brisbane, Australia, now is the time to disembark."

Lyza tuned her out by mentally organizing and reorganizing her things to do list.

"You are on our Qanta's 747-400 offering a myriad of features for long flights such as this. You can choose movies, music, and games on the screen in front of you..."

I must remember to drink only water and lots of it. Let's see, now... What else helps with jet lag? She remembered her mother telling them to always get up and walk as much as possible to avoid getting a blood clot. The good news was that the more she drank, the more exercise she got from running to the head. She hated those tiny restrooms.

Lyza glanced over at her trusty laptop. With business reports and articles she had downloaded for research regarding commercial real estate law, she could be plenty busy. She had memos to write and her calendar to update. Sleep could wait awhile longer.

Before the flight took off, she sent an e-mail to the Australian office with her itinerary and instructions. She would need a limo to pick her up, and a corporate secretary to work with. She would also need office personnel and a helicopter reserved for visiting the property. In addition, she wanted vehicles to meet the helicopter at the site.

She would inspect the real estate in order to properly represent it to whomever might be interested. Lyza kept in mind that she always had another option. If she considered the property advantageous as investment potential for L. L. Lane Unlimited, she had authorization to purchase the land outright to go into company inventory.

At least I'll be flying into Brisbane. She enjoyed the Gold Coast when the family went there for vacations. Visions of beaches, zoos, museums, and kangaroos filled her head as memories flooded her thoughts. *I'm so glad I'm flying into Brisbane instead of Melbourne. Melbourne had cold and rainy days last time I was there. The property is outside Brisbane, actually in the outback. Brisbane is as near as I can get. Nothing is close in Australia, but as the locals say, "No worries." It's going to be a good and fruitful trip.* When Lyza decided, it was so.

***

"Praise the Lord!" Cook looked around the room at her prayer partners. "We have answered prayer this week. This is wonderful. God is so amazing. I know He can do anything. Why am I always surprised when He performs a miracle?"

Doris got up to get a cup of coffee from the small table in the tiny kitchen a few steps away. She called over her shoulder, "We want to hear all about the orchids benefit."

Jack held up his hand to stop Doris. "I don't need to know about the orchids benefit. What answered prayer do you have? That's what I'm interested in."

Evelyn, a short, fortyish woman with wiry black hair, winked at him. "Jack, that's what we're all interested in. However, the orchids benefit report is just the icing on the cake."

Cook raised her hands. "I'll talk about the benefit first. I suppose they're all connected. The orchids benefit was way over the top."

"I heard Bingo and his Amazing Rock Band were there." Jane leaned forward.

"Oh, yes. Bingo and other celebrities, but the answered prayer news has nothing to do with them. Honestly, there was so much going on that I barely could take it all in. I was there to see that the kitchen staff carried out their assigned jobs. And I must say they did a terrific job. I gave them a glowing report."

Doris laughed. "Oh, Beverly, you'd give Granny Clampett's vittles a good report."

Jack's deep voice broke through the women's laughter. "My nephew got arrested during a drug bust."

Immediately the room fell silent.

Finally Evelyn spoke. "We've been praying for him to be free of his drug addiction. I'm so sorry this happened."

Jack brightened. "I believe with all my heart that this arrest is answered prayer."

Doris confronted Jack. "Just tell me how getting put in jail on a drug charge is answered prayer. I mean, he's just a boy. Didn't you say he is nineteen?"

"Yes, he's nineteen, and this time I didn't bail him out. It's the third time he's called me to rescue him. And let me tell you, he was shocked that I didn't bust my chops getting down to the station to pick him up. I decided that the Lord had a better plan for him. So far everything I've done for that kid has blown up in my face. I've turned it over to the Lord. He's really the only one who can rescue him."

Jane pursed her lips. "I think you might be right. He'll get off drugs in jail, won't he? The book of Isaiah says that God's ways are not our ways."

"It was hard. He actually cried over the phone, but I stood my ground. The Lord was right beside me saying to stand firm with Him and that He would take care of it." He broke out in a brilliant smile. "Praise the Lord!"

Jane spoke up. "I have praise, too. My granddaughter got into the private school they wanted. They worried because they've been on the waiting list for months. Praise the Lord!"

It was Doris's turn. "My brother got out of the hospital yesterday and everything looks good. He is feeling better than he has for years. Praise the Lord!"

Everyone else had shared; they looked at Cook for her turn.

"I have a lot of answered prayer to report. There's something going on in the Lane household—I mean Lawrence and Lana's home. The Lord is drawing them. I know this because Lawrence contacted his pilot to take them to Tel Aviv. When I asked their housekeeper about it, she told me that they are going to visit Yad Vashem."

Doris looked puzzled. "Yad Vashem? Isn't that the Holocaust museum in Jerusalem?"

"Yes, and you know both their parents were killed in the Holocaust. I know God is drawing them. Some soul searching must be going on. Why else would they travel to Jerusalem—the city of God? Praise the Lord!"

Evelyn smiled. "I thought you had something about the girls. We prayed specifically for husbands for them."

"Oh, yes, I have more to report."

Everyone at the table leaned forward in rapt attention.

"The night of the orchids benefit, I got home late. I was in my quarters, which gave me a clear view across the yard to the front door of the main house. I had turned off my light when I heard the white limo come up the driveway. I saw Leesa jump out and run in the house. A few minutes later I saw Lyza and her date walking closely together. And they were walking slowly. It looked to me like they were hugging."

Jack raised his eyebrows. "You spied on them?"

"I was already there. I just looked out. I couldn't help but see."

Evelyn shook Cook's arm. "What did you see? There's more. I can tell."

"They stood at the door for a moment." Cook's voice lifted. "Then he kissed her! No, I mean they kissed each other… on the lips. It was so romantic."

Jane laughed. "I'm surprised she didn't slap him, from what you've told us about how those girls are so proud and proper."

"Well, that's just it. She didn't slap him or scream at him. That's when I thought I might be needed in the main house. I slipped around back through the patio into the kitchen. I peeked around the corner and that's when I saw her."

Doris almost came up out of her chair. "What did you see?"

"I saw her leaning dreamily against the closed door with her eyes closed. I made no noise and she didn't know I was there. Just a few minutes later, she went up to her quarters."

Jack shook his head critically. "You did spy on her."

Cook shrugged. "Oh, whatever, maybe I did—a little. Anyway, praise the Lord!"

Chapter Thirteen

"Tim, I had a great time at the benefit. Did you notice Conner and Sandy waving at us when we were drinking champagne in the foyer?" Leesa remembered to ask after forgetting twice that night to mention it.

"Oh, yes, I did see them. You didn't see me wave back. Sandy was wearing last year's Yves St. Laurent."

Shocked at Tim's fashion knowledge, she exclaimed, "She was? I didn't notice."

He laughed. "I'm teasing. Seriously, what's going on?"

Leesa felt the need to bat her eyelashes. "Well, after our conversation the other night about architecture, I had an idea. I'm sort of in the early stages of a development fantasy. But I'm thinking this may work, because you seem to be in the early stages of a commitment to your father's business."

For a second, he appeared confused at her flirtation, but he evidently passed it off as a misinterpretation. "I'm listening."

They sat in Leesa's office, on the leather chairs surrounding a large marble coffee table. He had arrived shortly after her call, asking him to come over.

"I'm going to Seattle to take a look at an old fish cannery. Ever heard of Kramer's Kanning Factory?"

He remarked, "No, but please tell me why I would be interested in canning fish in Seattle?"

"It's located on a small island off the coast. The island itself could be a tourist attraction with a small Morro Bay type shopping district with curios, coffee shops, and restaurants. The canning operation shut down for obvious reasons. They went broke."

"Too bad." His eyes focused on the oil painting of Monet's water lilies on the wall behind her.

Her enthusiasm quickened her words. "I have a vision of Kramer's Kanning Factory rising out of the ashes like the Phoenix. With the proper redecorating, adding a small café and curio shop, then adding a dock for fishing expeditions, this could be the next Knott's Berry Farm or Disney park."

Tim's eyebrows shot up. "Where do I come in?"

"Well, you talked about how you liked the artistic side of architecture, and I'd like you to come along and check it out with me. You might be able to help me create something out of nothing."

"When are you going?"

"Tomorrow morning."

"Tomorrow morning? Let me check. Hold on." He brought up his calendar. "I think I have something."

Rats!

"Well, no, I guess I'm all yours. What time should I meet you at LAX?"

Good. "Our flight leaves at ten o'clock. I'll have our office set it up." She stood up. "See you in the morning."

He left and Leesa went back to her computer. *Tim's the perfect one to go along and check out this new site. I love Seattle. Someone once said that it's the kind of place where you can find fishermen lunching alongside top surgeons.* The more Leesa thought about Seattle, the more she wanted this project. *Seattle is such a beautiful city, surrounded by fascinating sights and attractions. Puget Sound and Lake Washington are only about ninety-six miles from the Canadian border. I could live there.*

She searched the Internet and found that Seattle's population ran about six hundred thousand residents, with over three million in the metro area—about the same as the city of Los Angeles. "Hmm... What other interesting things about Seattle would draw visitors?" Leesa often found herself talking out loud to herself. "Obviously I'm looking for something other than the Space Needle."

When she got to the information about a Duwamish Indian chief named Chief Seattle, she imagined being a settler in the nineteenth century and invading the territory of Native Americans who had settled there some four thousand years earlier. Leesa decided life was much more adventurous back then. Fortunately, Chief Seattle maintained a good relationship with the European settlers, and even at times protected them from attacks of neighboring tribes.

When I think of Seattle, I think Starbuck's, or Tully's, or Seattle's Best Coffee. I don't think about Indians and settlements. I think of rain forests and islands, whales and seafood, and ferries and sea planes.

Leesa spoke aloud again. "Really? Over fifty percent of Seattle residents over twenty-five have undergraduate degrees? Well, educated people like museums. Maybe I should consider a museum on the island." She continued her research. If she invested in the cannery, she wanted to have a solid argument to support her decision.

As a child, Leesa loved to explore the islands around Seattle. She perked up when she got to the section about San Juan Island. She remembered the rocky shores and the sandy beaches. She remembered walking the pasturelands there and exploring the lakes and forests. *Friday Harbor mirrors part of my dream for the Kramer's Kanning Factory Island because it's laid back, small enough to walk around, and offers everything tourists like in a vacation town.*

It's not that hard to get to. San Juan Island's only a ninety-minute drive to catch a one-hour ferry ride, then visitors explore the island by taxis, shuttles, rental cars, mopeds, and bicycles. I think I could get a ferry to Kramer's in half an hour, and people wouldn't need taxis. I'd make golf carts and bicycles available for transportation because the island is really too small for cars. This would make Kramer's Island a cheaper and greener vacation destination for families.

Leesa dreamily pictured Kramer's Island with a bed and breakfast, a tiny museum, no fewer than two restaurants, a farmer's market, shops, galleries, and a performing arts center. Perhaps she could offer whale-watching tours for the Orca whales often seen offshore.

She remembered watching whales. *I always loved Puget Sound. The Eisner boys taught me a lot about how wildlife survives here.* She smiled when she remembered the caution signs warning to tread lightly and 'Leave Only Footprints.' *Nature lovers enjoy watching porpoises, sea lions, seals, river otters, and hundreds of different birds, including bald eagles. I resolve to make sure everything is done to protect wildlife.*

Leesa shut down her computer and prepared to go home. *Yes! San Juan Island is my picture of what the precious canning factory island could be. If I can't include a heavenly lavender alpaca farm on the island, maybe I could include a winery. The one on San Juan Island has a camel. I could think of something equally unique for my island.*

She took the elevator to the parking garage. Walking to her car, she remembered when she and Lyza had stayed at San Juan Island for a long weekend, years before—Leesa couldn't remember if it was five or ten. But the one thing she remembered about that particular trip was the resident of Friday Harbor they'd met. Dressed in biker leathers, the gray-bearded, pot-bellied fortyish man had parked his motorcycle next to their rented bicycles.

Leesa had hung back when Lyza'd approached the man. "Hi, can we take your picture? We want to get a picture of someone who lives on the island."

He'd grinned a toothless smile. "Well, sure, you can. I was born on this island, and I've lived here my entire life."

Leesa hadn't been able to imagine living on a small island. "Whatever did you do for fun? I mean, are there movies or malls?"

"The nearest is Seattle. We can take the ferry when we want to go."

"That seems like a lot of travel just to go shopping."

He'd laughed. "I'm not a shopper. I find plenty to do here just keeping my place up and working at the general store." He had stepped back and eyed the two of them. "It depends on your lifestyle."

Leesa smiled at the memory, and made note of the fact that in addition to San Juan Island, captivating to say the least, there were Orcas Island, Bainbridge Island, Harbor Island, Vancouver Island, Lopez Island, and more Seattle islands. The area was filled with potential.

The beauty of the Kramer Kanning Factory is that it's on a small private island, Kramer's Island. I hope Tim loves these ideas as much as I do. I'm confident this place will excite him and bring out his creativity.

Leesa's limo arrived at the airport early the next morning. She found Tim at the ticket counter.

She came up behind and tapped him on the shoulder from behind. "Good morning."

He turned about and smiled. "Hi, Leesa. Looks like a beautiful day to go see Seattle. I can't wait to see your canning factory!"

"You're gonna love it!" She laughed.

***

Lyza's long flight streaked through the skies toward Brisbane. During the flight, she couldn't sleep much and kept busy with her laptop. Then she couldn't resist and took time off to enjoy a *Star Wars* movie. The excitement of watching spaceships flying while she was in flight gave Lyza a thrill. She laughed out loud more than once. She chuckled to herself. *I can't believe 'sophisticated me' is watching* Star Wars. *Glad no one can see me now.*

As the flight came to an end, Lyza felt exhaustion drape over her. She wanted to sleep, but she knew better. *The longer I can stay awake during the day, the sooner I can overcome jet lag. Of course, I don't plan to be here that long anyway, so what difference does it make? I just want to get to the hotel soon.*

She followed fellow passengers to baggage claim, where she found the person waiting to meet her. The tanned blond Aussie wore a tan linen suit with a red tie for identification. He held a large "Welcome Lyza" sign. When he saw that she recognized him, he removed the tie.

He held out his hand. "I'm Clete Collins. Welcome to Australia, Miss Lane."

She shook his hand. "Thanks. It's a long flight."

They stood in silence until the red lights flashed on the conveyor belt indicating the luggage had arrived. He picked her bag off the carousel, and they headed toward ground transportation, where a black stretch limo waited. She had been sitting for hours, yet the soft leather seats felt good.

"I'm exhausted. Take me to the hotel," she directed.

Clete got right down to business. "You've got a reputation for hitting the ground running, but I thought you might want to get a bite of breakfast first, then go over the details for our excursion."

She leaned back in the seat and folded her arms. "Food I don't need. Right now, I want some good sleep."

He leaned back in the seat and folded his arms, copying her posture. "Yes, ma'am."

She looked at him as though she could throttle him. "What? Did you call me ma'am?"

He looked her direct in the eye. "I did."

Irritated, she glared. "Well, I want you to know I don't consider myself a '*ma'am*,' thank you very much. I'm not old enough for anyone to be calling me '*ma'am*.' Don't do it again." With that remark, she opened the fully stocked bar and poured herself a diet soda. *This conversation cooks me. After the long flight, I don't need a little company pipsqueak insulting me. Welcome to Australia, indeed. What was his name? I won't ask. All he needs to do is accuse me of short-term memory loss, and I might fire him.*

Twenty minutes later, the limo pulled up to the hotel, and the young man opened the limo door for her. The driver fetched her bags and passed them to the doorman. At the registration desk, she collected herself enough to sign in, pick up the correct key, and follow the bellhop to her suite. Within seconds after he left the bags, she flopped unceremoniously on the king-sized bed.

Wonder what Gary's doing? What do I care what he's doing? Her thoughts turned to the night of the benefit at the Malibu Club. *Mother did surprise everybody.* She smiled to herself. *Bingo. How did she it do it?*

Mentally, Lyza was back there, back at the Malibu Club on the night of the benefit. *Everything's so beautiful.* She'd reached out to touch a white orchid on the table next to her dinner plate.

She was standing in front of her home with Gary kissing her.

She drifted back to the present. *Gary hasn't called. He could have called yesterday. How many years have we been friends, and he doesn't have the guts to call after what happened Friday night?* Mostly she thought of the kiss. *We've gone places together for years as friends. Okay, I'm willing to admit that he is good looking. What is he up to? Well, whatever it is, I'm not interested. I'm not going to let a few hormones run my life.*

With that declaration, Lyza curled into a fetal position to sleep. *I don't think he meant anything by it, and I'm not going to be the one to ask about it. As of this second, it never happened. Well, it did happen, and it was exciting, but it wasn't real, and it isn't going to happen again. Where does Gary get off? He knows better. There's no room in my life for this silliness. I'm making a name for myself in the business. I refuse to end up like Mother, giving ridiculous benefits to keep herself occupied.*

As much as she loved her mother, Lyza never respected the way she spent her time. Lana dropped out of the business years ago, finding more satisfaction in doing things she could now afford to do. Socializing, shopping, planning the benefit, traveling, and doing a variety of hobbies kept her busy. Lyza could not imagine being connected to anything that didn't generate income. Her mind flitted from one subject to another.

She wanted to get another half hour of sleep, but her mind kept giving rise to thoughts of the past. How she won the college debate competition her senior year at Stanford, how she and Leesa vied for her father's attention as they grew up, how Cook came into their lives as the nanny. *Oh, if only my mind would shut off and let me sleep.*

But thoughts kept attacking her until it was nearly noon.

***

The limo waited outside the hotel when Lyza emerged from the lobby. Clete, the young man who had met her at the airport, jumped out and opened the door for her.

Lyza put on her business tone and best obvious fake smile. "Good afternoon, Clete."

"Yes, it is a good afternoon, and I have news for you. You may have made this journey for no reason." His voice picked up speed. "You see, this morning we received confirmation of a bid on the property you are here to inspect."

"Really." She drew the word out as long as she could. "What kind of offer? Did you bring documents?"

He handed her the folder. "Here they are. You see how the offer sounds reasonable, considering the state of disrepair the property is in."

She read the contents of the folder. The offer was from one Charles B. O'Malley. The one million AUD offer, with a three hundred fifty thousand AUD down payment offer, stipulated that he would accept the property as it was, with no liability for unreliable property fixtures. The seller would consider the offer a windfall because the property had been abandoned for the last ten years. And now, just out of the blue, an offer appeared. She had that gut feeling something wasn't right.

"Clete, I want to inspect the property anyway."

"But… Oh, yes, we can do that. I already arranged for the Hummer to meet us. I believe it's over two hours by helicopter. I held off canceling everything until we talked. The Hummer out of Moomba already left to meet us at the property. We have time to go to the office while I get everything confirmed."

Lyza started grumbling. She felt awful. "You can do that from here. Take me to breakfast... a... er... lunch. I need coffee."

"Yes, ma'am—oops, I mean, Miss Lane."

She put her palm to her forehead. *Ooo—ooo, I'd like to smack him.*

Three hours later, their helicopter landed on the small deserted airstrip in the middle of nowhere. They loaded into the waiting Hummer. The Hummer wasn't as agile as the Swiss Pinzgauer Clete played with when traversing rocky trails around Brisbane. But it was air-conditioned. Their ride ended sooner than they expected. They stopped to inspect some old buildings at the end of the airstrip.

Lyza and her team got out of the Hummer below a short rise that would reveal a view of the entire landscape. Trudging up the short hill in her heels, she attempted to look 'professional' for the underlings with her. They crested the hill and surveyed the rambling ranch house, the wranglers' quarters, and out-buildings.

Lyza looked down at the scene. "It looks like we can drive down here. See these tracks? Someone's been out here. We can follow them. Go get the Hummer."

The recent wide tire tracks looked like the tread of heavy equipment. "What's been going on down here?" she demanded of Clete.

"Nothing, as far as I know." He looked around, and he pointed toward what looked like an abandoned campsite, far to the west. "I think we'd better check this out."

The Hummer pulled up, and they piled in, directing the driver to the place where several types of tread came together. Lyza commanded, "Clete, call the LA office. Talk to Bill. I want to know who's been out here."

"It's ten thirty at night in LA. I doubt he'll be in."

Lyza answered flatly, "They'll find him."

Clete shook his head and dialed the Brisbane office. "Hi, this is Clete Collins. Lyza Lane would like you to patch this call through to the LA office."

Clete turned on the speaker so Lyza could hear, and in seconds, the operator in LA answered, "Lane Unlimited." Clete explained that Lyza wanted to speak to Bill. "One moment, please. I can contact him on his cell phone."

Lyza thought about it while she listened to the ring. Perhaps Bill had more information than had been forwarded to the Brisbane office this morning.

After five rings, a drowsy voice answered, "This is Bill."

"Sorry to disturb you, sir. This is Clete Collins from the Brisbane office. I'm here with Miss Lane at the cattle station site. We believe there may have been some activity going on around the property. Can you tell us anything about it?"

Bill sounded like he was still clearing the cobwebs from his head. "Uh… Just a minute. Let me wake up my computer and take a look at the file. Just a second… Here it is. No, there's no activity here. Let me see whether I can find any additional information elsewhere."

The Hummer arrived at an abandoned campsite. Clete glanced over another small rise where wide tire tracks converged. He opened his window and smelled oil. "Never mind, Bill. Sorry we bothered you."

Bill came back on the phone and apologetically reported, "Clete, there's just nothing here. No one has reported any activity out there for years. The only recent thing that's happened with this property is that there was a bid on it this morning for one million AUD as-is. That's all I've got."

Lyza frowned and folded her arms across her chest.

Clete's face looked as if he had solved the Rubiks cube. "I think we've figured it out. Miss Lane will get back to you later."

Lyza followed Clete's gaze out the window. "What's going on? What are you thinking?"

He got out of the Hummer, carefully watching his step. "Miss Lane, look at the ground. You don't want those expensive shoes walking in this."

What is he talking about? Lyza started to push herself out the car door.

Clete stopped her with a hand on her shoulder.

"What are you doing? I'm not going to let a little dirt keep me from finding out what's going on here."

He kept his hand on her shoulder. "Don't. It's not dirt."

"What is it?"

"It's crude oil."

"Crude oil?" she repeated incredulously. "You've got to be kidding. You're not serious."

He tried to unscramble her questions. "No—I mean, yes. No, I'm not kidding; and yes, I'm positively, one hundred percent serious. I'm standing in crude. And we're about to find the well. I'll bet they capped it until they could get the property legally in their name." He walked down the small rise and came back smiling. "I believe the price on this little piece of property just went up significantly!"

Lyza grabbed the file off the seat. "What fool tried to put one over on L. L. Lane Unlimited?" She was furious. The sun beat down on them and Lyza was getting hotter by the second, in spite of the air-conditioned Hummer.

Lyza bristled. "If I have my way, someone's going to pay for this, and it's going to be a whole lot more than the purchase price. No wonder they wanted the property with no inspection."

Clete observed from his laptop screen that, "A Charles O'Malley, out of Brisbane, made the offer."

"I think it's time we paid Mr. O'Malley a visit. As far as this property goes, I am taking my option to purchase the land and mineral rights. As of right now, L. L. Lane Unlimited will purchase the land for the asking price. When we get back to the office, I want to sign the papers. They are to be dated last week. You got that, Clete?"

"Yes, ma'am."

She glared at him. The Hummer turned and ambled back to the helicopter. Lyza was so angry she couldn't wait to get to the office. *What kind of doublecross did this O'Malley think he could pull?*

She pulled up her computer screen and Googled, "Charles O'Malley, Brisbane, Australia." She couldn't believe what popped up. "Charles B. O'Malley, Information Technology, IBM." *Are you kidding me? A crooked IBM employee… Who does he think he is? This could be more fun than Germany.* Lyza thought of a hundred ways to punish the man she had yet to meet.

She got on the phone to Bill, unconcerned about the time change. "Bill, do you have anything else on this O'Malley guy? He's in deep trouble and I want to be sure I have all the facts before I confront him."

Bill sounded sleepy and reacted slowly.

"Lyza, that's all we've got. What's going on there? I just now got word that L. L. Lane Unlimited purchased the property outright. Is that true?"

Poor Bill sounds confused. "It is." Lyza hung up.

She was still exhausted from her overseas flight, but the added adrenaline from what had happened that day had fired her up. The occupants of the helicopter rode in silence the rest of the way to the office, each of them dealing with their own thoughts. Lyza's mind clicked away as she formulated her plan for meeting with Mr. Charles O'Malley.

When they arrived at L. L. Lane Unlimited Brisbane headquarters, Lyza ordered the secretary to contact Mr. O'Malley. She instructed the secretary to pretend it was in response to his offer on the property.

Chapter Fourteen

Chuck called George just to hear a friendly voice before he returned the real estate company's call. He had listened to the brief message three times already. He wanted to fill George in, although come to think of it, it wasn't any of his business. The land would be Chuck's and Chuck's alone. *It's all mine.*

"George, I just wanted to thank you for getting the crew together and getting me a good price on the drilling operation."

"Sure. Have you told anyone about it yet?"

Chuck dreamed up another lie, vaguely aware that it was getting easier to devise something at a moment's notice. "No, I'm going to savor the good taste of success on my own for a while."

"Man, I don't understand it, but it's your deal."

Chuck knew George was interested. But George had gotten into the situation by accident, and George wasn't driven by greed. The man only wanted a case of beer for his finder's fee. Chuck was amazed that George had not even considered that he would benefit from the deal in any monetary way. He was glad just to get some of his buddies a few days of paid work.

Chuck conjured up an amused laugh. "I also need some time to decide who is going to get my business."

"I have some names."

"Great. Why don't I get those tonight? See you at the pub."

Chuck's line beeped as he was hanging up, indicating an incoming call. He glanced at the caller identification and saw L. L. Lane Unlimited. He smugly smiled. *Eager?* "Hello, this is Chuck."

"Hello, Chuck, this is Daniel Grey from L. L. Lane Unlimited."

"Yes, I got your message. I was about to call you."

Daniel read from the notes on the yellow pad in front of him. "I called to let you know we received your offer on the property. I wanted to confirm that it's the property about two hundred miles east of Moomba, located in Queensland. Is that right?"

He leaned back in his chair. "That's right."

Again, Daniel referred to the notes in front of him. "That property is being sold as a small cattle station of six thousand acres."

Chuck had done the research. "Correct."

"Mr. O'Malley, you should be aware that the property has been unused and abandoned for many years."

"Oh, yes. I am aware of the situation. That's the reason I made the offer that I did."

"One million AUD."

He held his breath for a moment. *Are they going to reject my offer?* He maintained his tone. "That's right."

"Mr. O'Malley, we have stipulations. If you cannot accept these conditions, we will not be able to sell the property to you."

"Well, I will do my best. What do you want? Is it more money?"

"No, it is not additional money."

Inwardly, Chuck breathed a sigh of relief.

Daniel continued, "Because this property has been vacant many years, and because of its remote location, we would like to seal the deal with cash."

Chuck panicked. "You mean I have to come up with a million AUD cash?"

"No, we are asking that you bring the down payment of three hundred fifty thousand AUD in cash to our office. As I said before, this is an unusual stipulation. However, there is one other condition."

"I guess I could bring it. What is the other condition?"

Daniel straightened. "The other condition—and this is major to us—is that the closing be held in our offices here in Brisbane at two in the afternoon tomorrow."

"Tomorrow?"

Daniel looked up at Lyza standing next to him. She nodded to him and he continued. "That's right, Mr. O'Malley. Those are our only stipulations."

Bring cash? How strange. That place must be a real loser. "Two o'clock tomorrow doesn't give me much time." His heart was already racing. *It's all mine.*

***

L. L. Lane Unlimited's private jet touched down at Tel Aviv's Ben Gurion International Airport at four o'clock in the afternoon local time. Armed soldiers in a desert camouflage jeep accompanied the black limousine on the tarmac.

The limousine driver opened the door as Lana descended the few steps from the jet with Lawrence behind her. "Welcome to HaEretz. I am Aaron; I will take you to the King David Hotel in Jerusalem. Your friends, the Levis, will meet you at the hotel."

Lawrence knew enough Hebrew to thank the man in his native language. "*Toda raba.*"

They spent the next forty minutes looking this way and that, trying to watch the scenery on their ride to Jerusalem. Heavy traffic made it difficult to believe they were finally in Israel. Gridlock meant horns honking and drivers motioning to one another like every one of them were directing traffic. None of them looked angry or prone to road rage, but merely like they were trying to figure out how to get where they were going.

Israel. Lana couldn't help thinking of her parents. *How they would have loved to be here. This is the land of their forefathers; the land of my forefathers. The land of Abraham, Isaac, and Jacob, received from God as an inheritance. I already feel the hand of God on me.* Her eyes filled with tears.

She looked over at Lawrence opening his briefcase.

"First thing in the morning, we should go to Yad Vashem. That'll probably take most of the day. Then we'll dine with the Levis. They want us to come to Karmiel, but that'll be impossible this trip. The day after that, you have to yourself, for sightseeing. I'll be in meetings most of the day. Our last day will be in Tel Aviv. I have a short meeting there. Then we can return to our happy home in the good old USA."

Lana looked out the window. She dabbed her eyes, not wanting him to see her disappointment. *What's this trip really about? When he said three days, I thought he meant three days of taking in the Land together.* She kept looking out her window.

They came in sight of the ancient walls of Jerusalem's Old City. Both Lana and Lawrence looked at the majestic ancient walls with wonder. The walls represented Jewish suffering in ancient times as well as the present age. Within minutes, they pulled up in front of the hotel on King David Street. The pink quartz exterior blended with the surrounding buildings. Once inside, the Lanes delighted at the 1920s motif in the foyer and adjacent public rooms. They checked in and took the elevator to the sixth floor Royal Suite. Their modern suite offered every convenience.

Lana took a nap while Lawrence made phone calls in the sitting room. She awoke at four o'clock in the morning, Jerusalem time. She was wide awake. Outside, a noise sounded like a siren. The siren stopped. Then strange chanting came from loudspeakers throughout the city. Lawrence slept peacefully across from her in the king-sized bed. She waited, and the noise stopped in a few minutes. *Sounds like the Muslim call to prayer.* She went into the sitting room, turned on the lights, curled up in an overstuffed chair, and read a hotel magazine about the attractions in Jerusalem.

An hour and half later, Lawrence came into the room. Lana had begun reading a novel she'd brought, and his appearance surprised her. "I thought you were asleep, my love."

"I've been awake for at least an hour, trying to fall back asleep. It's not too early for breakfast." He picked up the phone and called room service.

They feasted on a classic Israeli breakfast created from fresh, local vegetables. They had Israeli salad, scrambled eggs, white soft cheese, and fresh bread.

Soon it was time to leave for Yad Vashem. Lana felt dread wash over her as they made their way to the waiting limousine.

I can do this, Lana thought, then decided to make small talk. "It looks like a lovely day."

Lawrence looked at the bright-blue sky and smiled. "It does, indeed."

The ride to the Yad Vashem museum took half an hour and people-watching was as interesting as their arrival in Jerusalem yesterday. Their destination was *Har HaZikaron,* a ridge on the western outskirts of Jerusalem. They would visit several commemorative monuments, a historical museum, a central archive, and a research center for the documentation of the Holocaust.

The streets were already jammed. Drivers paid no attention to traffic lanes. Although drivers did pay attention to traffic signals, everything else was unstructured.

Lana noticed drivers stopped near them. "All this traffic and I see no sign of road rage or impatience. Everyone seems set on helping each other so everyone can get where they need to go."

"Well, take a look around you, darling. Armed soldiers stand on every corner."

"Yes, I am aware of the presence of soldiers. Everywhere I look, I see soldiers carrying rifles. Look at all the women soldiers."

Their limousine pulled up to the entrance of a cold-looking concrete building. Inside, they checked in and went through security. Lawrence picked up a brochure and Lana read over his shoulder about Yad Vashem, the national Authority for the Remembrance of the Martyrs and Heroes of the Holocaust, established in 1953 by act of the Knesset to commemorate six million Jewish men, women, and children murdered by the Nazis and their collaborators during the years 1933–1945.

Lawrence folded the brochures. "This place is here to make sure no one ever forgets. Future generations must learn from this tragedy. Otherwise it was…" He choked.

Outside the entry building, they made their way down a tree-lined walk to the Hall of Remembrance. Lana noticed the trees planted to honor non-Jewish men and women who, at the risk of their own lives, attempted to rescue Jews from the Holocaust. More than twenty thousand received honor with the title "Righteous Among the Nations."

Lana put her hand to her mouth. "Non-Jews took us out of Germany and saved our lives."

Lana grasped Lawrence's hand as they entered the severe concrete-walled structure with a low tent-like roof. The empty room surrounded an eternal flame. Engraved in the black basalt floor, she looked at the names of twenty-one Nazi extermination camps, concentration camps, and killing sites in Central and Eastern Europe. The crypt in front of the memorial flame contained ashes of victims. They had been inside Yad Vashem fewer than twenty minutes, and Lana wanted to leave. She took a deep breath. Tears rolled down her cheeks.

Lawrence looked up from the lists of camps and killing sites grimly. "Let's move on."

They walked a short distance to the Holocaust History Museum. Mostly underground, the museum presented the truth of the Holocaust from a Jewish perspective, emphasizing the experiences of the individual victims through original artifacts, survivor testimonies, and personal possessions. Each exhibit appeared more shocking than the previous one. Lana tried to relax by breathing deeply and focusing on gaining information to block her emotions.

Watching old film footage showing Nazi soldiers yelling at Jewish men and women, as they herded them onto cattle cars, broke Lana's heart. Lawrence cringed when he heard Nazi soldiers yelling, "Christ-killers! You are going to pay for what you did to Christ."

"How could they believe that, Lawrence? That happened almost two thousand years earlier."

"They believed anything Hitler told them."

They spent well over two hours in the building that cut through the mountain like a spike, its uppermost edge–a skylight–protruding through the mountain ridge, affording a view of the valley below. Galleries on either side provided original footage of Jewish families dancing and celebrating Jewish holidays. They watched as the footage switched to pictures of men and women being forced to board railroad cars. Children were torn from their parents, and Lana's heart wrenched. She attempted to hold memories at bay.

Next, they viewed videos of the anti-Semitic propaganda preached across Europe by the Christian Church. The worst of them was of Christians turning in their Jewish friends in order to protect themselves.

Lawrence's jaw set. Lana's eyes welled up.

At the last exhibit, the Hall of Names, Lawrence viewed the Pages of Testimony of millions of victims. "It says here that the 'Yad Vashem Archive collection is the largest and most comprehensive on the Holocaust in the world. It includes fifty-five million pages of documents, nearly one hundred thousand photographs, film footage, and the videotaped testimonies of survivors.' This is simply overwhelming."

Lana remembered something she'd been told by her foster parents. "Lawrence."

He turned to look at her with his red eyes. "Yes, darling. What is it?"

"Do you remember what Eisenhower said when Auschwitz was liberated?"

"How could I forget? He told his men and the press to take all the pictures they could and make all the films they could, because some day in the future people would say this never happened."

"He was right. Already some people say this didn't happen."

He put his arm around her. "It's too horrible for a normal person to understand. It's too much for the human mind to take in. No wonder they want to deny it."

She looked ahead. "The next exhibit displays the original architectural blueprints of Auschwitz-Birkenau and original plans for the structures of the concentration camps that were prepared in the fall of 1941. Oh, Lawrence, that's where our parents died."

"Look, they haven't had these long. The plans were found in 2008 in an abandoned apartment building in Berlin. Then they were sold to a German media corporation Axel Springer, publisher of the newspaper *Bild*. This man gave them to Netanyahu in August of 2009."

Lana's attitude had turned around by now. She wanted to know more. "We have three memorials yet, and it's getting late."

Lawrence picked up his pace and strode to the Valley of the Communities monument. He started reading aloud the engraved inscription. The names of over five thousand Jewish communities that were destroyed made it impossible to read all of them. He stopped reading and ran his finger down the list looking for the name of the village he came from. He also kept his eye out for the name of the small community where Lana had been born.

He frowned. "Everything's looking the same. All the names are beginning to look familiar."

"I can't look." She stepped away and moved on to the Memorial to the Deportees, an original cattle car used to transport thousands of Jews to the death camps. She noticed it was perched on the edge of an abyss facing the Jerusalem forest.

She pointed to the valley below. "Lawrence, see how this car is about to fall into the abyss? It's supposed to symbolize the impending horror, and the rebirth that followed the Holocaust."

Sadly, he replied, "I don't see the rebirth. Our parents are gone. They didn't get a chance to see rebirth. Besides, Jews are still targeted and murdered everywhere, even in Israel, even in Jerusalem. As in the days of Esther and Haman, Gentiles still covet our property and our land. ”

On their way out of the memorials, they passed the Children's Memorial.

Lana peeked into the cave filled with flickering candles. "Nearly one and a half million Jewish children died in the Holocaust. These tiny lights represent the light of children in the prevailing darkness."

They left the museum and rode back to the King David Hotel in silence.

***

The meeting was set for two in the afternoon. Lyza wanted to catch the next flight out. Fifteen minutes for the meeting would leave her enough time to go back to the hotel and pack.

Ten minutes early, the secretary buzzed Lyza's borrowed office. "Mr. O'Malley is here for his appointment."

Lyza rested her five and three quarter-inch platform pumps on top of the bare cherrywood desk. "You can tell him I'll be with him in a few moments."

He could wait. She flipped through the paperwork again. Her temper flared again, and she resisted the temptation to go out in the foyer and kick him where she knew it would hurt.

She took a deep breath and walked out to the foyer. "Mr. O'Malley, I'm Lyza Lane." She sweetly extended her hand, which he shook. "Please follow me to my office."

They shook hands. "Of course, Miss Lane."

He doesn't look like a crook. I suppose most crooks don't. Maybe they are all good-looking; otherwise they couldn't get away with doing crooked things. He has kind eyes. Eyes, she noticed, filled with expectation. Upon reaching the office she offered him a seat and coffee, tea, or water.

"No, thanks, I'm fine."

"If you don't mind, Mr. O'Malley—"

"Please call me Chuck."

She spoke in her sweetest tones. "All right, then, Chuck. Please bear with us, as we, according to law, must have a witness to what transpires here today." She was setting him up and enjoying every second of it.

She pushed the intercom button. "Clete, could you come in here for the O'Malley transaction?"

Clete entered the room and took a seat next to Chuck. Lyza nodded in Chuck's direction. "Clete, this is Chuck O'Malley." The men shook hands.

"Now, Mr. O'Malley, I believe it's time we got down to business." Lyza's original script fell away, completely forgotten. She operated on gut level, something she never did. Her mantra rang in her ears: *Have a plan, and stick to it.* Staying cool took most of her concentration.

He was too eager. "Yes. I'm ready to do that."

"You were told to bring cash, right?"

Clete's eyebrows shot up at the mention of a cash transaction.

She looked Chuck straight in the eyes. He nodded toward the black briefcase sitting on the floor next to him. "Yes, I was. I felt that it was somewhat out of the ordinary, but it's all here."

She smiled. "Let's take a look at it." *Now the fun begins.*

Chuck placed the shiny black briefcase on the spacious desk. They stood as Chuck clicked open the locks. Slowly he opened the briefcase, revealing stacks of banded cash. "Here it is. Three hundred fifty thousand AUD in cash. That's the most cash I've ever seen."

"I want you to take a good look at this cash, Chuck." She moved the briefcase to the top of the credenza behind the desk. "I want you to say good-bye to this cash. You will never see it again."

She closed the briefcase and turned to face them.

Clete's mouth dropped open.

Keeping up his pretense for purchasing the property, he responded, "Oh, it's worth it. I love the place, and it doesn't hurt one bit to spend my life's savings on it."

Lyza's expression turned cold. "Well, Chuck, that's not exactly what's going to happen today."

A slight frown crossed Chuck's brow. "I thought we were here to close the deal."

"We are going to close a deal. It's going to cost you three hundred fifty thousand AUD, but you aren't getting the property." There, she said it. Now all that was left was the explanation.

"What's going on here?" Chuck looked toward the closed briefcase.

"What's going on here," Lyza began calmly, slowly, and distinctly, "is a little justice."

"What do you mean?" Chuck was on his feet.

"It's like this, Chuck: You don't drill for oil on property you don't own without permission and written authorization. It's illegal. What would happen if we didn't have such laws?"

She started speaking in a high-pitched, sing-song voice. "People would go out and drill for oil anywhere they wanted to. People would have no respect for other people's possessions and property. That's not civilized, now, is it?" Her fists rested on her hips.

"So you know." Chuck dropped his head. "Could you tell the property owner I can up my offer somewhat? It's obvious they don't care about the property."

"You don't care about the property either, Mr. O'Malley. All you wanted was to get your hands on that oil. And for your information, the owner cares about that property. The owner is L. L. Lane Unlimited, thank you very much."

"What are you going to do?"

"We could press charges. People are going to prison these days for lesser crimes. White-collar crimes are being rigorously persecuted because of recent security scams. I'm thinking you would get at minimum ten years, at maximum perhaps twenty-five years. So, here's my proposal to you."

She walked to the front of the desk and leaned back against it. "For thirty-five thousand AUD a year, because right now I'm thinking your approximate minimum sentence is ten years, you can stay out of prison. What d'ya think? That's cheap, considering the difference between what you earn compared to what a prisoner earns." Her confidence level was off the scale.

The color drained from his face. "I think you're screwing me over." He pointed at the briefcase. "I told you this is all the money I have to my name."

"Well, Mr. O'Malley, I guess you'd better get an extra job." She walked to the back of the desk again. "You're not a very good crook. We're done here." O'Malley looked white, the same color as Clete's face. Lyza turned, picked up the cash, and walked out of the office.

Lyza left the building. Her limousine made one stop on the way to the hotel: St. George's Bank.

Chapter Fifteen

Chuck O'Malley stood motionless for a full minute. He slowly turned toward Clete. "I don't know what I'm going to do. I don't know what to do. An attorney will do me no good. I can't fight L. L. Lane Unlimited. I'm finished."

Clete paused, then he muttered, "I guess you should have thought of that before you tried to defraud us."

They walked to the exit together. Chuck pressed the elevator button. Clete made his way to his own office.

Chuck rode the elevator to the first floor entrance. Still in a daze, he tried to take in what had just happened. *What a horrible woman. She set me up, and all the time it looked like she was enjoying it. She was enjoying it. She took it all, all the money I have, and I can't do a thing about it. She loved every minute of it. What just happened?* He wondered who told her about the oil well. *How did she find out about the oil well?* He stumbled out of the Lane Building onto the pavement into the glaring sunlight, trying to get a grip. Blinking, he leaned against the building. *I need to sit down. I need to be alone—No. I need someone to talk with. I need to be alone.* He noticed his hand shaking. He pulled out his cell phone and called George.

"Hello, this is George."

"George, this is Chuck. Meet me at—"

The recording on the answering service cut him off. "I'm not available to take your call right now. Please leave a message and I will return your call."

Frustrated, Chuck yelled into his phone. "George, this is Chuck. Meet me at the Watering Hole Tavern. We need to talk."

Chuck found his car and drove to their meeting place, the Watering Hole Tavern. He ordered a beer and sat alone, waiting for George's arrival.

Four beers later, he punched redial. His voice slurred. "George, this is Chuck. We need to talk. I lied to you. I didn't own the property, and when I went to buy it, they doublecrossed me. They knew all about it. I'm at the Watering Hole. Please call me."

Two hours and fourteen calls later, Chuck realized George was not going to show. He ordered another beer. He just knew George got his messages, each message deteriorating exponentially with the amount of beer ingested. Chuck felt deserted. *Well, what could I expect? I lied to him.*

I lied to him to protect him. If he knew we drilled illegally, he could've been in a world of trouble. Yeah. Like I'm in now. I did him a favor.

He really didn't know George all that well, but he was disappointed. He wanted someone to talk to and admitted for the tenth time that night that George was his only friend.

He didn't know what time it was, but Chuck could see out the front door that it was dark. He wasn't going to call anybody. *I don't have any friends. George, you let me down like everyone else I've ever known. I'll go home and dig out that bottle of Jack Daniels under the sink. Jack's a great listener.*

Once under the street light in front of the Tavern, he fumbled for car keys and searched the area for his parked car. It was across the alley. He staggered along the storefronts until he reached the darkened alley crossing.

Chuck heard his nose crack. A hooded figure shoved him into the alley. Chuck stumbled, dazed, before adrenaline pumped life into him. He threw his fists into the dark, getting only air.

Then the pounding began with a blow to his midsection. It knocked the wind out of him. Too shocked to react, he grabbed his stomach. He counted two, maybe three young hoodlums taking turns slugging him over and over. Sticky liquid impaired his vision.

He blinked away the blood running down his face in time to see another fist come at his jaw. He curled into a ball and hit the ground. The last thing he saw were two large gold crosses hanging from one thug's neck, as he leaned over to take Chuck's wallet and spit on him. One of the others gave him a sharp kick in the kidneys, and everything went black.

Three days after the mugging, Chuck O'Malley opened his eyes to unfamiliar commercial grade white ceilings. The pain was excruciating. He tried moving his head to survey his surroundings. His neck shot a message to the brain not to move.

He groaned and closed his eyes again. "Oooh." He waited. He wanted to go back to sleep. After what seemed like hours, a voice startled him.

"Mr. O'Malley?" The young woman dressed in a white uniform looked down at him while changing the drip hanging above him. "Mr. O'Malley, are you awake? It's all right. You're in the hospital. You're going to be all right. Now breathe deeply."

O'Malley complied.

"That's good, breathe again. Take some deep breaths. Relax. You had some surgery, and you're going to be just fine. Are you in pain?"

He grunted.

She smiled and looked at him with compassion. "I can give you something for that. Here." She punched the syringe needle into the tube from his hand. "Now you rest. The doctor will see you when he makes his rounds this afternoon." She closed the door and walked out.

Chuck stared at the ceiling and drifted into a deep sleep. His dream seemed all too familiar. It was dark. An ornate gold cross swung back and forth in front of his eyes. For a second he thought he was seeing double, but yes, there were two crosses. *God help me!* He screamed. The crosses swung back and forth, and with each swing, he felt pain erupt within him. *Oh, God, help—help me!*

Paralyzed by fear, Chuck woke up yelling. "God help me!'

The nurse heard him. "Mr. O'Malley, wake up. You've been dreaming. Are you all right? Can I get you a drink? Here, have some ice chips." The bright light made him squint. She held a Styrofoam cup to his lips.

"Oooh," he groaned and blacked out.

That afternoon, Chuck wakened at the sound of footsteps striding into the room. Two police officers approached his bed.

The tall burly one spoke first. "Mr. O'Malley, we're from the Brisbane police department and we need to ask you some questions."

The short thin one leaned down. "Can you answer some questions?"

The words tumbled out slowly. "Uh… Okay, I guess."

The short officer continued. "You were found in the alley behind the Watering Hole Tavern. Somebody beat you up pretty badly. Do you remember anything about what happened? Can you tell us anything at all?"

Chuck wanted them to go away. He wanted to sleep. "They jumped me and dragged me into the alley. I didn't see their faces."

The taller one pushed for more information. "You said *they*. How many were there?"

"I don't know, two, maybe three. It was dark, and it happened so fast."

The nurse came in to check his vitals. "Gentlemen, I told you he couldn't talk to you. He hasn't even seen his doctor. Now please come back tomorrow." She held the door open. Not speaking, they filed out.

Doctor Washington arrived shortly thereafter, reporting that O'Malley had sustained life-threatening injuries. Two cracked ribs, a ruptured spleen, and a broken nose topped the injury list, not to mention numerous cuts and bruises.

"We operated as soon as you came to emergency. Luckily, our team just finished a previous surgery, and everyone was still here. It was either go in then, or risk fatal internal bleeding. You lost a lot of blood. We gave you two transfusions. You're going to be all right, but you'll be here awhile."

The doctor lifted O'Malley's open eyelid to use his scope. "In six to eight weeks, you should be as good as new. Internal stitches heal beautifully, but you can't do anything strenuous. Is there anyone we should contact?"

O'Malley thought for a moment. *Work! Oh, no.* "How long have I been here?"

"It's been three days. You had no identification on you. The bartender at the Watering Hole pointed out your car. That's how we identified you. Whoever did this simply wanted your money."

"I need to call my boss…"

***

Leesa smiled brightly. "I never promised you the weather would be good in Seattle. At least the rain feels like a fine mist instead of the torrents we get in LA."

Tim agreed. "Yes, rain in LA is different. This seems pleasant."

Leesa liked the feeling of comfort she had with him. "The only time we ever get together is when I call you to be an escort for something like the benefit last week. What's that about?" *Okay, so I'm being assertive.*

"You're always so busy. You can't blame me for that. I used to call you all the time, but I have to admit I finally gave up."

She laughed too hard. "That doesn't sound like the Tim Young I know. But I accept the excuse."

They caught the Four Seasons shuttle bus that delivered them to the front entrance of the hotel, where they checked in. Tim held up his key card. "I'm on the fourth floor. Where are you? Oh, never mind. I'm sure you're in the penthouse."

"The Royal Suite. Meet me in the coffee shop in about thirty minutes. We can go over today's schedule."

He pushed the elevator button. "Sure, see you then."

Leesa finished checking in and made her way to the penthouse. When she got to the Royal Suite, she dumped her bag on the bed, made a couple of phone calls, freshened up, and went to meet Tim.

She scooted in next to him in the small booth, just inside the coffee shop. "I have a surprise."

Leesa bumped his arm, and he balanced his sloshing cup of coffee before it spilled. "You are full of them. What's the plan?"

She laughed. "Don't order anything. We're going to the pier."

Tim took a drink of his coffee. "I figured we'd get there sometime today because we're going to an island."

Leesa took the cup out of Tim's hand and set it down. "You know Gil Bates?"

Tim reached for the cup. "Of course."

Leesa scooted the cup further from him. "Gil was on the phone with Father as I was telling him we were coming to Seattle. He offered his yacht and crew for the exploration of Kramer's Island."

In fewer than twenty minutes, they walked up the gangplank of the *Winsome*, Bates' eighty-five-foot luxury yacht.

The captain welcomed them aboard. "Greetings."

In unison, they returned, "Greetings."

"Make yourselves comfortable," the captain ordered. "If you need anything, the steward will be around soon to serve you. It's about half an hour to Kramer's Island. Enjoy the ride."

He tipped his captain's cap and disappeared. Soon they were in the middle of the bay heading for Kramer's Island, one of the small islands off the coast of Washington.

Tim lay back in the lounge chair and gazed at the clear blue sky. The mist had given way to a lovely day.

The sun feels good. Leesa took off her cashmere jacket. She leaned back and closed her eyes. After thirty minutes, they docked at Kramer's Island.

Leesa shouted into the wind and pointed at a tall dilapidated building, surrounded by a few smaller ones in similar condition. "This is it!"

They walked on weather-beaten docks and strolled into the rundown, tiny gathering of buildings.

Tim stuck his hands in his pockets and looked around. He shrugged as he listened to Leesa's dream.

Leesa began describing her vision for the island in excited tones. She waved her hands all over while explaining. "This little area could be renovated or reproduced to look new and upscale. I picture little shops here and there—curios, cafès, ice cream shops, and chocolate factories all along the walk to Kramer's Kannery. Can you envision sort of a theme park with the cannery at the center?"

Ragged trees and brush lined the dirt road they walked on. When they reached the cannery, Tim frowned. "Slow down, Leesa; give me some time. To tell you the truth, this is much worse than I imagined."

"Here's the main cannery building."

Tim's gaze traveled from the peeling paint at the foot of the building to the warped metal peak, perhaps forty feet above them. All he said was, "It's tall."

Panic flashed across her face, replaced instantly by a look of resolve. "I know it needs work, but it has real potential. Families could come have fun here. There are so many possibilities. I'm so excited about this and I need your input."

Tim paused. "Let me have a look, girl. I know you're excited, but don't rush me. Don't get mad at me, but this place looks like a dump, and it smells like dead fish." He wrinkled his nose.

Leesa giggled. "Of course it smells like dead fish. That's what they do at canneries. Have an open mind. Let's consider the impossible; that's how great things are accomplished."

Tim followed her to the front door of the cannery. "Oh, now I'm going to get a lesson in philosophy."

Leesa pushed it open, and the rusty door blew a hinge and fell, diagonally blocking her entrance.

"Oops!" She laughed. "This could be dangerous."

Tim stepped back. "Dangerous is putting it lightly. Like I said, this place is a dump. Do you think we should go in there?"

Leesa couldn't stop smiling. "Oh, man up, Tim. Help me get this thing out of the way."

Tim pulled the door out of its other hinges and laid it against the rusted siding. They stuck their heads in the dark building. Sunlight, peeking through cracks in the tin siding, revealed a spacious building with little inside. The building was at least three stories high, but only a ground floor and a ceiling towered over them. In the center of the room there was a weird contraption, probably some kind of canning machine, standing rusted and useless.

Leesa's eyes shone brightly, her excitement overflowed. "Isn't it huge?"

Tim surveyed the scene before him and asked slowly, "What do you see here?"

"Oh, Tim, it's nothing like what we're standing in now. What I need to know is if it's physically possible."

"All right, tell me what you see."

"I see this building as the center of something like a theme park, a cheerful village that would be a fun place to shop and eat. A little passenger train could circle the island. But this building we are standing would be the principal attraction. I picture a red-tiled roof with red-painted tin siding, with bright yellow signage. The ground floor would have the cannery—but no actual canning would be done here. It would just look like it, and they could offer canned smoked salmon for sale. The attached shed outside could be the place for the little café that served the catch of the day or whatever."

"Leesa, do you have any idea what a project like this would cost?"

"I know, I know, but what I really want to know right now is—is it possible? Because if you say it's possible, there is much more in my vision."

Tim looked at the floor, then up at the ceiling. He put his hands in his pockets. "Leesa, you know how it is. Yes, it is possible, but is it worth it versus the cost? Would it pay off?"

He made a three-sixty turn, spreading his hands out. "Did you happen to notice how many people are currently visiting this island? Us."

Leesa sounded desperate. "Tim, listen to me. The second floor would attract families with children. It would have arcades and a theater with puppet shows and gentle clowns. The top floor would be an observation deck where people could come and watch whales and ships and ferries go by. And one more big thing, Tim; I want a dock with an old-fashioned steamboat for families to ride and dine with entertainment."

Tim rolled his eyes. "Is that all?"

Leesa ignored his tone and angled her head toward him. "No, it's not all, but those are the important thoughts. You think I'm crazy, right?"

He laughed. "Well, I think you're crazy, but I'm not sure that has anything to do with what's going on here." He shrugged. "Let me think about this. I need to put it to pencil and paper and make some drawings and notes while we're here. You can get me blueprints when we get back, right?"

She pulled a white cylinder from her backpack. "Here they are."

He shook his head and took the blueprints. "Always prepared, aren't you?"

"Well, I thought if I could get you to listen to me, I should at least have the tools you might need. Oh, there's one other thing I thought would be fun."

He pulled a small notepad from his inside coat pocket. "Slow down. I won't be able to remember all this."

"Let's go outside in the sun."

She kept talking as they walked back across the threshold. "I want an outdoor center stage for live performances on summer weekends. Then a little Ferris wheel and carousel for the children and a dress-up room for taking pictures."

"Hold it. Let's slow down. Stop talking so I can start writing. I won't be able to remember all of this."

"Only one thing more: a zoo." She saw his look of impatience. "Okay, okay, I'll stop. We'll talk about lodging later."

The wind turned cold. "Is there more I need to see now?"

"I think you've seen enough. I've shocked you. It's cold. Let's get back to the yacht."

He noted the setting sun, grabbed her hand, and they hurried toward the yacht. "It's getting dark. I don't want you to stumble."

Once aboard, Leesa went to freshen up. Then she met Tim on the deck where the steward was serving hors d'oeuvres with white wine. The yacht sliced the dark water, and the moon came from behind a cloud. The wine, the ocean, the quiet, and the release she felt from sharing her dream all calmed her. The cruise seemed to relax Tim, too. The steward served a tasty salad, fresh-grilled fish with baby red potatoes, and steamed asparagus.

Leesa teased Tim, "Am I going to have to explain a billion-dollar project to my father?"

He laughed. "The first billion will be for the Kramer's Island project. The second billion will be my fee. I'm sure he'll understand."

The yacht docked. They leisurely finished dinner, then packed to board their waiting ride.

They returned to the hotel about ten o'clock. As they walked through the hotel lobby, Tim nudged Leesa. "I hear music; want to go to the bar?"

"Sure, let's see what's going on." The band pounded out a tune as the lead singer sang old rock songs. Soon Tim and Leesa were playing music trivia by trying to guess the original artists.

Tim grinned. "That's Bob Seger's 'Old Time Rock and Roll,' one of my favorites. Let's dance."

He held out his hand, and they started dancing the night away.

They stayed on the dance floor until the end. The last song of the night was a slow dance to Roy Orbison's "Only the Lonely." They had been on the dance floor since they came in. The slow dance was a welcome change of pace.

As the song ended, Tim gave her a long hug. They walked back to their table and collected their things and rode the elevator up to the penthouse, where Leesa got off. Tim said good night, and the elevator doors closed behind her.

Chapter Sixteen

The next morning, Leesa and Tim flew back to the LAX airport where the L. L. Lane Unlimited limo picked them up and took Tim to his condo.

After letting him off, Leesa chose to go home for the day. Excited about the prospect of creating a world of fun and escape for certain privileged people who would visit Kramer's Island, she began to plan her presentation to Father. *I think Father will be surprised at my plans for Kramer's Island. Lyza's not the only one who can make creative deals. I know I can get the price down. It certainly isn't the turnkey-ready factory the listing claimed.*

After the deal Lyza closes in Germany, I should be able to dig deeper. I can instigate projects, too. I don't always have to react; I can lead. What is the matter with Tim? He can't see my vision? Maybe not, but that doesn't mean he won't work with me. I can convince him.

In retrospect, she realized that the more she talked, the more she saw Tim's opinion changing. The more she thought about Kramer's Island, the more things she wanted to add. *This little island is my baby, and I have the authority to purchase it for Lane Unlimited if I believe it's a profitable project. I think it is, but I should lean on the side of prudence before making the purchase. Tim will give me some solid numbers soon. I'll sit tight for the moment.*

Leesa dressed for bed, wanting to sleep. Just a short nap would revive her for the rest of the day. She thought sleep wouldn't be easy because of her vivid imagination, but she fell asleep immediately.

She dreamed of being in Kramer's Kannery, enjoying the view from the observation deck, watching the whales and the sailing regatta. She could hear children laughing at the puppet show, hear the ringing bells of the arcade, and smell the cotton candy and popcorn. She could see herself walking through the zoo, looking at exotic animals. She drifted through curio shops, cafés, ice cream shops, and the chocolate factory. She took a ride around the small island on the smallest, cutest steam engine in the world.

Finally, in her dream, she walked the dock behind Kramer's Kannery and boarded the Kramer's Island Steamboat. The huge paddle wheel started turning. The red, white, and blue banners on the railings rippled with a slight breeze. She stepped up to the top deck and looked back at Kramer's Island. The bright colors made her smile.

She felt happy! *Could this little island end up being my paradise? I'm going to do it. I'm going to make the purchase.* Her heart soared in the dream. She desperately wanted to break out in song!

Leesa awoke in the afternoon. She dressed for the office and ventured down to the kitchen looking for a snack. A turkey sandwich on rye filled her up.

She reached for a Diet Pepsi and sat at the bar. Cook had left a basket of fresh fruit there, but she was full after eating her sandwich. Leesa watched the flowers out in the gardens and looked out toward the sea. Faraway barges and cruise ships dotted the ocean.

She would go to the office and begin a serious mapping of her project to present to her father. *Making Kramer's Island look like my vision seems impossible. True, much work is to be done. I'll never regret one moment of this labor of love. It is going to happen.* After a few more moments staring outside, she picked up her coat and backpack. It was a ragtop day, so she left the top down on the yellow Bimmer.

Traffic was light on the I-5 as she tuned in the radio. "Hello, everybody. This is Talk to Me Radio."

The deep male voice introduced his daytime radio talk show. "This is Bert Helms with Crystal Stevens. Glad you joined us this hour. Today we're talking with you all about the lengths people will go to for attention. Crystal, what are you cooking up for today's show?"

Crystal started, "Well, Bert, you know many lonely people out there in our listening audience desire attention."

"Yes, Crystal, I can tell you from experience that some people will do anything for attention. Many people, as you well know, try to get on my show, and some of the stories we hear are absolutely unbelievable! Luckily, I have a very efficient staff checking these stories out before we invite someone on the show."

"Bert, you know that doesn't always work. I remember a couple of times people slipped through the cracks. Like that author. Now what was his name? He sat there and lied to your face the whole hour."

Leesa started laughing out loud. Crystal Stevens had it right. Leesa remembered the big flap over that unfortunate episode.

"Thanks, Crystal, you didn't have to remind me. But I was thinking of the very same thing…"

Leesa pushed the seek button for another station.

"So, Dr. Gina, do you think I should tell my friend I know her husband is cheating on her? I mean, what kind of friend hurts another friend by telling her such a thing?"

"You should tell her," Dr. Gina ordered. "What kind of friend keeps a secret like that from her friend? So tell her. Good-bye. Next caller, please."

"Hello?"

"This is Dr. Gina. You're on the air."

Leesa slipped a sixties rock and roll CD into the CD slot. The rest of the trip she spent in Surf City, USA.

About four o'clock, she walked into her office. A few employees remained on her floor. She pulled out a blank sheet of paper and began drawing pictures of what the footprint of the Kramer's Island project might look like. *There's the cannery, the village, the center stage, the train, the zoo, and spots for flower carts. We need kiosks throughout the village to sort of 'cute' it up. Old-fashioned gas streetlights would be neat. No, not like that.* She crumpled up the paper and threw it in the trash. Retrieving another blank page, she started again. After several tries, she felt she was making good progress.

Leesa didn't notice it had gotten dark outside. Her work was truly becoming a labor of love. She continued into the night, thoroughly enjoying herself. About one in the morning, she arrived at what she considered a good depiction of what she wanted to present to Tim for estimates and refining.

She couldn't call Tim at that late hour. It would have to wait until a decent time in the morning. She drove home and went to bed, feeling as if she had put in a productive day. *Tim might be impressed with my work tonight. A sound plan, that's what I created on black and white this evening. I know this plan will make an impact on him. I can't wait to see the look on his face.*

***

Lyza boarded the flight back to the States and took her place in first class. She loved Qantas airlines.

She still couldn't believe how Mr. Charles O'Malley had tried to drill for oil on land that did not belong to him. She shook her head. *Are people that stupid? Or I suppose the question is 'Are people really that careless?' Did Mr. O'Malley not think anyone would inspect the property before the sale?*

Lyza smiled at how Mr. O'Malley had actually showed up with *cash. What a putz!*

The astonished look on Clete's face when I walked out? She chuckled out loud. *Priceless!* All in all, it had been a fun afternoon. She couldn't let that crook get away with his con. *Truth be told, I had no choice other than to purchase the property for the company. What a coincidence that Gary just said he was newly interested in his father's business, gas and oil. There might be a fit here.*

As the flight left the runway, she had peace that the deal was over and done with. *How it will eventually turn out will take months to calculate. No one knows how much oil is under the property.* She had meant for this to be a short deal, one that might barely break even. She had taken the loser property so that Leesa could outdo her for once. *It's tough when you have the Midas touch. Yes, always being right isn't easy. I wonder how Leesa's deal turned out.* She slept part of the way home.

***

Lyza's flight landed in LA midmorning, and a Lane limousine picked her up. She wanted to go home for more sleep.

The car dropped her and her luggage off at the front door, where the butler came out to carry her bags upstairs. She went to the kitchen and enjoyed an ice cold sparkling water, then went upstairs to run a hot bath. Lyza added baking soda to help combat jet lag. *There's nothing like a soak bath to relax me enough to sleep.* When she got out, she went directly to her familiar soft mattress. It felt good to be home. She fell asleep instantly.

Lyza awoke early. Birds serenaded her with their morning songs in the trees outside her open window. *I love that sound, the waves and the birds. It's like a natural symphony.* She dressed, gathered her papers and attaché case, and walked downstairs to the kitchen for coffee and whatever delights Cook might have prepared. That morning, cantaloupe and fresh strawberries looked good. Leesa sat at the bar reading the paper.

"Lyza, you're back!" Leesa held her arms open and they hugged. "How was everything in AussieLand?"

"AussieLand? Please. You're so funny! Australia was successful. I'm pleased so far. It's going to take some time to figure out the profit margin."

Leesa couldn't wait to fill Lyza in. "Oh, it sounds kind of like my deal turned out. Mine looks like a long-term commitment, but I'm up for—"

Lyza interrupted. "Listen, Leesa, you would not believe what happened."

"What happened? You made the sale, right?"

"Oh, we had a buyer. But the guy tried to rip us off. Some people have no brains. This joker drilled for oil on the property, then he tried to cover it up. He made an offer on the land before I arrived in Brisbane. I'm so glad I made the trip to inspect the property."

"It's a good thing you did. I would have been tempted to skip that part."

"The place is so remote, I considered not going. Once I heard there was already an offer on it, I had to know what was so interesting about an abandoned cattle station. I hate to think of it. O'Malley could have easily wound up a multi-millionaire on our dime." Lyza omitted the justice she'd enacted; Leesa wouldn't appreciate it.

"He tried to rip us off, but you were on top of it. Lyza, you are so good!"

They high-fived over the breakfast bar. "I'm excited about the property in Seattle. I took Tim with me for his opinion on some of my ideas. It's the cutest little fish cannery!"

Lyza wrinkled her nose. "Cute fish cannery? I can't believe you said that. Isn't that an oxymoron? Help me understand what a cute fish cannery looks like!"

"The cannery hasn't been in operation for years. It's my dream for it that makes it cute. Tim is going to look at the sketches and give me an idea of how much an investment it will be, but I think this is really going to be big."

"I want to see the sketches. Tell me. What's your dream?"

Leesa eyes brightened. "I want to convert the cannery into a café with an area for a curio shop and a place to learn about the old cannery and how it operated. Patrons will be able to buy canned smoked salmon. Upstairs will be an arcade and gift shop with lots of stuffed animals. You know, like Mr. Ted."

She shot Lyza a look and continued. "The top floor will be an observation deck where people can whale watch and just look at the boats on the ocean. A small-scale steam engine will give rides around the perimeter of the island."

"Leesa, it sounds as though you're planning to take over the entire island."

Leesa looked at Lyza and grinned. "That's right. I'm going to buy the island. What I'm proposing is a mini Disneyland—very mini. I want a little zoo, flower bins, and kiosks throughout the village, which will have to be designed. It's a huge, long-term project, but once I get it rolling, I'll be free to work on other projects. Until then, I am consumed with Kramer's Island."

"Kramer's Island, eh? Don't you think that if you buy it, the name should be Lane's Island?"

"Nope, everything is centered on the old Kramer's Kannery."

"I can't talk you into naming it 'Leesa's Island,' can I?"

"Nope."

"How about Leesa's Folly?"

***

Cook laid a copy of the Wall Street Journal on the kitchen bar. The headline read "German Pharmaceutical Company Contaminates Rhine." Lyza picked it up and read about Müller and Sons Pharmaceutical Company being charged with contamination of the Rhine-Main-Danube Canal. Lyza smiled when she read the exorbitant fines involved. She especially enjoyed reading about the prison sentences possible for the owners and other important parties involved. She could not have planned it better. Her intention was to report suspicions of such infractions in about a year. Evidently, someone beat her to the punch, but that was all right with her. In fact, it was even better.

Looking further into the article she read, "A concerned group of citizens demanded a thorough inspection, which revealed the contamination. Local officials applaud the actions taken." She let out a giggle. *Germans reporting Germans, I love it.*

That Nuremberg deal brought justice for those Nazis who killed our grandparents at Auschwitz. I will never tell Leesa, or our parents for that matter. Justice is sweet. I see Klaus Müller was treated in a German hospital for heart disease. I hope he dies. He deserves it, he and all those Jew-killing Germans.

"Anything interesting in today's news?" Leesa asked, looking over her shoulder at the paper.

"No, not really."

"Well, I'm off to the office today. Are you going in?" Leesa asked.

"I am, but not until this afternoon. I'm trying to contact Gary Wagner. I want to get his advice on the oil find."

"Ooo, that's right, he's working with his father. How timely for your deal. I'll see you later, then. Have a good morning." Leesa picked up her keys and walked out the door.

Lyza punched the number on her cell phone for Gary Wagner. Three rings later, she got his voice message. "Hi, this is Gary. Leave a message."

That message always managed to tick her off. She left a curt message. "This is Lyza." Then she hung up.

Picking another strawberry, she resigned herself to the notion that Gary would call when he could. "All right, Gary. It looks like you're going to make me wait on this. Might as well change clothes and go into the office."

Once in her dressing room, she changed her mind. *I feel like blowing off work today and celebrating.* She dressed comfortably, in cream-colored velvet sweats. The Armani style fit her perfectly. Her pink accessories matched, of course. *Perhaps I should go shopping instead.* She used the intercom and called for the limo. After three minutes, the driver pulled up the circular drive to the front door. The driver opened the limo door. "Hello, Miss Lane."

"Hello there. Take me to Rodeo Drive."

"All right, Miss Lane."

The white stretch limo journeyed down Wilshire Boulevard on the south, then turned north to Santa Monica Boulevard, cruising the three short blocks of Rodeo Drive like a moth circling a flame.

Those three short blocks of Rodeo Drive made up the most famous shopping district in America and perhaps the most expensive three blocks in the world. *Why do we go to Paris? I love to shop here, too. There's Armani, Gucci, Christian Dior, Coco Chanel, Ralph Lauren, and Valentino, among others, here. The Cartier and Tiffany jewelry stores alone could burn the entire afternoon if I let them, not to mention a small fortune, should I spy anything I fancy.*

Lyza viewed Neiman Marcus, Saks Fifth Avenue, and Yves Saint Laurent, but couldn't get in the mood. *I wonder if I could get into Bijan's without an appointment today.* She especially enjoyed Bijan's because it was touted as the most expensive store in the world, and shopping was by appointment. Lyza's power card itched, and she knew she had enough clout to get in without an appointment.

The limousine crossed over to the newest addition to the famed boulevard, Via Rodeo. *These romantic versions of old Europe always intrigue me. It's almost like Paris with the romantic archways, bubbling fountains, Italianate piazza, and charming balconies.* Black wrought iron streetlamps with polished brass fixtures and ornate planters filled with colorful flowers and trees reminded Lyza to take some time to enjoy her surroundings. The small outdoor mall, Two Rodeo, created the illusion of freestanding storefronts faced with brick, stone, and marble.

Lyza spotted a sidewalk café that had provided rest and refreshment for the twins on many of their joint shopping trips. Today she wanted to walk the streets to see whether anything on window display appealed to her.

Her driver slowed. "I'll get out here. Wait for me."

She hopped out of the limo and walked the outdoor mall, peeking in the store windows. *What is wrong with me? Nothing looks the least bit interesting.*

Leesa's enthusiasm for shopping is what's missing. Lyza studied her reflection in the store window. She pulled a strand of hair back around her ear. *Maybe we'll go later this week. But for now, perhaps a little bling.*

Stepping into Tiffany's, she again felt disappointment at their offerings. *I guess I'm not in the mood to shop. Mostly I want to walk around amongst the throng.*

She remembered the Nuremberg deal. *I set him up for the fall. It was perfect. I knew that the former business there had contaminated the canal and some residue was probably left.*

New contamination would be suspected from a pharmaceutical company. I doubt they can prove the contaminant was already there. Revenge is best served cold. Justice has been done. Now I can forget about it. Just like the deal with O'Malley. Justice is done.

She was through with O'Malley, but the property remained a concern. *If Gary would return my call, I know he could help with how to proceed. His family's oil company's been in business for more than a hundred years. His recent interest in his father's business seems like a perfect match.* Anxious to talk with him, she called Gary's number again.

This time he answered. "Hey, Lyza, what's up? I was just going to call you."

Sure, you were. "Gary, when can we meet? I have a proposal for you."

"Really?" he drawled. "I can't imagine. You want to meet now?"

"I'm at Gucci's on Rodeo. Can you come this way?"

"Meet me at the café on the corner. I'm on my way. Ten minutes."

She sauntered to the nearby café and found a shady spot on the patio. The waitress brought iced tea, and Lyza gazed at passersby until she saw Gary briskly walking toward her.

His jogging shorts and tank top showed off the strong physique of his six-foot lean frame. "Lyza, you look fantastic. Where are we going this time? I enjoyed our date."

"Sorry, Gary. It's work, not a party."

He turned to leave. "No party? You got the wrong guy."

She grabbed his arm. "Gary, I'm talking about something I think you're going to be interested in. It's about one of our properties in Australia."

He smiled at the waitress and took a seat, ordering a glass of tea. "Australia? I like Australia. All right, let's hear your proposal."

"I just got back from an inspection of an abandoned ranch in the Australian bush. I found a capped well on the property. The find is new, and the well is drilled—never used, just capped." She knew how stupid that must sound, so she shrugged her shoulders.

"Did you say *capped,* because that sounds suspicious to me." He leaned forward. "There's something you're not telling me."

She didn't want to tell him any more than she had to, but realized she was going to have to give Gary more information eventually. After all, she was asking him for a consultation. "I caught a prospective buyer drilling on the land illegally. He capped the well hoping no one would suspect if there was no visible sign of drilling. However, crude oil all over the ground made it rather obvious. In short, I need to know what to do with my new well."

Gary slapped his thigh and laughed. "You caught a poacher! I didn't know they had those in the oil drilling business. Or is he a rustler?"

Lyza frowned.

He stopped laughing. "I can help you. First, we need to get as much information as possible. If you want to know how big the find is, I'll get some men into the field right away. If it's a small pocket, you may not want to pursue it."

"Let's do what we need to do to find out whether it's a viable project. Give me quotes so you can get started."

Suddenly she remembered the kiss. It didn't embarrass her. It was something that happened. *And it's not going to happen again.*

Much to her dismay, Gary began explaining the basics of oil exploration to her. "Oil exploration depends on highly sophisticated technology to detect and determine the extent of the deposits. Exploration geophysicists subject the area to a gravity survey, magnetic survey, and passive seismic or regional seismic reflection surveys to detect large scale features of subsurface geology."

Oh, please, Gary. I do not need to know the details. She flashed him a charming smile, trying to look interested while he kept going.

"Then we do more detailed seismic surveys using reflected sound waves traveling through matter, usually rock, creating a profile of the substructure. It's sort of like how a doctor uses a sonogram to examine an unborn baby."

Finally, he wound down. "What we need to do initially is identify a reputable crew down there that passes our company's selection criteria."

Lyza hoped she could stop Gary from telling her everything he knew about the oil business. "If that's what we need to do, you have my authorization."

Your family's been in the oil business for over a hundred years, and someone in that company will know what they're doing.

Gary frowned slightly. "Are you sure? This is a huge commitment."

Lyza's back straightened. "Am I sure? Look, Gary, I get that oil exploration is an expensive, high-risk operation. But the fact that they've already drilled must be of some advantage. Let's get your people to talk to my people and get started on the project."

Gary gestured toward the sky. "You've got it, Lyza. From your lips to God's ears."

"I'll alert Bill at the office. Have your people contact him tomorrow morning. Will that work for you?"

Now she was ready to move on to the next subject. "By the way, Gary, I want to address that kiss the other night."

His tanned face slightly blushed. "Lyza, it was no big deal. It wasn't planned on my part." He winked. "Can I help it if you're irresistible?"

She hesitated and started turning red. "What do you mean, on your part? Are you insinuating it was planned on *my* part? Because if you are, let me make it crystal clear to you—that will not happen again. A little champagne, a few laughs, that's great, but you and I are friends and friends don't kiss like that. I don't want it to happen again."

His expression softened with his voice. "Lyza, it won't happen again. But let me explain to you, it was the moment. I was feeling good after a fun night at the benefit. You seemed so soft and loving, and so—" the tone of his voice turned hard— "different from what I know you are. You fooled me for a minute."

She sniped back, "There's no need to get bitter. I'm sure you get more than your share of stolen kisses." *Now this is more like it. This little tiff is more like brother and sister, and that's the way I like it. No romance, not with Gary or anyone else. There's so much more to life.*

All business again, Lyza ended their meeting. "Listen, I need to get to the office today, so sorry to leave you, but I must update Bill on the project. Thanks for meeting me."

Not waiting for a good-bye from him, she gathered her Gucci bag and walked around the corner where the limo waited. She saw the driver slumped in his seat with his cap pulled over his head, taking a snooze. She knocked impatiently on his window, and he started.

"Oh, Miss Lane. I'm so sorry." He scrambled out of the limo to open the rear door for her.

She frowned at him and stepped in.

Chapter Seventeen

Lyza directed the limousine driver to drop her off in front of the Lane building in spite of the fact that it was nearly noon and she still wore her casual velvet sweats.

Riding up the elevator, she devised a plan. *It might be fun to update Bill on the Australian situation.* She found him poring over pages of statistics at his desk.

She loved setting him up. "Bill, remember that questionable property you tried to warn me about in Australia?"

He looked genuinely concerned. "Yes, Lyza, I do remember. Is there something you want to tell me about the deal?"

She tried to put on a disappointed face. "Yes, there's something I need to tell you, and then I need you to do something."

He sat up straight. "You know I'll do whatever it takes to get you out of this mess. Just tell me what you want me to do. I know you authorized purchase of the property by narrowly outbidding the prospective buyer and paying the asking price—rather generous, if you ask me."

Bingo! She shot back, "Well, as a matter of fact, I didn't ask you. Here's what I want you to do. Last week while I was in Australia, I discovered oil on our newest little property. What do you think about that?"

Bill's eyes popped wide open. "Oil? You mean like an oil well?"

She talked down to him. "Yes, Bill. Now, you understand that there is still a lot to do before we start making money. I want you to get with Gary Wagner and work with him about what must be done. I've already told him I would have you waiting for his call, but I want you to call him right away. You know how I like fast results."

Bill readily agreed to her orders. "Sure, I'll call Wagner Oil. I can't believe it. Only you could take a loser of a property like that and discover oil." He gave a silly grin. "I don't know how you do it. You are one lucky woman."

She thought he looked like the Cheshire cat in Alice in Wonderland. *Bill thinks I'm a lucky gal. But I'm a working gal and I'm a thorough gal and I'm a planning gal. I wish I could wipe that silly grin off his face. I know he just can't wait to fill Father in on this news.*

She gave him a grimace and shook her head. "You know, Bill, I work at it."

She left his office and headed to her own. She began leafing through listings left in her mail inbox.

Wanting to find something that required travel, she looked at European offerings. *My love-hate relationship with travel frustrates me. I love to visit other places. I hate all the stuff you have to take, all the lines I have to wait in, and all the stupid people I have to deal with. At least my love-hate relationship with travel has benefited me and the company.*

She looked at her e-mail and smiled at a note from Leesa that said, "Seattle's gonna be my dream come true." *She sounds as though she's found her true love. All I can do is generate income. Oh, that I could fall in love with a project.*

Her attention shifted back to the listings. *This one in Zermatt looks promising.* The listing read:

"In the shadow of the Matterhorn, this unique property boasts a ski lift with a restaurant at the top of the lift. Near the bottom of the lift, one can relax at the spacious and inviting lodge."

She noticed the property had been on the market two years, making it ripe for a renovation. *Leesa's having fun with her dream island project. I wonder how much fun a ski attraction in Switzerland could be?*

She's absolutely having a ball with the fish cannery. Then there's the Tim factor. I think she's having more fun working with him.

Lyza dreaded Leesa's Monday morning meeting. At the last meeting, Father made Lyza look good and hurt Leesa's feelings. *I can take it, but Leesa's sensitive. I don't want to be the reason she gets hurt, and I sure don't want her embarrassed in front of the other agents. Father can be such a jerk!*

Lyza hated family conflict—unless, of course, she was the one doing the confronting. *I don't want to hurt Leesa's feelings again. On the other hand, I don't want anyone to know that the unexpected oil discovery on that loser property in Australia couldn't have surprised anybody more than it surprised me.*

Bill's reaction made Lyza angry. *It's true that I was lucky, but this time the luck worked against my plan. My plan was to make Leesa look good, not to get involved in the oil business. Some things happen. I am in control of my own destiny, but sometimes things just happen.* She punched the intercom to the reception desk.

"Has Leesa gone for the day?"

The receptionist stretched across her desk to look down the hall as Leesa stepped into the elevator. "She just now caught the elevator. Do you want me to go after her?"

Lyza decided to catch a ride home with Leesa. "Never mind. I'll catch her on her cell."

Leesa answered on the first ring. "Lyza, what's up?"

"Is it too late to catch a ride home?"

Leesa's cheerful voice slightly annoyed Lyza. "It's not too late to catch a ride to Café de Leche for a latte and a sandwich."

"That sounds good to me. I'm walking out of my office as we speak. I'll meet you at the parking elevator."

Leesa stayed on the phone. "I'm here and waiting. What did we do before cell phones?"

Lyza's damp mood lightened. "You mean people didn't always have cell phones? I'm so glad you suggested Café de Leche. It feels like the perfect ending to the week."

"You said it. Hope you don't mind Tim meeting us there."

Oh, crumb. I wanted to relax. If Tim's coming along, I have to keep my public face on and be nice to him. I thought it was going to be just us. Lyza wanted to relax and talk with her sister. That wasn't going to happen until after dinner, it seemed.

She had no control over the Tim situation. "Oh, Tim, yeah, sure." She couldn't complain. *At least I got invited.*

They hopped in Leesa's yellow Bimmer. Leesa's taste in colors sometimes mystified Lyza. *Isn't this bright yellow something like a Big Bird from Sesame Street color? Oh, well. It's Leesa, and I love her, so it's all right.*

Tim was waiting in front of Café de Leche and held open the door for them. "What a nice surprise. I'm graced with the presence of two beautiful women tonight."

"Oh, please. You know you're going to have to pick up the tab," Lyza joked.

"I know it now."

They followed the hostess to a table near the windows. Within moments, their waitress appeared and took their order. All of them ordered Perrier and Greek salads.

Tim accepted his water from the waitress. "Leesa tells me you just got back from Australia. Do you plan any more trips soon, or are you satisfied to hang around sunny California for a while?"

"I might go to Switzerland."

"What?" Leesa sat up. "I haven't heard about this. What are you up to this time? You know, Tim, she just came back from an amazing deal. The property she went to inspect in Australia turned out to have oil."

Lyza enjoyed the look on Tim's face. "You are kidding me! How does that happen?"

The waitress delivered their food, and Lyza put her napkin in her lap. "It was a fluke. I can't take all the credit. Well, I had a hunch something was going on. The find shocked everyone at the Brisbane office."

Tim probed for more information. "How did you know to look for oil on the property?"

Leesa's ears perked up. "Yes, Lyza, how did you know to look for oil on the property?"

Shut up, Tim. I'm not telling that I already knew about the oil before our purchase. Change the subject. But the only story she could come up with quickly was about Gary's involvement. "Oh, I talked with Gary about the property, and he gave me some good advice."

"Good advice, you call it? Well, I guess so. Leesa, remind me to ask Gary for some good advice."

Their table cleared, the waitress took orders for dessert. Lyza and Leesa ordered lattes. Tim ordered the cheesecake with his latte.

Lyza finally thought of a way to change the focus. "You understand about coincidence. Look at you and Leesa working on the Kramer Island project." The waitress brought their lattes and Tim's cheesecake.

Leesa broke into a bright smile. "Isn't this just the best weather tonight?"

Tim lifted his cup. "Sunny California, that's why we live here."

Leesa sipped her after-dinner latte. "Mmm. This is the best. Looking forward to the weekend?"

Lyza leaned back in her chair. "I am so looking forward to it. I can tell by the look on your face that you have something up your sleeve."

"Yes, I have a great idea. Let's take a drive up the coast tomorrow. I'd like to visit a little art gallery in Morro Bay. Do you have anything else planned?"

I am so ready for some meaningless fun. "Road trip! Yes, I'm in! Let's leave about nine o'clock. I'll have time to enjoy my coffee and read the paper before we go."

Tim frowned. "What am I, chopped liver? Or is this a chick trip?"

Leesa gave him a light punch on the shoulder. "Sorry, it is definitely a chick trip."

Lyza broke in. "And, for fun, I'll drive. I need to get some miles on my Mercedes."

Tim looked interested. "How many miles have you got on it?"

"It's just at six thousand."

"You sure don't drive much. How long have you had that car?"

"Five years."

Chapter Eighteen

Leesa awoke early, excited about the trip. She chose her pink-and-black rhinestone-studded backpack. Then she walked into her closet and tossed in her silk teddy and designer black jeans with flower appliqués down the sides. She added a pink halter top with a net covering plus a pink T-shirt. In case of a change in the weather, she put in a pink hooded sweatshirt. She wore a yellow sweatshirt with Ralph Lauren pants and her cork heels. As a last thought, she threw in her Reebok running shoes.

She took a five-minute shower and washed her hair. Pulling her wet hair back, she tied it with a yellow scrunchie. A dollop of moisturizer and sunscreen later, she dashed downstairs to the kitchen for a bite of breakfast. No one was in the kitchen, so she found a bagel and some strawberry cream cheese with a cup of freshly brewed coffee.

Lyza came down carrying her stylish gray overnight bag and matching gigantic purse. Her light blonde hair fell on her shoulders, topped with a gray cap that matched her velvet top. Her designer blue jeans fit tightly and, with her five-inch heels, made her look like a teenager. "Coffee smells good. Where's the paper?"

Leesa reached for the television remote as she handed the paper over. "Here it is; enjoy. Mind if I turn on the news?"

"Go ahead. It won't bother me." Lyza started browsing *USA Today*.

Leesa turned off the TV. "The weather report looks good; I think we're ready to roll."

Lyza grabbed her keys. "Okay. Remember I'm driving."

Leesa joked, "Of course I remember; we've got to get some miles on your car."

They walked out to a perfect California day. After filling the trunk with their bags, they cruised out the tall, black iron security gates of their property onto the busy streets.

Turning north onto U.S. 101, Lyza sat back to enjoy the stupendous coastal view for the next four hours to the strains of U2. Traffic seemed sparse for a weekend drive up the coast.

They left the Simi Valley and traveled up the coast through Santa Barbara and into Santa Maria. "Lyza, look, there's a cute place for lunch. Let's stop."

Lyza glanced into the rearview mirror. "Okay, okay. Let me pull over here. That guy behind me is right on my bumper."

Leesa turned as the car roared around them. "Here, let's park. That guy must be late for something."

They sat on the patio, and both ordered the Portabello Avocado Croissant special with a glass of white wine.

The shady patio, surrounded by an explosion of various flowering plants, offered a view of doves drinking and bathing in the three-level fountain in the courtyard below.

Lyza wanted to know more about Leesa's new project. "So tell me, where are you on this Kramer's Island project?"

Leesa smirked. "I thought we had a rule about talking business while on vacation."

Lyza tried another approach. "All right, then. Where are you on the Tim Young project? And I don't mean business."

The waitress brought their order, and Leesa picked up her sandwich. "You know Tim. I like working with him."

Lyza sipped her water. "Dinner yesterday didn't look like work to me."

After chewing her bite, Leesa answered, "Wow. You are snoopy. Let me assure that there is nothing there. I mean, I do like him. I like him. I guess I feel more comfortable around him than any other guy."

Lyza dug into her lunch. "That's interesting, Leesa. He seems very attentive to you."

Leesa wiped her mouth. "I guess so. I don't know. Let's talk about something else."

Lyza leaned forward. "You're thinking about Tim in a new way." She shook her head. "I can't believe it. You have a thing for him, like, overnight."

Leesa threw her napkin into her plate. "Stop it. I said I want to change the subject."

But Lyza kept at her. "No, I'm not going to change the subject. What happened in Seattle?"

Leesa's eyes flared. "Nothing happened in Seattle. Absolutely nothing. Are you happy now?"

Lyza leaned back in her chair with a satisfied look on her face. "Oh, I see I hit a sore spot. All right, we should probably get back on the road. I'm going to let you off the hook this time."

Leesa motioned to their waitress for the check. "I think it's a little late for that. But you got what you wanted, didn't you?"

Lyza frowned. "What are you talking about?"

"You got me to admit that the situation between Tim and me is not what I would like it to be. And you got to see me react." Leesa pulled cash out of her purse and put it with the check under her water glass.

Lyza stood up. "Oh, forget it. So Tim's stupid if he doesn't fall for you. He's just playing hard to get. Let's hit the road."

At San Luis Obispo, they stopped to look around and stretch their legs. They sauntered past the famous Madonna Inn, then Lyza peeked in the Fremont Theater to get a look at the historic art deco theater. Built in the nineteen forties, it still played first-run movies on a huge screen.

She nudged Leesa and pointed at the main theater walls decorated with murals with neon swirls lighting the ceiling. "We should come back and spend an afternoon here. "

Leesa pulled Lyza away to a display of brochures in the lobby. She picked up a brightly colored one about Bubblegum Alley, where people had been sticking their ABC (Already Been Chewed) gum since the 1950s.

Lyza shook her head. "Are you serious? Bubblegum Alley, a place to memorialize your chewed bubble gum? What is this world coming to? I think I needed this. It gives me a whole new perspective on how I'm living my life."

Leesa pulled out another brochure. "Look there's a Frank Lloyd Wright building here."

Lyza found one for the San Luis Obispo County Historical Museum. "Let's take a look at the museum."

Leesa opened the door for Lyza, and they stepped onto the sidewalk. "Lead the way."

Leesa and Lyza spent an hour at the San Luis Obispo County Historical Museum. After leaving the museum, they found their way back to the car and drove onto Morro Bay Boulevard to find the gallery Leesa wanted to visit.

Lyza followed Leesa's direction to turn up Embarcadero Street and park in front of 601 Embarcadero Street at a gallery called *Showcase by the Sea.*

Leesa's big smile gave her excitement away. "I think we're in for a treat. I've admired the works of this artist for months now, and today he is making a personal appearance at this gallery. We really made it. I can't tell you how many of these public appearances I've missed because of one thing or another."

"I'm sorry, who is this artist?" Lyza looked genuinely confused. "Where is he from?"

"The man is from California. How cool is that? His paintings are so inspirational and so life-affirming! His paintings are all about light and different shades of lighting. That's the name of his tour, the Share the Light Tour."

"What do you mean it's all about light?"

Leesa responded thoughtfully, her eyes kind of glazed. "He uses special techniques to emphasize light and depicts a simple way of life that appeals to me."

Lyza opened her car door. "So, let's go meet him."

They walked up to the gallery and saw it full of people buying prints and standing in line to visit with the painter. Lyza frowned. "Where are the originals?"

Leesa explained to Lyza. "Thomas Kinkade is America's most collected living artist when it comes to painting scenes depicting light. They should have some originals in the special gallery."

Leesa spoke to a woman standing in the crowded room holding a child. "What did we miss?"

The woman stepped out of Leesa's line of vision. "Only the most wonderful, life-affirming message. He grew up in a small town in California and talked about the important values nurtured throughout his childhood. So moving, I'm sorry you missed it. But he's still signing books and autographs."

Leesa shopped the store and triumphantly found the painting she'd come for.

Lyza inspected the painting of light filtering through leafy branches and reflecting off a dark green pool. Soon Leesa was shaking Kinkade's hand. He took a few minutes to visit with her while Lyza hung back.

Leesa, eyes shining, took in every kind word the man spoke.

Afterwards, they chose to have dinner in a quiet seaside restaurant. Lyza admired Leesa's chosen painting. "It's marvelous. Where are you going to put it?"

"Oh, it has to go in my sitting room. Don't you think it would look good above the settee?" Leesa munched on her tofu salad.

Lyza took a sip of her white wine. "I think it would look good anywhere. He was such a delightful man. I'm so glad we did this. You can tell he loves what he does."

"Oh, yes, you can. He has a glow about him."

Lyza's practicality kicked in, and she began planning for tomorrow. "Let's see if we can get a room at the Blue Sail Inn. It's close, and all we need is a place to sleep before we head back in the morning." She suddenly wanted to get back and make arrangements for her flight to Switzerland.

"Shame on you!" Leesa teased. "You're already at the office, aren't you? This is our road trip. We'll be back in time for the Monday morning meeting."

Lyza shook her head. *I don't want to think about the Monday morning meeting. Leesa's right; I need to focus on the moment, not the future. It's been a wonderful day. Let me bask in it now.*

They parked the car in the Blue Sail Inn's small parking lot, carried their bags to check-in, and found that no penthouse suites existed. They registered, then walked up to room 214. They stood on their balcony facing the ocean and beach to enjoy the scene. The full moon illuminated the beach and the huge rock just off the coast, mimicking one of Kinkade's paintings.

***

Morning arrived, and the plan to leave first thing in the morning got scrapped. After a Starbucks latte and breakfast bagel, eaten overlooking Morro Rock, Leesa got curious about Morro Bay State Park and asked Lyza to take a turn through the park to see what was there. They found a lagoon and natural bay habitat. Morro Rock dominated the beach, but on the bay's northeast edge, they found a pristine saltwater marsh supporting a thriving bird population.

Lyza decided their choices were sailing, fishing, hiking, or bird-watching. For what they had with them, it had to be bird-watching. Lyza pulled the field glasses out from inside the console. They got out of the car, walked a short distance on the trail, and shared the field glasses.

After the magnificent bird show, they visited the museum, where they learned about the local natural features and cultural history. Time flew by, and soon it was time to begin the drive back to LA.

They stopped at Pismo Beach on the way home for a sandwich and soda as a farewell to their soon-to-end road trip and fun weekend. Again, Lyza appreciated the light traffic because she enjoyed driving the coastal highway. Sometimes she found it difficult to take in the scenery and watch the road. Normally she was an impatient driver, shouting and gesturing to other drivers on the highway. Today she relaxed, yielding to other traffic, and sometimes slowing for cars entering the highway from an entrance ramp. She felt a peace, somehow, an inexplicable peace.

They pulled into the estate at eight o'clock. The twins immediately went to change into their pajamas and met again in the main kitchen.

Lyza went through the refrigerator. "What a great trip! I'm hungry."

"It was a great trip. But the weekend isn't over. Let's watch a movie."

Lyza found a tray of sliced cheese and fruit. "Sure, but make it something light. I don't want to have to think tonight."

Leesa raided the pantry, finding a bag of chips. "*Dave's* in the media room."

Lyza stopped midbite. "Dave? I didn't know someone was here. We're in our pajamas. Why didn't you say something, for crying out loud?"

"No, no, *Dave*. The movie starring Kevin Kline. It's stupid and senseless, but not to the point of irritation."

"Perfect."

Each girl curled up on her own dark leather sofa in the media room, and Leesa started the movie.

Chapter Nineteen

Lyza hated the redundancy of Leesa's Monday morning meetings. She could hardly sit through the weekly update and review meeting. *Everyone who needs to know already knows all that happened last week, and everyone has their plans for the week in mind. If they don't, they're fools. It's a public display of victory or despair.*

These stupid meetings are business as usual from the nineteen sixties. They should be replaced by e-mails and technology. She was the last to sit down at the conference table.

She caught a look from Leesa as Father walked in, asking if she knew what was going on. She shrugged in answer. *Don't tell me he's taking over her meeting again.*

Lawrence went to the front of the room and spoke directly to Leesa. "Leesa, I hope you don't mind. I have some concerns to discuss today. I promise not to usurp another meeting after this."

He opened the meeting. "Last week's bottom line looks positive. And it's a good thing, too, because L. L. Lane Unlimited acquired two significant properties last week."

Lyza's eyes met Leesa's.

"Furthermore, both of these properties will take considerable investment and substantial time for our initial costs to be regained. Every agent in this room added revenue to the bottom line this week. Congratulations to all of you on a job well done. However, two agents have put us in a precarious position regarding the profits for the week and only time will reveal whether they made the right decisions."

Father had made his point to the group. His girls made some important decisions without consulting him. They had the authority to do that, since he was going to turn the company over to them one day, but it was the first time either of them had taken such liberties.

"Both of the properties in question are risky. I don't know whether I would have taken them on, but as a corporation, we have taken them on and will do what it takes for them to come to fruition."

He turned to Leesa. "Leesa, your Kramer's Island plan sounds like pie in the sky, and I have to be honest with you, I don't think you can make it work. I'm not shutting you down. I'm saying you have a lot of work ahead of you."

Leesa stood up. "I know there's going to be a lot of work getting it set up, but you watch. I believe with all my heart that you'll be surprised." Leesa sat back down and asked, "Have you looked at the architectural report?"

"Not yet." He looked toward Lyza.

His stern voice got softer. "Now, Lyza, I see you've found another barn-burner. You picked up an abandoned cattle ranch in the Australian bush for the price of a song. Then how did you find oil on the property? Do you care to explain to me why Wagner Oil Company contacted me Friday afternoon regarding an oil rig for the property?"

Lyza stood up. "I'll be happy to explain. When I went to inspect the property, I stepped into a pool of something I suspected was crude oil. I took it to a professional. He absolutely swore to me that it was crude oil and recommended that I investigate the possibilities. I immediately contacted Gary Wagner, who advised we get a crew out there as soon as possible. His crew confirmed an oil find. Now we are waiting for a report as to how big the find is." *One of my best lies,* she thought.

Lawrence visibly puffed up. "Lyza, honey, that's the way to go. Agents, take a look at what it takes to be a success. Get a look at your assigned listings and get busy. This is your model. Lyza, again you have surpassed all expectations. Good job! This meeting is over." Lawrence Lane walked out of the office.

Drat! Lyza thought. *This didn't turn out the way I wanted it to. I wanted Leesa to shine today. What on Earth is the matter with Father?* Leesa approached with a big smile on her face. She looked genuinely happy.

"Congratulations, you did it again! Good for you. Don't look so surprised; I really mean it. Your deal will make the most money the soonest, and I'm happy for you. My project is a labor of love, and if it happens to be profitable, that will be the frosting on the cake—don't tell Father!" She winked and turned to go to her office.

Lyza sat at her desk. *I wonder how she really feels. But then she doesn't hold her feelings in well. Well, good, then maybe I can let Leesa take care of herself. Now I need to contact the people in Zermatt and set up a meeting for an inspection of that ski property on the Matterhorn.*

Later that afternoon, Lyza buzzed the travel department asking about arrangements for the flight to Switzerland. *Packing is going to be different.* Her white ermine fur was in the cold storage closet on the garden level of the twins' home.

My white fur boots with the little bows at the top will work with the black and white suede skirt and matching top. I have that new white alpaca hat. Yes. That will be warm as well as stylish. I'll be there a couple of days. But for sure I want to take my white fleece pajamas and fuzzy slippers.

She ordered a room with a fireplace. Her flight was set for nine in the morning. She left the office early because she couldn't wait to get home and start packing.

She walked in the house and caught a glimpse of Cook's reflection from a mirror in the sitting room. "Cook, I'm here to pack. I'm going to Switzerland."

Cook stuck her head out of the kitchen. "Switzerland sounds cold to me."

Lyza ran upstairs to grab the new luggage set she had received from Neiman Marcus. She'd bought the gray luggage with silver piping to match her car. *I'll probably never use this with my car. I forgot about it last weekend.*

But it also matches my traveling velvet sweatsuit. I don't get many chances to wear furs in LA. She enjoyed going through her cashmere sweaters and wool pants to whittle her choices. *As fun as this is, I refuse to pack two bags for a few days.* Finally her clothes were packed, and she was ready to choose her jewelry. *White diamond pendant with matching dangling earrings and tennis bracelet, definitely! A fifteen-carat ruby pendant with ring and matching earrings and bracelet, and I think I'll pack a gold ankle bracelet in case I ever get out of my boots!*

At ten o'clock, she wandered down to the kitchen. Cook had left a shrimp cocktail with wheat crackers and Brie for snacks. She sat at the bar and started surfing the TV channels while digging into the shrimp cocktail.

"Hey." Leesa popped her head around the corner. "Ready for your jump across the pond?"

Lyza wondered what project Leesa had picked this week. "Oh, yeah, I'm packed and ready to leave in the morning. How about you?"

"I'm headed back to Kramer's Island for a few days." She picked up a banana. "See you next week. Have a good trip."

"Is Tim going?"

Leesa dashed up the stairs without answering.

***

Arriving the required three hours early for international flights, Lyza breezed through the VIP security line. She ordered a bagel and latte in one of the terminal coffee shops. Then she strolled to her gate and spent the next hour and half surfing the Internet and reading *Winning Through Intimidation.*

Passengers lined up to board the Swiss International Airlines flight to Zurich. Her first-class seat looked acceptable. After awaking at four o'clock and taking the limo to the airport in the dark of early morning, she was ready to snuggle in for the long flight.

"Welcome to Swiss International Airlines Flight 687 to Zurich," the flight attendant spoke over the PA system. "Please fasten your seat belts…"

Lyza fell asleep before the attendant finished the announcements. She slept almost the entire flight and felt rested when awakened by the flight attendants handing out customs forms. Before landing, she went to the facility to freshen up. *You have to be a contortionist to change clothes in one of these bathrooms. Do they need to be this small?* She wiggled into black suede pants, five-inch heeled black leather boots, and black mink jacket with matching mink hat. Opening her toiletries bag, she reapplied her faded make-up. Some twenty minutes later, when Lyza opened the door, a waiting flight attendant hurried past her into the bathroom.

Lyza stepped off the flight looking like a *Vogue Magazine* model. From Zurich, Bill had booked her a limo to Zermatt instead of the train, per her instructions. The driver picked up her luggage and led her outside.

"Welcome to Switzerland, Miss Lane."

She hugged her fur around her and stood next to the limo. "It's cold."

He opened the door. "Yes, it is brisk. You are in Switzerland."

I love riding European trains, but it didn't fit my schedule. Maybe next time. This isn't vacation. I need to focus on work.

Less than an hour later, Lyza's limo stopped in front of the Grand Hotel Zermatterhof. After her long flight and limo ride, she felt surprisingly energized. She registered and the hotel manager escorted her to the luxury suite, the requested fireplace already lit.

After walking through the rooms, making sure she was alone, he backed out of the suite, bowing slightly. "Please call if we can make your stay more pleasant."

Lyza thanked him absently and closed the door. She turned and looked out the window, viewing the majestic snow-covered Matterhorn in front of her. She called room service and ordered dinner, a small cress soup with pine nuts, sea bass with artichoke, and chocolate mousse for dessert. Relaxing on the soft sofa, she picked up the local tourist magazine and read about Zermatt, which was evidently known for its constant snow.

Oh, right. Constant snow means constant cold. I'm a California girl. I can only take this for a few days at a time.

At least there's clean air. That's something we California girls aren't used to. She smiled to herself and kept reading.

With twelve headwaters and eighty-six springs, I should enjoy drinking water here. It's ninety-five percent pure spring water, according to Swiss Food Law requirements. All right!

Room service delivered her order. She was surprised how fast she ate everything on the serving tray. She snuggled on the sofa again and picked up another brochure about Zermatt.

After a while of reading, the crackling fire stole her gaze and sucked her into the flames. Moments later, she fell asleep.

Lyza shook her fist at a darkening afternoon sky as a fat raindrop smacked her between the eyes. Muttering, she shook it off and trudged down a street littered with rubbish. Wearing a dirty black coat, she pushed a grocery cart filled with trash bags. Her filthy face and cracked hands yearned for soap and warm water. A gust of wind blew a ragged scarf off her itching head. As raindrops splashed on the pavement, people hurried past, not seeing her. She seemed invisible. Heaven and Earth ignored her. The air reeked like the dress she wore, and her stomach grumbled. A volunteer nodded a familiar 'Hello' as he opened the door to the rescue mission.

Lyza shuddered and jerked awake.

She jumped up and hugged herself for a few seconds, looking around the strange room as reality swept in. She began pacing the room. *I am in a five-star hotel suite in Zermatt, Switzerland. I am not on skid row.*

She drew a hot bath, unpacked her white fleece pajamas, and brushed her teeth. After a few minutes, she relaxed in the warm bubbly tub and concentrated on the next morning's meeting. *I'm glad I e-mailed them at the Zurich office. At least the secretary, attorney, and assistant will arrive early. They have a heads-up on what I intend to accomplish here.* She sighed. *I do my best planning in the tub; a ski resort just outside Zermatt, who would have guessed I would decide to pick up a project like this? It's no cannery, but it is exciting.*

The warm bath did its job. She felt warm and relaxed enough to get a few more hours sleep before morning.

When the sun poured into the room, she leaped up, rested and ready to hit the ground running. She chose her black-and-white large-checkered suede suit with the white fur for the day's events. Because she would be outside during the property inspections, she dressed accordingly, not forgetting the high altitude and low temperatures.

She glanced out her window. The sun reflected off the majestic Matterhorn. Lyza stopped short. *What an amazing sight!* For a few seconds, she forgot the meeting and took in the view. The knock at the door brought her back.

Lyza opened the door to a man and a woman, both carrying briefcases. The tiny woman wore her black hair pulled back. The tall thin man had a pale complexion, with short black hair and a scar across his chin.

Lyza nodded to them to come in and pointed them to the cherrywood oval table in the middle of the suite. "Come in. Take a seat."

Then Lyza directed the woman, "Call for room service: coffee and rolls. Then we can get started."

"Of course I will do that, but you should understand I am Olga Svenhof, your international attorney. This is Jan, my secretary. Pronounce it *yawn*." Jan stood and extended his hand, which Lyza ignored.

Lyza redirected her command. "Very well then, Jan, if you would call room service." Jan immediately picked up the phone.

"Let's get started. Olga, what I need from you is obvious. What kind of hoops are we going to have to jump through to get this property should I decide it's something we want? What rules and regulations need to be met before this ski area can be reopened? How long will it take, and how much will it cost? Give me all the information you can now. I expect you will know more after we meet with their people."

Lyza was on a roll. "Jan, I want this meeting and all meetings you attend to be recorded. You will need to inform all participants they are being recorded, understand?" Jan nodded. "Not that you need to know why, but this procedure is used in case any misunderstandings arise in the future. Language and cultural differences sometimes block progress or redirect outcomes. I don't want any mistakes."

She turned toward Olga. "I expect you to stop me immediately should I propose anything that doesn't fit within the parameters of international law." Olga nodded.

Jan answered the room service tap at the door. Coffee and rolls were served while Olga produced sheaves of documents to review.

Olga focused on business before her coffee. She spoke with a heavy German accent. "This property is a choice investment. The owners are three brothers. When their parents died, they inherited the property. All three of them live out of the country and have no interest in the business. When they closed the ski slope, even though it is the smallest one near Zermatt, people fiercely objected. The community in general eagerly awaits the reopening of Slope 20—"

Lyza interrupted. "Why is the name Slope 20? That will be changed unless it has local significance."

Olga read the file in front of her. "Slope 20 came out of the personal experience of the couple who started it. They were twenty years old when they came here to open one of the first ski slopes. That's why they called it Slope 20."

"Well, that's just ridiculous. The name will be changed. I can come up with something much better."

Olga continued, "In any case, all the lifts, all the equipment, including the restaurant and ski rental shop, are intact. Here are the inspection reports. They could be restarted with little effort and minimum investment."

After hours of review and strategizing, Lyza felt ready for the eleven o'clock meeting. They walked to the hotel conference room and met the seller's people. It seemed the sellers were eager to get out from under the burdens of keeping the property intact. Even though the little resort was closed, there were many expenses in addition to property taxes.

After only ninety minutes, they decided to make the physical inspection, the final phase of the meeting. Lyza boarded the snow tractor with the others for their thirty-minute ride to the buildings. The bright sun and blowing snow contrasted each other.

How can it be so bright with all this blowing snow? She pulled her fur hat further down over her ears. Their vehicle shook at a sudden blast of wind. Her mink coat kept her warm, but she longed for heat from the vehicle. *What is the matter with these people? Are they not warm-blooded?*

Finally they arrived to walks that had been shoveled for Lyza's sake. She stepped out of the cab. Cold air stabbed her lungs, and vapor escaped from her lips when she exhaled. The small group surrounded her, blocking some of the wind. *I can't wait to get back to LA. It's warm there.*

The icy wind made inspections go quickly, but Lyza was thorough despite it. *I refuse to let this cold keep me from finding anything I should see. I can do this. I can tough it out.* She steeled herself and continued going through cold empty rooms in cold empty buildings. *Have I discovered anything more than I learned within the confines of the warm hotel?*

I need to figure out why they really closed it down. A profitable business would have been easier for them to sell. Oh, it is so cold.

Her assistant and secretary made notes and, as Lyza had directed earlier, recorded comments as they went through the cold, vacant buildings. Finally, the inspection done, they boarded the snow tractor vehicle, which looked like a limousine built on Sherman tank treads.

Back at the hotel, Lyza wanted to huddle next to the fire, but she resisted and went down to the hotel shops. *I cannot leave Zermatt without buying something besides real estate.*

A wool knitted hat with a derby-type bill, a white quartz necklace, some Swiss chocolate, and a fine woolen sweater accompanied her back to her room. *My flight leaves in the morning, so I'd better pack tonight.* She began repacking her bag. *It's getting dark. Before I forget, I need to e-mail the LA office.* She brought up her laptop. She informed the office of her purchase and business plan to get the resort running before reselling it. She intended to present her plan to the directors immediately upon her return. The idea excited her.

Then she got a short note off to Leesa. "Deal is closing. See you tomorrow —Lyza." She collapsed into the fluffy, goose down bed and fell asleep within minutes.

Lyza awoke in time to get dressed for the flight and checked her e-mail. She discovered she could make the directors' meeting regarding the property if her flight arrived on time.

She called for the limo to take her to the Zurich airport. Forty-five minutes later, the driver loaded her luggage and apologized for taking so long, muttering something about snowdrifts blocking the road. The morning darkness combined with blowing snow made everything surreal. *I feel like I'm on Mars.* Lyza hurried to get into the warm vehicle. They drove off at a snail's pace. Once they were moving, visibility was more difficult.

Is this a blizzard? It wasn't like this when we came. Obviously he's driving as fast as he can in this horrible snow. Lyza took a deep breath and tried to relax. *I need to move. I need to stretch.* The spacious limo gave her plenty of room to stretch, and she flexed her muscles. Then she pulled her fur coat around her and tried to get warm.

Chapter Twenty

One hundred miles on frozen highways took more than four hours. Lyza's tension had worn her out by the time she exited the limo at the airport. Exhausted, she made her way to the ticket counter through stranded travelers.

"Checking in for the flight to Los Angeles."

The young agent staffing the ticket counter frowned at the computer screen.

Lyza could tell from the overhead screen that lots of flights were cancelled.

The agent informed her of the latest news. "Authorities have recommended closing the airport due to the storm. But if you hurry, you might make the flight. They are almost through boarding. It's across the terminal." He pointed toward the gate.

Her five-inch heeled boots made sprinting difficult, but Lyza was determined to make the flight. *Yes! The plane is still at the gate!* She pushed her way through a group of men dressed in suits.

Presenting her boarding pass, Lyza started to walk onto the jetway.

The gate official stopped her. "Sorry, this flight is closed."

There must be some mistake. "What?" She pointed out the terminal window. "There's the aircraft. I'm looking at it. It's sitting right here."

The official was firm. "Yes, that's true; the aircraft has not left the gate. However, they have shut the aircraft door. Passengers are not allowed to board once that door is closed. You are not getting on that plane."

Her blood pressure rocketed. *How dare he? I'll miss the directors' meeting!*

She used her most authoritative voice. "Do you know who I am?"

"It doesn't matter who you are. Regulations are regulations, and you're not getting on this flight."

She watched the aircraft pull away from the gate and shouted, "I'll have your job!"

He muttered, "I doubt you could handle it."

"What did you just say to me?"

He turned and walked quickly away.

Frustrated and angry to the point of tears, she found the nearest restroom. Once inside the tiny stall, she began to plan.

After a moment, she lost it and began sobbing. *What is the matter with me? I'm tired. I'm angry. I'm going to get even; right now I need to get to LA.* Then she composed herself and marched to the ticket counter to see when the next flight left for Los Angeles.

The ticket agent took forever, typing on the keyboard, then looking at the screen and typing again. "Flights are being canceled. We may close the airport, in which case you will be stranded overnight."

"It's not closed yet. When is the next flight?"

"If everything goes according to schedule, the next flight for LAX is in four hours. I'm not promising anything. Have you seen the weather outside?"

Lyza held back a strong retort. "Yes, I have. Please schedule me on that flight."

Her temples throbbed. She would try to reschedule the directors' meeting. She desperately wanted to be there to explain her fantastic plan for the ski resort. Six e-mails and two phone calls later, she succeeded in rescheduling the meeting. *The next flight will put me in LA before five o'clock.* She avoided the gate where the rude official had been. At the last minute, she went to get her boarding pass.

The PA system announced boarding for first class passengers on her flight, and she headed for the front of the line. It was the same official as last time.

She showed her ticket. "First class."

"Yes, I see."

Why did I have to get this jerk again? She tried holding back her hate for him.

"It's a first class ticket, but no first class seats are left."

"What did you say?" Lyza felt her anger peaking. "Don't you dare do this to me."

He looked her in the eye. "You can fly coach or you can wait for another flight. It's up to you. What's it going to be?"

She clenched her teeth. "I hate you! I absolutely hate you! I have no choice and you know it. Just assign me a seat, please."

He smiled. "Sure, and thank you for flying Swiss Air."

She snatched the ticket off the counter and glared at his name badge. *Sven Burkhart, no need to write it down. I will remember you.*

She wanted to kill him. She boarded with coach passengers struggling with back-packs and carryon luggage.

Seat 16E, a middle seat, of course. That schlemiel is going to be so sorry. She sat next to a young man staring out his window. He obviously he wasn't going to give up his window seat. *Maybe the aisle seat will be empty,* she hoped.

One by one, people walked by. Nearly all the passengers had boarded when a young woman carrying a baby collapsed in the aisle seat. *Oh great, just great.* Leesa mentally slapped her forehead.

The baby started fussing. The mother rocked her gently, shushing her. "There, there, little one." She kissed her baby on the forehead.

The woman turned to Lyza. "Hi, I'm Silvia, this is Tammi. Sorry, Tammi doesn't fly well. We'll do our best to keep quiet. How are you doing?"

Lyza tried to contain her anger. She spoke through tight lips. "How am I doing?! How am I doing? Let's see now, I missed my flight more than four hours ago. I traveled from Zermatt in a blizzard this morning. I may miss an important meeting in the States. I guess I'm not doing well right now."

The woman brightened and cheerfully responded, "You know, whenever I feel like things are out of control, I remember that everything happens for a reason and that God is in control."

Lyza felt the statement was a slap in the face. She straighted her posture. Her voice cracked. "Why am I even talking to someone like you? You haven't got a clue!"

Lyza snapped her head toward the front, grabbed a magazine out of the seat pocket in front of her, and stuck her nose in it. *How am I going to survive this miserable flight?* The baby started crying.

Lyza squinted, concentrating on the magazine advertisement for touring Egypt. *Oh God, if there is a God, just get me through this flight.*

The flight attendants began their pre-flight litany. "Welcome to Swiss Air flight 688 to Los Angeles, California. Please pull out the safety card in the seat pocket in front of you…"

Lyza ignored the safety procedure instructions and leaned back in her seat, closing her eyes. The baby snuggled next to her mother's breast and fell asleep. The aircraft reached cruising altitude at 38,000 feet. Flight attendants began serving drinks. Hoping to ease some of her misery, Lyza ordered white wine. She had barely ordered when she noticed flight attendants putting away serving carts before finishing their service to the rest of the passengers.

The cabin intercom spoke. "This is the captain speaking. We are experiencing some mechanical failure and will be returning to Zurich. Please remain in your seats and keep your seat belts fastened."

I'm going to miss my meeting because of this inept airline company. Someone is going to pay. Lyza slumped back in her seat, helpless.

The aircraft shook convulsively.

The captain's reassuring voice returned. "Folks, this is the captain speaking. A—" The PA system crackled and stopped.

The aircraft took a nose dive. The interior lights went out. Yellow oxygen masks dropped out of the ceiling. The aircraft lost altitude rapidly. Passengers grabbed for masks, terrified. People screamed and cursed.

Lyza fumbled for her mask in the dark. She felt the cord, but she couldn't get the mask to her face. Panicking, she felt darkness surround her. She screamed with her last breath. "God help me!"

Lyza felt herself falling. Not falling fast, but falling slowly, as in a dream, as if she were floating. Free floating, as if she fell free from the confines of the aircraft. Through closed eyes, she felt the brightest, warmest light she ever imagined.

Although slowly falling, she realized panic had left. Fear dissolved into nothingness. A strange sense of peace filled her. She felt strong arms supporting her. She felt loved for the first time in her life.

The most caring voice she ever heard spoke gently into her ear. "Lyza, you can come to Me now. I want to give you life and life more abundantly."

A thought rushed through her brain. *How can I have a more abundant life? I have everything in the world already. Am I dreaming?* She watched a bag lady pushing a grocery cart in front of her closed eyes.

The warm voice spoke again. "Yes, Lyza, I've called you again and again. I chose you for a life of true abundance, a life in Me. I am drawing you to Me. And although you already belong to Me, now I want you to become part of Me. Thus, your life will truly prosper."

A light went on in her brain and suddenly Lyza realized that the bag lady in her recurring nightmare represented not her lack of earthly riches, but her spiritual poverty. And she knew. She knew she was destitute. Tears crept from beneath closed eyelids.

The warm voice said, "I am the Way, the Truth, and the Life. No one comes to the Father except through Me. Lyza, I am your Salvation, your Messiah. I was with you from the beginning. I created your inmost being. I knit you in your mother's womb. You are fearfully and wonderfully made. I made you and I love you." Time stopped. Hope welled up in her. Only she and He existed in this private dimension.

All of her pride and arrogance melted. Her hardened heart softened and yearned to be cleansed. Tears flowed like a river, and bitterness, ambition, and selfishness flowed out of her at the same time. Her desire for Him overwhelmed her. In desperation, her heart cried out, *"Lord, forgive my unbelief."*

The Lord embraced her. "You will be spared, my child, for you have work to do. Do not be anxious for anything, but in everything, by prayer and supplication with thanksgiving, present your requests to God. And the peace of God, which transcends all understanding, will guard your heart and mind in Me, Christ Jesus, your Salvation, your Yeshua." She fell into a deep sleep as He gently placed her on a piece of floating debris.

A fishing rig's crew witnessed the loud explosion and watched in horror as pieces of aircraft, bodies, and luggage fell from the sky. Immediately the captain swung into action, ordering his rig into the floating debris, searching for survivors floating in the frigid waters of the North Sea. One by one, they frantically pulled frozen, dead bodies from the sea.

Seconds after her descent, a lifeboat reached the piece of wing Lyza rested on. One of the fishermen pointed and yelled, "She's alive? Be careful. She's alive!"

The other man yelled back over the icy wind. "You sure? I haven't found a live one yet."

***

Cook entered Doris's living room. "Thanks for getting everyone here."

Doris addressed the prayer group. "Only in times of crises do we call emergency prayer meetings. I want to thank all of you for getting here in less than thirty minutes. That is a record and I'm proud of your quick response. I've barely had time to let you all in, so I don't know anything specific about the emergency."

She looked at Cook. "Look how upset she is. Everyone's here, so start talking, Beverly. Tell us how we need to pray."

Everyone looked over at Cook. She was visibly shaking, on the verge of tears.

Evelyn's nearly inaudible voice asked, "Dear Lord, what has happened?"

Cook tried to control herself. Her voice cracked. "I don't know much. It was more than thirty minutes ago. I heard a news report a Swiss airliner crashed into the North Sea. They don't expect to find survivors because of the extent of the damage and the cold waters of the North Sea."

Tears filled her eyes. "One thing I do know." She choked. "When I heard the flight number, I remembered that Lyza was on that flight. The only way I know is that she missed her first flight and had to do some rescheduling. She called me during a four-hour wait to make sure I would have the limo meet her at the airport.

"She had tried to contact the driver, but he didn't answer. She was so angry. I could tell she was under extreme pressure. Her voice sounded hard. She said something about this being the worst day of her life. I told her not to worry, I would take care of it."

Tears came down her cheeks. Her voice faded. "Which I did immediately."

Jack handed her a tissue. "Come on; let's pray."

All five of them got on their knees. Cook attempted to gain control of her tears.

Doris began. "Most Gracious Heavenly Father, we come to You today on bended knee. You are the Creator and Sustainer of the universe and everything in it. You control the heavens and the earth.

You created us and You love us. In fact, Lord, You instructed us to come to you in our times of concern and need. Instead of worrying, You tell us to bring all our concerns to You. So here we are today, Lord. We come seeking Your intervention, Your power, and Your peace. We don't know the details, Lord, but You do. A plane crashed. Lyza was on it. Lord, we are praying for her deliverance and for the other passengers, as well."

Jack shook his bowed head. "Lord, we trust You for all of our lives, for whatever happens, for every part of us. Lord, we ask for mercy. Please be with the parents and comfort them in this unexpected time of loss. You know how hard it is to lose a child. Please draw them to You, the only true source of comfort in a loss such as this. And Lord, please be with Leesa, the more sensitive sister. I can't imagine what it would be like to lose a twin. Perhaps You can use this to wake Leesa up to the knowledge that life is short and sometimes shorter than we expect. Help her realize that riches cannot protect her or console her. We continue to join with Beverly in praying for her salvation."

Evelyn's soft voice picked up where Jack left off. "Lord, we know this life is all about You. How this will glorify You is a mystery to me. Help us understand. I pray for the family and for You to put Your Heavenly arms around them and Beverly at this time of loss. We've prayed salvation for the family, Lord, I pray that because this happened, it will bring all of them to the foot of the cross, to the saving power of our Lord Jesus, whom You sent to save us. Reveal Yourself to them, Lord. They need You so very much."

Evelyn stopped and the room was silent for a moment as each prayed in their spirits. Then Jane began praying aloud.

"Dear Heavenly Father, be with us now and help us know how to pray. You say in Your Word that wherever two or more believers are together, that You are there in their midst. We are five, Lord, and we know You are here. Magnify our prayers, Lord. You are God. You can do anything. Do we dare ask for a miracle? Do we dare ask for the undoable? We ask for the comfort, support, and salvation for the family. Do we dare ask for Lyza to live? And if she should live, that she be healthy and well? Do we dare even ask when we already know not one is expected to survive? By faith I do ask, Lord, knowing that with You all things are possible."

Cook's sobs broke through Jane's prayer. Jane continued. "And we pray for Beverly, Lord. Please comfort her. Give her strength, peace, and wisdom so she can be a witness to the Lane family of Your power."

Cook prostrated herself to the floor. "Oh, God, You know I have been faithful. For more than thirty years, I have prayed for this family's salvation. And it has come to this? Lord, is this what it takes for them to stop and acknowledge You? Lord, is this what I've been praying for?"

She sobbed into the carpet. "This is not what I wanted. This is not my design. It's Yours. It's Yours and I must accept it. Help me accept it. If this be Your will, help me accept it. If it is not Your will, help me understand how to deal with it."

She took a deep breath. "Lord, I want to honor You and I represent You on Earth. I feel immense responsibility now in how to conduct myself in difficult days to come. I'm going to need all You can give me to shore me up and be a source of support for the Lane family."

She rose to her knees. "Be with me now, Lord. Thank You for those who join me today. If I need to pray in a different way or for something not mentioned, I ask the Holy Spirit to intervene and pray for us. It's in the Name of Jesus, our precious Lord and Savior, that we pray all these things. And Lord, I am reminded that we don't deserve any blessings You shower down on us. It's through the blood of Christ that we have relationship with You, the Almighty God. I am eternally grateful. Amen."

And in unison the group restated, "Amen."

They got off their knees and one at a time came to give Cook a hug.

Evelyn hugged her long and hard. "God help us all."

Jack hugged her, too. "It's going to be all right, Beverly. I know He has His hand on you."

Doris wiped her eyes. She hated seeing her friend in such pain. "I love you, Beverly. He loves you. It's going to be all right. Please call if I can help."

Jane chimed in. "Yes, if there is anything we can do, please let us know."

"You were here today. Thank all of you. The Lord listened to us. He is on His throne, and that's what matters."

***

Lawrence Lane had called the directors of L. L. Lane Unlimited to a planning meeting to discuss strategies for the next year. His front shirt pocket vibrated. The call had to be from Lana or one of the girls.

He looked around the room at the eight directors sitting around the conference table discussing business matters among themselves. For a moment, he considered ignoring the call. He watched as Bill readied the computer and screen for his PowerPoint presentation and decided he had a free minute. He pulled the cell phone out and looked at the caller identification. *Just as I thought; it's Lana. What's she up to today? I have a minute.* "Hello."

Lana screamed into the phone. "Lawrence! Oh, Lawrence."

The sound of her voice made his heart leap. "Lana, what is it?"

Lana was sobbing and trying to speak at the same time, making it difficult for Lawrence to understand her words. "The plane crashed. Lyza's in the hospital in Amsterdam. Come home. Come home now."

The color drained from his face as he grasped the meaning of her words. Without saying a word to the group he had called together, he pulled his suit coat off the back of his chair and dashed down the hall toward the elevator, his heart pounding.

He yelled into the cell phone as he rushed. "What?! What else do you know?"

"More than two hundred are dead. But she's alive. We must go to her now."

Lawrence shouted as he ran past the receptionist's desk. "Get ahold of Leesa, and tell her to call her mother."

He spoke into the phone as he waited impatiently for the elevator. "I'm coming, darling. Try to relax and get a grip. I'm on my way. Don't do anything until I get there. Here's the elevator. I'll call you when I get to the car."

Down in the parking garage Lawrence ordered the attendant to get the limo, "Pronto!"

He didn't think he could drive. His heart rate was off the charts. As much as he didn't want to wait the three minutes it took to get the driver, he decided it was the better decision. While he waited the eternity of those three minutes, he couldn't help himself. It wasn't that he didn't believe Lana, but he had to try. He called Lyza's cell.

Each unanswered ring confirmed the worst.

The other person he called was Cook. He punched the twins' estate number.

A housekeeper answered. "Lane House."

"This is Lawrence Lane. I need to speak to Cook."

"Oh, so sorry," the Oriental voice returned. "Miss Cook is not here."

"You find her and tell her to get to our home as soon as possible. This is important. Do nothing else until she gets this message. You understand?"

"Yes, sir. I understand."

***

Helicopters had transported survivors to AMC, Academish Medisch Universiteit van Amsterdam for emergency treatment.

Lana and Lawrence Lane arrived in Amsterdam within hours of notification with a full medical staff, headed by Dr. Eckstein, to take Lyza home.

The Dutch woman doctor spoke to the lead doctor of the Lane medical staff. "Incredibly, she has no broken bones. As far as we can tell, there is no internal damage. Currently, she remains in a coma."

Dr. Eckstein examined Lyza's pupils. "You approved her stability for transport, as we spoke of by phone?"

The woman smiled at Lana while speaking to Dr. Eckstein. "Yes, we will release her to you. Her family has contacted the administrator. Everything is in order."

The medical team immediately transferred Lyza to the medical transport jet. For the next few hours, Lana held Lyza's hand. Nurses checked IVs and her vital readings. Doctor Eckstein stared at his computer and studied reports from the hospital in Amsterdam. Lawrence sat and watched, uncertain what to do now. Everything seemed surreal.

They touched down at the private airport near the Lane estate and were met by the ambulance. The Lane limousine carried Lana and Lawrence behind the quiet ambulance to the Lane estate where Lyza had grown up. Medical personnel met them at the front drive and ushered them into Lyza's old room, which had been transformed into what looked like a hospital room.

Leesa met them at the door, tears in her eyes. "Is she all right?"

Lana hugged her. "She's in a coma."

Once settled in the hospital bed, Lyza's family stood around her. Lawrence felt it necessary to voice what they already knew to reassure himself and the others in the room: Leesa and Lana, three nurses, Cook, and Dr. Eckstein's colleague.

He raised his voice so he wouldn't tear up again. "There will always be someone here with her. The doctor is on-call twenty-four seven, and two nurses are on duty at all times. Whatever she needs, we will do."

Leesa took Lyza's hand. "She looks so helpless. I refuse to leave her in this room alone with strangers. I'm staying."

Lawrence started to speak, but Lana touched his lips with her forefinger. Then she faced Leesa. "You can stay. I'll stay with you tonight. Lawrence, ask Cook to get us some blankets."

She turned back to Lawrence. "I think it will be best if Cook and Leesa stay here as long as it takes."

Lawrence nodded. "Absolutely."

Leesa got upset. She stood at Lyza's bed repeating, "Lyza, wake up. Wake up, Lyza." Leesa's tears kept coming. "Why did this have to happen? Why? I knew something was wrong. I could feel it."

Lana and Lawrence Lane didn't speak. Lana held Lyza's other limp hand. Lawrence put his arm around Lana's waist.

Doctor Eckstein entered the makeshift hospital room. "Hello, I need to take a look at our patient."

Lawrence spoke the question they all wanted to ask. "How is she?"

Dr. Eckstein quickly glanced at the informational chart in Lyza's medical file. "She's—well, she's a miracle. I can't imagine surviving an explosion and the fall, then to survive those frigid temperatures. It's nothing short of a miracle. You don't fall seven miles and survive."

Bitterly, Lawrence remarked, "If it's such a miracle, why is she lying here not able to communicate with us?"

Dr. Eckstein handed Lyza's file to the nurse who accompanied him. "She's in a healing coma. I believe she'll come out of it. But Lawrence, you know I cannot make any guarantees."

Lawrence frowned. "Boy, have I heard that enough times the last few hours."

Dr. Eckstein put his hand on Lawrence's shoulder. "We have to wait. She has no broken bones, no bruises or contusions. Internally, the X-rays look good. Her recovery will take time and patience on your part. I haven't seen the other five survivors, but from information received in Amsterdam, she is in the best condition of all the survivors. Be thankful for what you've got here. It's a miracle."

Lawrence whispered softly in his wife's ear, "I am thankful."

Leesa burst into tears again and went into the adjacent bathroom. Lana clung to Lyza's cold, limp hand while she slept.

Cook went to the sitting room and prayed.

Chapter Twenty-One

To the world outside, Lyza looked unconscious, but she was experiencing a most astonishing phenomenon. Her days were filled with the presence of Yeshua as He revealed His never-ending graciousness to her. She sat at the foot of the King of the Jews learning of His eternal faithfulness to His people. His enduring love enveloped her. He taught her that He came to save the world, not to condemn it.

She learned how to communicate with the God of the Universe as He revealed Himself to her each moment, each hour, every sleeping day of her coma. This, indeed, was a time of recovery in much more than the physical. He taught her personally, as though she was the only being in the entire universe. Day and night He spoke words of love to her:

"Give thanks to Me, because I am good.
"My love for you endures forever.
"Give thanks to Me, the God of gods.
"My love for you endures forever.
"Give thanks to Me, the Lord of lords;
"My love for you endures forever.
"I alone do great wonders
"My love for you endures forever.
"By My understanding I made the heavens
"My love for you endures forever.
"I spread out the earth upon the waters,
"My love for you endures forever.
"I made the great lights —
"My love for you endures forever.
"The sun to govern the day,
"My love for you endures forever.
"The moon and stars to govern the night;
"My love for you endures forever."

Each time she heard Him say His love for her endured forever, she felt her heart fill with warmth from His very breath.

"I struck down the firstborn of Egypt
"My love for you endures forever.
"And brought Israel out from among them
"My love for you endures forever.
"With a mighty hand and outstretched arm;
"My love for you endures forever.
"I divided the Red Sea asunder
"My love for you endures forever.
"And brought Israel through the midst of it
"My love for you endures forever.
"But swept Pharaoh and his army into the Red Sea;
"My love for you endures forever.
"I led My people through the desert,
"My love for you endures forever."

Memories of childhood Passover celebrations flashed through her head. Even as a girl she had understood how God had delivered His people out of slavery. Over the years other events trumped religious feasts. The Lanes hadn't attended the Passover feasts for more than twenty years.

"To strike down great kings,
"My love for you endures forever.
"And kill mighty kings —
"My love for you endures forever.
"Sihon, King of the Amorites
"My love for you endures forever.
"And Og, King of Bashan —
"My love for you endures forever.
"And I gave their land as an inheritance,
"My love for you endures forever.
"An inheritance to My servant Israel;
"My love for you endures forever.
"Give thanks to Me, the One who remembered Israel in its low estate
"My love for you endures forever."

The realization that the God of the universe loved her specifically, individually, relentlessly, and unconditionally made Lyza's heart overflow with thanksgiving. She recognized she had done nothing to receive His favor, it was only by His Grace that He came to her.

"And freed them from their enemies,

"My love for you endures forever.

"And who gives food to every creature.

"My love for you endures forever.

"Give thanks to Me, the God of heaven.

"My love for you endures forever."

***

Each hour Lyza lay in the hospital bed was pure torture for Leesa. Her twin sister, her other half, her only friend, seemed as though she was as delicate as a China doll, frozen in place.

After two weeks, Leesa spent less time in the room where she had been every waking hour after they brought Lyza home. The two nurses spent their days on their computers or playing cards and chatting. In the beginning, Lyza required little care other than bathing and changing IVs. Every morning, the physical therapist came in to exercise her arms and legs.

Another week passed. Leesa continued staying at the Lane estate, but began resuming some of her duties at L. L. Lane Unlimited. She spent whatever was left of each day with her sister.

"She's doing fine," the nurses would say. "Her vitals are good. She's been through a traumatic experience, and it will take time." The medical staff seemed confident that one day Lyza would wake up and everything would be normal.

Leesa didn't have the same confidence. She struggled constantly with her sister's mortality, as well as her own. Even when she was out of the room, Leesa might as well have been there in the hospital bed next to Lyza, because that's where her heart and mind stayed.

Leesa's cell phone vibrated. She checked the caller identification to see 'Gary Wagner.'

Leesa could tell from the sounds that he was driving. "Hello, Gary. I guess you're calling about Lyza."

"That's right; I wanted to see how she is doing."

Leesa wondered why he hadn't called sooner. Perhaps he'd kept informed through other sources. "Not well. I'm sorry. I wish I could give better news, but nothing has changed. She's still in the coma."

"I wondered if it would be all right for me to stop by and see her."

Leesa's voice went flat. "You can come, but she won't know you're here. She can't see you or talk to you."

Gary refused to be shut down. "I want to come by and say hello. I know she's in a coma, but maybe I could talk to her."

"Sure, you can talk all you want. She'll never know what you say. Come on over. Anyway, it might be good to have someone different in the room."

"I'm at the front gate."

Leesa straightened. "Oh. Uh. I'll call security to admit you."

***

Gary waited for the iron gates to open and reviewed the last three weeks. How alarmed he was when he heard Lyza was on Swiss Air flight 688. How relieved when Bill reported her survival. How devastated when he heard she was in a coma.

At first he tried to ignore the tug to call Leesa and ask about Lyza. He tried to ignore thoughts of her throughout the day. He went out on a few dates with old girlfriends to put her out of his mind. *I don't think I could date an invalid. What if she never comes out of it? She could be in a wheelchair for the rest of her life. She could come out of it and never be the same. Who knows how much brain damage she has?*

But thoughts of Lyza haunted him. *If she woke up today, and if she was all right, I would never forgive myself for giving up on her.* Then his brow wrinkled. *But she might have scars. If she's disfigured, I don't think I could handle that.*

He could wait no longer. He needed to see her. *I don't care whether she knows me or not, I will speak to her. And I will tell her that I love her. The game is over, if she's all right.*

The gray-haired nurse commented to the other that it seemed sad that Lyza had no visitors. "Have you seen anyone other than family?"

"No, I haven't, but I only work days."

Just then Leesa and Gary entered the room. He noticed bins filled with get well cards in the corner. Suddenly, he and Leesa were standing next to a tiny blonde princess in a hospital bed. He wanted to kiss her, for her to rise out of the bed and be restored. *Then we'll live happily ever after, just like Sleeping Beauty.*

He reached for Lyza's hand, but Leesa stopped him. "Pull up this chair and sit for a while if you like."

He looked at the nurses and felt uncomfortable. "Thanks, I'd like to stay awhile."

The younger nurse stood. "We can go for a walk. Be back in twenty minutes."

The nurses left the room. Leesa put her hand on Gary's shoulder. "I should leave, too. Call my cell if you need anything."

"Okay, I will. I would like a few minutes alone with her."

Alone. When Leesa left, he was finally alone. Lyza wasn't there, and he didn't feel anything. *I thought I at least would feel your presence.* He looked at her and took her cold hand. She breathed normally. She looked as beautiful as the last time he saw her, but it was as though she was dead.

His voice broke the silence. "Dear Lyza, what's happening to you? Where are you? What can I say to the girl who always runs away?"

He sat in silence for a few moments. He felt empty. He looked at the room filled with flowers. *It looks like a funeral home in here.*

He put his other hand on her forehead and her expression did not change. "I came to tell you that I love you. You didn't want to hear it before, and you're not hearing it now. Perhaps I've been a fool too long. Perhaps seeing you like this is what I needed to move on. Certainly you never knew how much I cared. You rejected me, but I couldn't let go. My heart is breaking for you. I will always love you."

He stood and pushed the chair back. Then he leaned over and kissed her on the forehead. "Maybe I can finally let you go now. If you ever do wake, you know where to find me." He choked on the last few words and left the room shaking his head, blinking tears until he reached his car. He opened the car door and looked up at Lyza's window. *Sorry, Lyza, I can't put my life on hold. Your situation is too precarious.Thank God you were always too busy for me.* Then Prince Charming drove off into the LA sunset.

***

Six long weeks passed.

The family met at Lyza's bedside. At Lana's insistence, flowers adorned the room and were changed every other day. Extra orchids filled the room that day, because it was Lyza and Leesa's birthday.

A cheerful Cook rolled the birthday cake in on a serving cart. The two-layered chocolate cake with raspberry filling was Lyza's favorite. "Here we are, girls. Happy birthday to you. Now let me light these candles."

She quickly lit them. "Now get ready to sing before all these candles set off the fire alarm. Thirty-two candles are enough to roast marshmallows over."

Leesa stood next to the bed to sing "Happy Birthday" to Lyza. Lana and Lawrence joined in, then sang the song again to Leesa.

"Now, Lyza, you know I need help blowing out all these candles." Leesa managed a chuckle. "You can help me. Make a wish. One, two, three," Leesa blew with all her might and the candles went out. Everyone looked at the smoking candles on the cake and didn't see Lyza open her eyes.

The nurse whispered. "Her eyes are open." She bent over Lyza. "Lyza, Lyza, honey, can you hear me?"

Leesa grabbed Lyza's hand. "Lyza! Lyza! You're awake! You're awake!"

The other nurse took ahold of Leesa's shoulders. "You need to leave the room if you can't control yourself. I've called the doctor. He's on his way. We have to check her vitals. You can stay, but please move away from the bed."

Leesa, Lana, and Lawrence stood in the corner of the room and waited for the doctor, who arrived in less than fifteen minutes.

Dr. Eckstein entered the room. "Everyone relax." Lyza's eyes had closed again. "Let's have a look here."

He lifted each eyelid, using the light probe to check her iris, then took his stethoscope and listened to her heart. "This is a good sign.

She may be waking up soon. Continue the same treatment. Call me if there is any change."

Lawrence wanted answers. "What does it mean?"

Dr. Eckstein smiled and patted Lawrence's shoulder. "It means she may be coming out of the coma. I can't guarantee anything. It looks good. It's going to be all right."

"Is it really?" Leesa's tears rolled down her face. "For sure?"

"You know I can't guarantee anything, but it looks good, very good. By the way, happy birthday."

Leesa wiped her face. "I'm thirty-two years old today. This morning I felt like a hundred, but now I'm feeling younger by the minute."

Chapter Twenty-Two

The Lord said to Lyza, "Soon you will be back in the world to do works that I planned in advance for you to do. Know that I will always be with you. I will never forsake you. You are my child and I will never leave you."

In the distance, Lyza heard voices singing "Happy Birthday." *Who is it? If I could get a look.* It took all the strength she could muster to lift her heavy eyelids.

She saw, just for an instant, Leesa, Mother, and Father standing in front of a flaming birthday cake. Lyza saw Leesa blow out the candles, and then her eyelids fell closed again.

The Lord spoke again. "I will always be with you, Lyza. Neither angels nor demons, neither the present nor the future, nor any powers, neither height nor depth, nor anything else in all creation, will be able to separate you from My love that is in Jesus Christ, your Yeshua."

She fell into a deep sleep. The nurses hovered around her, plumping pillows, straightening sheets, checking her vitals, anticipating her return.

***

"It's been two days now," Lawrence Lane complained over the phone to Dr. Eckstein. "Nothing's changed. What's going on? You said everything was going to be all right."

"Lawrence, I was there last night. It means there is no change. She will come around. Your job is to relax and make it easier for her. You can't force her to respond. This isn't a real estate assignment. It's life."

Exasperated, Lawrence responded, "What is *that* supposed to mean?"

"You know what it means. For years, I've watched you drive these girls to perform beyond expectation. I want you to stop it right now.

Accept the situation as it is, and learn to live with it. You're lucky. I honestly believe she'll be back soon."

Lawrence repeated Eckstein's mantra, "But you can't guarantee anything."

"No, I can't. I can say it looks good. Stop making her and everyone else feel like it's their fault and they should feel guilty. You can stop blaming yourself, too."

Lawrence's felt his blood pressure rise. He hung up. *Doctors think they know everything. They think they are God Himself.* He composed himself before going in to check Lyza again. She looked so beautiful. Her peaches and cream complexion, with a hint of blush on her cheeks, gave her youth away. She breathed regularly without help from a respirator as she rested peacefully. No stress or worry lines crossed her face.

She looks like a little angel. He saw the little girl he had taken to school on her first day. He began to search himself for the way he had raised the girls and the expectations he had put on them since they were in elementary school. *Perhaps Eckstein is right. I need to learn to back off.*

Dear God, if you bring her back, I will change. I'll change my attitude toward my family and the bottom line of L. L. Lane Unlimited. The business has already expanded beyond any successes I ever thought it would achieve. In fact, the company would go on if I never set foot in the door again. My involvement is something to do. What would I do if I couldn't go in and shake up the employees? But I could stop it. Please, God.

Lyza groaned.

Lawrence started bellowing at the nurses, "Get the doctor over here."

Lyza opened her eyes and gave a weak smile. "Hello, Father. How are you?"

He grabbed her hand, tears in his eyes. "I'm fine; I'm fine; and how are you, sweetheart?

"Well, I think I'm all right. Why am I here, in my old room?"

"You were in an accident. But you're going to be all right." *Where is Eckstein? He should be here by now.*

He spoke to the other nurse. "Go tell Lana that Lyza's awake." The nurse went.

Seconds later, Lana burst into the room. "Is she awake? Oh! Oh! Sweetheart, you're awake!" She ran to the bed to hug her daughter.

Lawrence grabbed her arm. "Stop! Wait until Eckstein gets here. You might injure her."

Lana jerked her arm away and bent over the bed, hugging her daughter. "Don't be ridiculous."

***

After Lyza awoke from her coma, she spoke more softly and seemed to respond more slowly. Doctors attributed the distinct personality change to the mental and emotional stress of recovery.

Three weeks later, Lyza and Leesa moved back to their estate. Lyza sat on the patio by the pool in the cool of the morning. Leesa left for the office early that morning, and Lyza was alone with Cook.

Cook brought a carafe of coffee and an avocado omelet with extra tomatoes, just the way Lyza liked them. "Here's your omelet, sweetie. Can I get you anything else?"

Lyza tore her eyes from the sea to accept the food. "No, I'm fine. Do you have time to sit a minute?"

Cook sat in the chair next to her. "I always have time for you, girl. What's going on? Are you all right—I mean as all right as you can be, considering what you've been through?"

"I think things are getting back to normal." She smiled and shrugged. "Anyway, the doctors say I'm all right."

"Doctors can discern your physical condition. But how do you feel?"

Lyza paused, and then sighed. "You always know what to ask because I feel weird. Everything seems normal, yet everything seems different. I know that sounds crazy. I can't put my finger on it, but everything seems as though I'm seeing it for the first time."

"Is it stressful?"

"It's peaceful."

Cook's eyes widened. "What happened out there?"

Lyza thought a moment before she answered. "It's not something I want to talk about yet."

"You know you can share anything with me."

"Yes, I do know that, and Cook, I appreciate it.

"Cook, you're the only person I feel at home with. You know, last time I spoke with Father, he was all business. He told me the Zermatt deal was a stroke of genius and lifts would be running in less than a month."

"He is so proud of you."

"I don't care about what happened in Zermatt. And I've tried, but I have no interest in going to the office."

"You have plenty of time to go to the office. No one is pushing you."

"Did you know he plans to sue Swiss Air? Like suing them would bring any victims back. It's not like we need money. I tried to talk him out of it."

"Oh, honey, that's just his way of looking out for you."

Lyza shook her head. "Swiss Air took care of everyone's medical expenses, and none of the other survivors sued."

"Isn't that amazing? The other amazing thing is that every survivor recovered. The federal investigators, the doctors, and—of course—the press are having a difficult time explaining how *that* happened."

Lyza laughed. "Imagine dumbfounding the press!" She sipped her coffee. "They're saying no one should have survived the crash. No one should have been pulled out of the icy North Sea alive."

"We are so thankful you are back with us."

Lyza's eyes drifted back to the ocean. "I'm thankful too, Cook. I'm thankful too. One thing keeps coming back."

"What is it?"

"I keep remembering the woman sitting next to me on that flight. She rocked her baby back and forth. I remember her saying, 'Whenever I feel like things are out of control, I remember everything happens for a reason and only God is in control.'"

Cook's eyes filled with tears. "God *is* in control. And everything happens for a reason."

Lyza's cell phone rang. "Lyza Lane speaking."

"It's Leesa. I wanted to let you know that I'm off to Kramer's Island for a few days." She sounded giddy. "Tim and I have to work onsite, so I'll catch up when we get back."

"Thanks for letting me know. He's a fine man." Then Lyza ended the call in an unfamiliar way. "Love you."

***

Lyza slept late. She wandered down to the kitchen where Cook was baking chocolate chip cookies.

She hinted to Cook, "Mmm, that smells good."

Cook extended the hot cookie sheet. "They're still warm, so be careful."

Lyza picked up the hot cookie and looked Cook straight in her kind, hazel eyes. "You know, Cook, you spoil us."

Cook laughed. "Yes, I do, and you love it."

With Leesa at Kramer's Island, Lyza had the estate to herself. She walked along the beach. She walked the nature trail. She sat in the sun on the beach. She sunned herself on the balcony.

She eventually wandered back to the kitchen and sat at the bar. She reached over and picked up the copy of *USA Today*. The headline read, "Memorial Planned for Swiss Air Victims." That was the first she'd heard of it. *A memorial?*

"A memorial to those who died in the crash of Swiss Air flight 688 will be held in Memorial Park. The memorial will honor the two hundred eighty-six passengers and crew who died in the North Sea crash. The six survivors, four Americans, a woman from Switzerland, and a man from Italy have been invited to attend. Many friends and families of the victims have contributed to this memorial, which will be held outside the city of the flight's destination, Los Angeles, California."

"Wow. Cook, they are having a memorial for the victims of flight 688 here in LA."

"Well, I should hope so. Memorials are important, especially for those left behind. A lot of those passengers were from here."

"I guess it's a good idea. I never thought about it before now. Maybe we should contribute."

"No, sweetie, you should be there. Contribute if you like, but you should talk with the other survivors. You also need to meet with the families of those who died."

Lyza trusted Cook's advice. She picked up a sweater and decided to go to the office. "You're right, I do need to see those families."

***

"What are you doing here?" Bill said as Lyza walked past his office. "Your father told me you are banned from the office."

She tilted her head. "Forever?"

"Probably not forever. It just seems like it." Bill opened his arms and gave her a big hug. "He doesn't need to know everything."

"You got any listings for me to look at?" Lyza asked. *Maybe being here will help get me back in the groove.*

"You're bored. You must be getting well. Sure, I'll bring them right in." He went back into his office and opened a file drawer.

She ambled to her office. *I miss this place.* She walked back to the empty break room to fix some coffee. She got her coffee and returned to her office to look through the listings Bill had left on her desk.

Nothing here interests me. What was I thinking? I thought coming here, seeing this place, looking at listings, would energize me. I feel flat. I told Mother I didn't need the psychologist, but I do need something. I need a direction that matters. It doesn't mean I need a shrink.

Flipping through more listings, her mind wandered back to when her parents pressured her to get professional help. She'd finally agreed to see the psychiatrist once. *The fool prescribed anti-depressants. Feeling contented and at peace is depression? He warned me of detached emotions. He said that without drugs and therapy, I might have trouble concentrating or getting interested in projects.* Lyza remembered taking all this advice with a grain of salt and getting out of the psychologist's office soon as she gracefully could.

Today she was indeed not concentrating on projects. *Can I help it if all the choices are boring?*

Since the accident, she saw things differently. Her crash memories were jumbled, but she *knew* in her heart there was a God. Before the accident, she didn't know for sure. Since the coma, she desired further knowledge of God, but she hadn't pursued it beyond praying. Praying in itself was different. Suddenly, she knew how to pray. She could talk to Him, and she knew He listened.

It crossed her mind several times to go to synagogue. When she thought of Jewish acquaintances practicing their faith, she shuddered at all the rules and traditions they observed. *Perhaps I could do without pork, but shellfish? No lobster? Out of the question. Anyway, I tried that years ago. Not eating pork didn't make me feel any closer to God.*

Her mind flitted to the coming memorial for the Swiss Air flight 688 victims. *I want to go. I want to honor those who died on that flight. I want to meet the other survivors.* She took a deep breath. *I believe I'm ready.*

Leesa will be home tomorrow. Maybe she'll go with me. It's being held not far from home, outside Los Angeles. It's as though the memorial is coming to me instead of me going to the memorial. In any case, I want my sister with me.

This Kramer's Island project means a lot to her; I hope the trip goes well.

As Lyza stood in the middle of her office, she looked around and was glad to be back. Yet, as far as trying to come up with any projects, or any interesting listings, she was at a loss. She decided to head back home, though she was there less than an hour.

She drove home slowly, parked the car, and went to her room. She undressed, took a shower, pulled on a pair of jeans, grabbed a white T-shirt, slipped on a pair of flip-flops, and walked outside. She wandered around the estate and wound up sitting on the ground under a maple tree. She looked into the clear blue sky and contemplated her Maker.

Lord, I know you saved me from the crash. You have revealed Yourself to me, but I don't know what to do. I know You are Yeshua and You told me that You are my salvation. I want to understand, Lord, but I feel as though I have so much to learn. Please bring me to the place You want me to be and help me understand You and Your ways. I feel You all around me now, as before. I'll never forget Your arms around me when You saved me from certain death. Please, show me how to love You.

***

At the airport, Lyza waved as she popped open the trunk for Leesa's luggage. After dumping her luggage in the trunk, Leesa jumped into the passenger seat. "You look wonderful! Did you miss me?"

"If you only knew how much. You wouldn't believe it. Did you eat on the flight?"

"I had a snack of, like, five peanuts."

They drove up the coast to a small café on the beach. Choosing the deck nearest the water, they ordered fish and chips. Their order arrived in red, oval, plastic webbed trays. The breeze fanned them, keeping them cool, in spite of the coverless deck.

Leesa cooed, "I love Kramer's Island. I love seeing the progress. On the outside, it looks like progress is slow. But that's because we're involved in the prep work, shoring the structures inside and that type of thing. The best part comes soon."

"I am so glad you're getting so much pleasure from this project. I never had a project that I connected with like you do with Kramer's Island."

"I was surprised, too, because to start with, it was just a cannery. Who would buy a cannery? I tried thinking outside the box. I thought of the furthest thing from a cannery. What would be far, far from a stinking, slimy fish cannery? I kept asking myself that question."

Both of them started laughing hysterically. Leesa continued. "The thing I kept thinking was escape. How could I get away from a stinking, slimy old fish cannery? It occurred to me that I should pick something I would like versus something I found repulsive, thus, an amusement park."

Lyza raised her hand for a high five. "Brilliant. My sister, the brilliant one."

"There's brilliant, and there's lucky. You're the lucky one. I'm so glad you're here. I love you so much. I don't know what I would have done if you were killed in that crash."

Lyza suddenly got serious. "The experts all agree, I should have died in that crash. Only God saved me. No one can fall seven miles, hit the ocean at terminal velocity, and survive."

Lyza never voiced this before. She had never acknowledged her experience that day. It all seemed surreal. She had difficulty thinking about it. *What is real and what part of it was imagination or a dream? My encounter with Jesus seems so real, but unbelievable. How do I choose between two unbelievable possibilities?*

Leesa had tears in her eyes. "You are so brave. You made it, though, against all odds."

"It wasn't me. I'm not that brave."

They turned to watch the waves on the beach.

Lyza turned to Leesa. "They're having a memorial for the victims of the crash. It's coming up soon, and I hope you will go with me. I mean, I could go by myself, but if you don't have anything going that day, I would like you to come with me."

"Sure, I'll check my calendar, but I'm sure I can go with you. I want to be there for you. What about our parents?"

"Oh, no, I don't want them there; too much publicity, too much fanfare."

"I understand. We could ask Tim and Gary; they would go with us."

Lyza couldn't understand why, but she teared up. "No, it's not that I don't like going places with them. I feel like the memorial is too personal. It is for me, anyway. Sorry. I'm more emotional since the crash. I don't want to see Gary."

"Don't you dare apologize."

Lyza wanted to explain what she didn't understand herself. "It's just that everything seems different now."

"How do you mean different?"

Lyza wiped her eyes. "Everything seems more important, more precious. People, situations, relationships, even some physical things have taken on new significance. For example, for the first time since I did it, I really am sorry about throwing Mr. Ted overboard. I'm trying to get it, but I have this deep conviction that it's going to take a long time."

Leesa leaned forward. "It's going to be all right."

"Oh, I know it is, but some things are bothering me." She grinned a sheepish grin. "One thing is about the Zermatt deal. When we signed the papers, I noticed they made a mistake and left out one of the smaller maintenance buildings. I mean, the building was on the schedule, but they forgot to assign the dollar amount. They made a mistake."

"You mean they signed off on a contract and basically gave you a building?"

Lyza nodded.

Leesa laughed. "That is so great. What a deal. They probably will never figure it out either. Father will be so impressed."

"I'm going to make an addendum to the agreement and pay them for the building."

Leesa's eyes widened in disbelief. "What? That's just nuts. They messed up. It costs when you mess up. It's not up to you to fix their mistake."

"No, that's the right thing to do," Lyza said.

"The right thing to do? Are you crazy? It's unfortunate for them, but it's business and you know it. It's not like they don't have money."

Lyza leaned back in her chair. "I don't think it's the way I want to do business."

"You're beginning to sound like some kind of saint. You know very well there's a reason saints aren't in the business of making money. Father taught us not to pass up freebies, and that was definitely a gimme. You should take the money and run."

"There's a problem with that kind of thinking. Just lately I have considered something. What if the shoe were on the other foot? How would I feel about a deal that I made and ripped myself off? No, I can't live with the deal the way it is. I'm changing it. End of discussion."

Chapter Twenty-Three

Cook studied the Scripture as she prepared for her quiet time with the Lord. She sat at the tiny desk at the end of her bedroom. Her green, spiral-bound journal lay open next to the Bible in case she felt the need to write a comment. Aloud, she read the passage from chapter three of Titus, beginning with verse 3. "At one time we too were foolish, disobedient, deceived, and enslaved by all kinds of passions and pleasures. We lived in malice and envy, being hated and hating one another."

The memory of her childhood roared through her mind like a black tornado. Her hands covered her eyes, attempting to block out the vision. The face of her father loomed in front of her and she gasped. His contorted face accused her. "Fool! You never do anything right. You never do anything right. You will always be a failure."

She cringed and blinked away the sight to focus on the picture of Christ hanging across the room above her bed. She was haunted by the sound of her father's voice still echoing, "You stupid brat. You're as dumb as a box of rocks. You'll be the death of me yet. You're weak and stupid. What a combo."

She winced, remembering him slapping her face with the back of his hand.

She could still feel the heat on her face when she touched her cheek.

How she hated him. He was probably the only human being she'd ever hated. She had wished him dead, and now she hung her head, remembering her fractured childhood. She remembered telling her mother that she wished her father dead. She had prayed to the Lord God Almighty that he would die. And on the day he died, she'd felt free for the first time in her life. The freedom was short-lived, crowded by guilt.

"Get Thee behind me, Satan. I rebuke you in the name of the Lord Jesus; in Jesus' Name, begone. I'm not eight anymore. You cannot accuse me for what God has forgiven." She looked back at the picture and felt reassured as she felt His presence in the room.

Cook looked back at the Scripture, "At one time, we too were foolish, disobedient, deceived, and enslaved by all kinds of passions and pleasures. We lived in malice and envy, being hated and hating one another." *It's true I was foolish, disobedient, and deceived when, at eight years old, I believed my mother's ranting, "Now you've killed your father, and I hope you're happy." But no more. Jesus freed me from the bonds of sin and changed my life. Thank You, Jesus, for bringing my cousin Susan into my life.*

Having rebuked the devil, she returned to her quiet time with the Lord. At the end of their time together, He gently suggested that she call her cousin. She dialed her cousin's number.

"Hey, Bev."

The happy sound of Susan's voice cheered Cook. "Susan, I'm so glad you picked up. Do you have time to talk?"

Susan sensed her cousin needed to vent. "I have plenty of time. What's going on?"

"I've been under attack this morning, and I felt like the Lord told me to call. Does that sound crazy?"

"No, it sounds right. We are to bear one another's burdens and comfort each other. You did rebuke the enemy, didn't you?"

"Oh, yes, and I immediately felt the presence of the Lord. But after my quiet time with Him, I guess I wanted to talk to someone. I keep remembering the day Dad died, and I keep reliving Mother shouting at me, telling me that she had told me to put my skates away and that I killed him. She said—"

"I remember exactly what she said. She said that he was gone because he tripped over your skates and fell down the staircase. She said that she told you to pick up the skates, and you didn't do it. And for that reason, she blamed you for his death. But, Bev, haven't you ever wondered why your mother didn't pick up her eight-year-old child's skates if they were situated at the top of the stairs? You were eight."

"Oh, I know it. I resolved this years ago. I'm certainly not trying to shift blame to her, either. It was an accident, pure and simple. It's just that it came up today during prayer time, and I could almost hear her say that I hated him and now he was dead, that I should be happy."

"That's just old garbarge. The day your father died, no one put an arm around a sad eight-year-old girl to comfort her. No one said that it wasn't her fault. He came home drunk again and fell down the staircase. You forgot about the skates. You didn't mean to leave them at the top of the staircase. You didn't kill him."

"But, Susan, I remember like it was yesterday. I felt peace for the first time in my life. I didn't mean to do it, but I had to admit that I was glad he was gone."

"Who wouldn't? He mistreated you."

Cook reached for a tissue. "All those years, the voices in my head asked me what kind of girl feels glad her father died. Mother agreed with the voices. Life with her became hell, but at least she wasn't hitting me. No one stood by me, and I carried the guilt like a smoldering boulder until you came into my life. When you and your mother took an interest in what was happening to me every day, I felt hope that things could change."

"You know what I remember?"

Cook wiped her eyes and blew her nose. "What?"

Susan's voice went soft. "I remember a little girl in the third grade who sat in the back of the classroom. She always looked at the top of her desk, afraid the teacher would call on her. She didn't have any friends and kept to herself."

"That's because the voice in my head kept telling me that no one would want to associate with a wicked person like me. I know now that it was the enemy, trying to destroy me."

"Well, I don't think it was just the devil. When my mom overheard your mom screaming at you, accusing you of killing your father, she told Dad that her sister had lost it since the death of her husband. They needed to provide a safe place for you. They devised a plan to start asking you to dinner and for sleepovers, even keeping you for days at a time."

Cook brightened. "The best part of it was that we became best friends. Cousins can be best friends. And when I started going to church with you, I felt like part of the family. You know, I really thought it was normal for families to scream at each other every day, and when you were different—well, at first I thought it was all an act."

Susan chuckled. "If we're going to reminisce, we can't leave out the summer we went to church camp."

"That summer changed my life."

Cook and Susan talked for over an hour about the summer of their sixteenth year when Cook and Susan went to church camp. They hiked and swam and canoed and had songfests beside the campfire at night. They sang about love and God and Jesus. One night, the Lord spoke to Cook, and she accepted His invitation. She'd prayed a prayer of repentance and asked Him for forgiveness. At that very moment, she'd felt the smoldering guilt boulder lift off her shoulders. The warmth of God's love filled her heart. Then she made a vow to serve Him in any way He chose for the rest of her life.

Cook sighed. "The Lord is so good. Thanks for listening to me this morning. I just needed to talk to someone."

"Call me anytime."

After Cook said good-bye to Susan, she thought about the events following her conversion. After returning to school, she took a job as a cleaning helper for a young couple immersed in building their business. When she graduated from high school that year, Lana Lane asked her if she would extend her work hours to full time and become a live-in housekeeper. Then Lana got pregnant and had twins. Cook became nanny as well as housekeeper.

The day the twins came into the world, Cook felt the Lord had commissioned her to lead the Lane twins to Him no matter how long it took. The Lanes became wealthier, and Cook got older. The Lanes hired more help, and Cook became their right hand at home. Overnight the twins grew into adulthood and built their own estate. They begged their parents to let Cook come with them. After weeks of waiting, Lawrence announced that Cook could go with them. Cook knew all the time that she would go. She had a mission.

Now I suspect Lyza's found Jesus, from her changed behavior. Jesus changes people. His love changed me from a beaten down, accused, guilt-ridden girl to a woman dedicated to serving Him.

Cook turned back to the Scripture and read the next verse. "But when the kindness and love of God our Savior appeared, he saved us, not because of righteous things we had done, but because of His mercy."

She stared at the picture of Jesus. "People can change. Glory be to God, the Father."

***

Lyza dressed for the office. A gray, mid-knee length Gucci suit with pink blouse and pink diamond-studded heels looked acceptable in the floor-to-ceiling mirrors in her dressing room. She grabbed the matching gray briefcase with silver trim. Before leaving, she stopped by the kitchen to get a bite of breakfast.

Cook gave her a heads-up, "Leesa left an hour ago."

Lyza poured herself a cup of coffee. "I thought I heard her leave. I have time for breakfast. I wouldn't want to show up too early and shock the staff."

Cook pulled out a tray of the largest, most beautiful fruit scones Lyza had ever seen. "Have a cranberry scone, just out of the oven."

Lyza savored the first bite. "Pass the butter, please… Mmm, these are to die for."

Cook teased, "Yeah, well, they will kill you if you have that much butter on them. Here, put some honey on them. That really makes them good."

"You are evil."

Lyza ate half the scone, drank most the coffee, and then decided it was time to leave. She was still savoring the scone while driving down to the freeway. Traffic was heavy. She relaxed and popped in the latest U2 recording.

She thought about the night of the benefit. *So much has happened since that magical night. The kiss from Gary. The flight to Brisbane. The meeting with O'Malley. The oil transaction with Gary and his father. The flight to Zermatt. The inspection of the ski area. Then the accident and my miraculous salvation.* Her mind stopped. *There it is. My salvation, body and soul, is a miracle. I'm getting more of that memory back.* It both comforted and frightened her.

Every Jew I know believes Jesus is not the expected Messiah, yet He revealed Himself to me. He is our salvation. Lyza tried to reason with herself. *I'm no theologian. What am I supposed to do with this information? I know Jesus is exactly who the Christians say He is. Am I supposed to go around proselytizing like those annoying Christians do? Am I still Jewish?*

Lyza tormented herself with these questions. She had so many questions, yet she had a different kind of peace than before. Her peace remained, especially at times like that one, alone and driving to the office.

She arrived late at the parking garage. It didn't bother her that day. In the past, she would've been frantic to be on time. Before the accident, she'd kept normal office hours like her parents did before her mother retired and her father spent his time meeting with the good old boys and flying his private jet to meetings around the globe.

Lord, I know You are God. I trust You. I called out for God and You saved me. I know You are real. You filled me with a peace beyond understanding in an unbelievably frightening situation. You protected me from seeing and hearing the violence. You gave me peace when my whole world was destroyed. I know You now, and I know You will answer every question in my heart. I know You will resolve the confusion I face daily. How am I going to tell my family? I trust You for the answers. And, Lord, You know trust doesn't come easily for me.

Her thoughts wandered back to the Australian cattle ranch turned oil discovery. As she rode the elevator up to her office, she began thinking about Mr. Charles O'Malley. *Surely, Lord, You know this man drilled for oil on land that did not belong to him. What a flagrant disregard for the law.* She remembered how angry she was at the time. Now she couldn't muster any emotion. Her anger no longer existed.

All at once she realized, *He must have been desperate to have done such a thing. I took every dime he had to his name to teach him a lesson. I'm not sure it was up to me to teach him a lesson. When I think of how gracious God has been to me in spite of the idol-filled life I've lived, I must respond by extending grace where I can. Maybe Mr. Charles O'Malley deserves a break. Or maybe he's like me, and he doesn't deserve a break, but he's going to get one anyway.* She sat at her desk.

She pressed the intercom button. "Bill, could you come in here?"

"Sure."

"Could you please bring O'Malley's original file? The one with his offer for the Aussie cattle ranch." *He's probably wondering what he did wrong this time.*

Bill immediately found the file and brought it into Lyza's office. "This deal is sewed up, Lyza. You bought it. I don't see the point. You know we don't do post-ops."

Lyza remembered how she had attacked Bill in the past for what she thought would have been an inappropriate remark. In the past, she took it as judgment on her abilities. She relaxed her shoulders. *Bill, you're about to get a pleasant surprise.*

She looked up at him and laughed. "Oh, Bill, I know we don't do post-mortems. I need some information on how to contact Charles O'Malley. I have some personal unfinished business, and don't get the wrong idea." She raised her eyebrows.

She spread the contents of the file on her spacious desk so both of them could look at them. "Do you see any leads on where he might be?"

Bill's face brightened. "The agent you worked with in Brisbane was Clete Collins. I'll bet he can find him."

She smiled at him. "Bill, you're amazing! I appreciate it."

Bill couldn't hide his delight at Lyza's compliment. "You're welcome, Lyza. You're feeling better, aren't you?"

She closed the filed and handed it back to him. "Much better, Bill. I'm feeling much better. Thanks for asking."

He took the file and went back to his office.

Lyza perused the recent listings, hoping to find something she would like to work on. Nothing jumped out for her, and it disappointed her, because she loved the business and wanted to find something to make her feel productive. That day, same as the last time she looked at listings, she simply could not get interested. She turned on her office terminal and began to surf the Internet, looking at expensive, but old, listings.

***

Clete Collins was startled to get a call from Lyza Lane. "Miss Lane, how are you? We were all so worried about you when we heard about the accident."

The sweetest voice answered, "I'm fine; I'm fine, thank you. Listen, Clete, I need a favor."

"A favor?" He was stunned. Who was this person trying to push herself off as Lyza Lane? "Of course, what is it?"

"I want you to get a message to Charles O'Malley. Remember, he's the man…"

He picked up the black ball point pen in the office set on his desk, poised to write on the yellow pad in front of him. "Oh, I remember him. How could I forget? What's the message?"

"First, I want this printed in script on stationery paper and hand-delivered. Second, this is a confidential transaction. I called you because I can trust you."

"As you wish." Curiosity got to Clete. *What is she up to this time?*

"Ready?"

"Ready!"

She spoke clearly and slowly, dictating at a rate Clete could maintain.

"Dear Mr. O'Malley,

"This letter is to remind you of our recent meeting regarding the property outside Moomba, in the Australian bush. The property was an abandoned cattle ranch and consisted of an estate with several out-buildings. When I inspected the property, I found a capped oil well. Since you had made an offer on the property, I assumed you had drilled on private property without permission. And it seems you did. You took a risk. You found oil, and then you wanted to buy the property. I explained to you at our meeting that we don't do business that way. Since then, the well has been put into full production.

"I refuse to sell the property to you under any circumstances, but I want you to know that, first, I am not going to press charges for the illegal acts you performed, and second, I am not an extortionist. Go to St. George's Bank on Market Street and ask for Mr. Terry Lindberg. He will present you with a check for three hundred fifty thousand AUD, plus interest for the time the money was in his bank. I deposited it directly after our meeting.

"I am not condoning what you did. I hope you never undertake another illegal plan. However, I am willing to conclude that you made a mistake. I don't want your money, but I do want you to understand what you did. Mistakes happen sometimes. Forgive me for my past actions in this matter. Your mistake does not justify me making one as well. It's not right for me to keep your money. I sincerely hope these last few months have not been unbearable.

"Lyza Lane."

Am I hearing things? Clete wrote every word as fast as he could, but his mind was racing. *Will the real Lyza Lane please stand up? This can't be her. The old man must have told her to do this. Wow. O'Malley is going to be shocked.*

"Did you get it? You have his address, right?"

"I'll find it. When do you want this delivered?"

"I'd like to do it today, as soon as you can find him. Thanks for taking care of this. I appreciate it."

***

Lyza took the scenic route to the Lane estate where she'd grown up. She'd called earlier to be sure Mother was there.

Mother sounded mystified. "Just coming for a visit? What's happened?"

"Nothing's happened. I just haven't come by for a long time. Is it all right if I come, or is this a bad time?"

"You know I always have time for you. Maria will make your favorite iced green tea."

The road curved through a canopy of trees leading to the main house. The trees filtered sunlight onto the windshield, making happy dances of light. Lyza parked on the red stone circular drive at the front door.

Her mother stood on the porch. "Lyza, so glad you came by. Come in, come in."

Lyza jumped up the two steps and gave her mother a hug. "You look wonderful, Mother. Did you just have a massage?"

Lana laughed. "As a matter of fact, I did."

They walked through the house to the back patio and sat at the poolside table. Maria brought a tray with iced tea and sugar cookies.

Lana couldn't hide her curiosity. "What brings you here today? I heard you were at the office."

"Yes, I was at the office, and that's what I want to talk with you about."

"The office?" Lana waved her hand. "I know nothing about what goes on at the office. In fact, office discussion is off-limits when your father is home."

"I know it. You never discuss business, yet at one time you were all about L. L. Lane Unlimited." Lyza bit into the cookie.

"That was a long time ago."

Lyza cut to the chase. "I'm having a hard time relating to the office. I just can't seem to get interested. Is that what happened to you?"

Lana vigorously stirred her iced tea, making tinkling sounds with the ice hitting the sides of the glass. "No, that is not what happened to me."

"Mother, I'm trying to figure out what's wrong with me. Is this another consequence of the accident, or is it burnout, or…?

"Sweetheart, I think it's the accident. It took a tremendous toll. It had to. I'm amazed that you're functioning as well as you are. Everyone's been amazed. It may take months to recover."

"Don't tell me that. I don't want to hear it."

"All right then, let me tell you about me and the business. Your father and I started out with nothing. He made a couple of good deals that gave us something to build on. At that time, the business was everything to me. We worked long hours. We talked business all day and all night. There was nothing but the business. It was our life. Then you came along."

"Did you have to quit then?"

"No, I didn't have to, but I wanted to because my focus changed. I was a new mother. I stopped going to the office for a while because I had two wonderful children and I wanted to be there to hold you as much as possible. I remember rocking you to sleep and holding you and rocking you hours after you drifted off. I loved having you all to myself. Well, Cook was there, too. In any case, nothing at the office could keep my attention."

Lyza smiled, "Until…"

"Yes, until the day Bill got a call from Israeli Defense Forces, requesting his services for two years. He had to leave immediately, and I knew it would be all right to go back and fill the gap Bill left. After all, you and Leesa had Cook, who rocked you almost as much as I did. I went back because I convinced myself that your father needed me there."

"If Bill hadn't gone to Israel, you would have stayed with us. I can't remember a time that you didn't work."

"Well, you were young when I went back. And, after being gone for over two years, I found the corporate world invigorating once again. Part of the challenge meant working as hard and doing as well as Bill did. I got caught up in it. I was your father's right-hand man, so to speak." She smiled. "The same will happen with you, dear. Perhaps you should stay away longer."

Chapter Twenty-Four

The day of the memorial arrived, six months from the day Swiss Air flight 688 exploded over the North Sea. Federal Aviation inspectors never established the cause of explosion.

Lyza dreaded attending the memorial, yet she was determined. She called Leesa on her cell phone to see what she was going to wear.

"What? It's today? Lyza, do you know where I am?"

"No, where are you?"

Leesa stammered. "I—I'm at Kramer's Island. There's no way I can get there. I thought it was next week. I'm so sorry. I feel terrible. What a mess! But Lyza, you'll be all right. Everyone there will treat you right—you're one of the survivors."

Feeling abandoned, Lyza worked up a cheerful response. "Oh, I know I'll be all right. Have a good trip. I'll see you when you get home."

Now she had to go to the memorial by herself. Leesa could have provided the moral support she felt she needed.

Little voices in her head argued as she walked in to her spacious closet, surveying her choices for the day. *No! I refuse to wear black. Black is for mourning. I know many will be mourning, but that day was more like a new beginning for me. Everything has changed for me. I can't mourn the day.*

I can mourn the dead. Oh, all right, I'll wear black. She chose a Ralph Lauren little black dress, knee length with a not-too-deep scooped neckline and elbow-length sleeves. For shoes, she picked the shiny black Christian Louboutin pair, with spiked heels. The black matching purse finished the outfit.

Oops! What does one wear for jewelry at one of these? She sat in front of the mirrored vanity lined with clear containers filled with every color in the rainbow on both sides. Reaching for the diamond earrings, she chose a small stone dangling from a one-inch gold chain. Wearing her tennis bracelet without the necklace made her feel properly understated.

She didn't feel up to driving, so she asked Cook to call for the limo. *At least then I know he'll wait, and I can collapse when it's over. I'm not looking forward to this, but I should go.*

She stopped by the kitchen and peeked in the fridge, looking for lunch, but nothing appealed to her. She grabbed a bottle of Evian as she went out the door to the car. She glanced at her watch. *Oh, no, I'm going to be early. This is a disaster.*

She went back into the kitchen and began to read the copy of *USA Today* lying on the bar. *No interesting news, just the usual boring stuff: wars, violence, politics.* She went back upstairs and looked for another pair of shoes, but the ones she had on were the best choice. Thirty minutes later, she went out and got into the limo.

At ten after two, she arrived for the two thirty service. Lyza sat in the limo a few minutes before joining the people standing around. The sun filtered through tall oaks, making shady places to sit on the edges of the sea of white chairs. Walking up to the lines of folding chairs, she saw a familiar face. *How do I know him?*

He smiled. "Hello."

Lyza smiled back. "Hello." She thought she knew him, but she couldn't remember his name or where she had seen him before—not that she would admit it, with her mother already wanting her to see a psychologist.

He said, "I'm glad you could come today. Are you doing all right?"

She stalled for time to remember. "Oh, yes, I'm doing fine. How about you?"

"I'm doing well, thanks. It looks like we got a beautiful day."

She looked at small groups of people chatting. "Yes, it is a lovely day. It looks like a good turnout."

She was drawn to this friendly man. He looked so familiar. She knew that she should know him, but she was racking her brain and coming up with nothing. Finally, she had to 'fess up. "I feel like an idiot. I can't remember your name. I apologize."

"Oh, I don't believe we have formally met. I'm David Gabriel." He held out his hand.

She shook his hand. "I'm Lyza Lane."

He held her hand an extra few seconds. He spoke as though he was concerned about her feelings. "Oh, yes, you're one of the survivors. I'm so glad to meet you. You went through a horrible ordeal. I hope this gathering will lift you up and not bring you down. Almost everyone here mourns a lost loved one."

"I needed to come." She confessed aloud to herself and to him. "I didn't want to come, but I couldn't stay away, either."

"Well, if you need anything, like if you want to talk or have any questions, please come to me. I'll be happy to talk with you anytime."

"Oh, thank you." She felt as if he really cared.

His kind eyes searched hers. "I notice you came by yourself. Was that intentional?"

Lyza smiled in spite of the grimace she felt. "No, my sister was supposed to come with me, but she's out of town." She held a hint of bitterness at being deserted by Leesa for Kramer's Island. "She's working on a huge project and got the dates confused."

By then, a large crowd had gathered. The folding chairs filled up. Men on the stage tested microphones. A young man came to David and whispered something.

David turned back to Lyza. "Sorry, I have to go, but I'd like to talk with you more. Please stick around; maybe we can talk after the service."

He walked away quickly, but not before Lyza noticed his naked left ring finger. Lyza found a seat on the end of a row in case she felt the need to flee.

The young man who'd whispered to David was on the stage. He spoke into the mic. "Good afternoon and thank you all for coming to this memorial for the victims of Swiss Air flight 688. First, let's bow our heads and I will open with a word of prayer."

"Dear Heavenly Father, we are gathered here today to acknowledge and memorialize the loved ones we lost that fateful day. None of us can understand what happened that day and why we had to lose people who were of great importance in our lives. You, dear Lord, only You, know the heartache and suffering they went through and what we are going through today. We ask that You be with us today as we honor them, and we ask Your blessing on this gathering. In Jesus' name, Amen."

"And now I would like to introduce the Reverend David Gabriel." David walked on the stage.

Lyza caught her breath. *A pastor! He is a pastor. I can't believe I was talking to a pastor. I thought I knew him. He looks so familiar. There's no way I know a pastor.*

David took his place in front of the glass podium. "Thank you, Steve, and thank you for that prayer and blessing. None of us would be here this afternoon if we didn't have a connection to someone on Swiss Air flight 688. We are here to honor the survivors of the flight, as well as remember those who died.

"The plane left Zurich on a stormy day. In fact, it was the last flight out of Zurich before they closed the airport due to blizzard conditions. None of the people who boarded thought they would be gone in the instant it took for that explosion to occur.

"The accident took them, and beyond that, it changed your lives forever. We had loved ones on that flight. People we will never see again. We are left with our memories and a hole in our hearts. Now is the time to remember the good times.

"Memories that aren't good, those we must leave behind. We must look to our own futures and make a conscious decision to lead the rest of our lives in a way that would make those who have gone on before us proud. Our loved ones look down and see how we respond to their absence. They want us going on with our lives. One verse in the book of Hebrews, chapter twelve says, 'Since we are surrounded by such a great crowd of witnesses…' We are surrounded by them and their love."

David Gabriel continued, giving a moving eulogy. Afterward, he had something personal to share. "You may wonder why they chose me to speak today. I'm a small-town preacher from Lakewood, California. I lead a congregation of about a hundred fifty people, and I'm not famous. Many pastors would have loved to come and share this memorial with you, but I was chosen for a special reason.

"I lost someone on Swiss Air flight 688. My sister Silvia and her baby daughter—my baby niece—were on that flight. My sister was about the friendliest person in the world. She didn't know a stranger, and I am confident that she died with friends around her. Aviation inspectors say they died instantly in the explosion. It's comforting to know they didn't suffer. Her husband Brett is here." David gestured to the man in the audience. "Brett, stand up." The gathering applauded.

Lyza's mind flashed back to the woman who sat next to her on that flight. She remembered the woman smiling and introducing herself, "Hi, I'm Silvia." Lyza burst into tears as she realized the woman sitting next to her with the baby was David Gabriel's sister. *Oh Lord, I survived, but this wonderful woman, the woman who tried to be kind to me, perished.*

Lyza started judging herself. *Why would God spare a selfish, spoiled woman like me instead of Silvia? And I was so rude to her when she was trying to comfort me.* Lyza sobbed uncontrollably.

She heard David continue, "Several survivors joined us here today. None of us can imagine what they have been through. Not only the explosion, but floating in the cold of the North Sea until those fishermen picked them up. We praise God for those men, and we praise God for sparing the lives of six people. Let us pray."

"Dear Heavenly Father, we thank you for those who survived this tragedy. We ask that you bless them with complete recovery. For the rest of us, Lord God Almighty, Giver of every good and perfect gift, we ask for healing. Please heal our hearts and help us never forget You are the God of the universe and You will bring out our best to glorify Your Name. May we avoid the quicksand of self-pity. Help us walk our paths of healing through loving others and performing good deeds to Your honor. In Jesus' Name, Amen.

"We want to take a few moments to remember each victim personally. As I repeat each name, take time to remember them and thank God for how they touched our lives."

Slowly and deliberately, he pronounced each name in its own space, pausing before voicing the next name.

"Christopher Anderegg, Adelheid Angst, Kay Austin, Donald Bane." His pause was barely noticeable. "Silvia Beemann"—his voice cracked—"Tammi Beeman, Cheryl Books, Carolyn Brooks…"

With much effort, Lyza managed to get control of herself, but when David started reading the names, she lost it all over again. Many people cried openly; no one cared.

He read the last name and quietly walked off the stage. After the orchestra played taps, people began moving toward their cars. They stopped and introduced themselves to one another and told others the names of whomever they were there to remember. Lyza wanted to meet some of the other survivors, but she had no clue how to find them. She had been practicing denial. She made a mental note to meet with each of them soon.

David walked to her. He put his hand on her shoulder. "Are you all right?"

She started sobbing again. She was far from fine, and he knew it. She sniffed and dabbed her face with a tissue. "Oh, I'm fine. I'm fine."

"It's going to be all right." He patted her on the back. "It really is going to be all right."

She searched her purse for another tissue to replace the saturated one in her hand. Not finding one, she looked up. "I'm so sorry. I lost it."

He offered his handkerchief. "Lyza, have you had any counseling for this?"

She dried her tears. "I did go to one session, but didn't go back," she admitted. "I couldn't explain how I felt. I wish I could meet the other survivors. I don't even know their names."

"I can arrange for a meeting if you like."

"I would appreciate it." She handed him back his handkerchief.

He shook his head. "You keep it. I'll be glad to contact you when I've set up the meeting."

She dug in her purse, found her card, and handed it to him. "Here's my card."

"Thank you, Lyza. I'll give you a call after I've contacted all the other survivors."

She got into the limo and rolled the black window down. "Thank you, David, I can't thank you enough. Your eulogy moved me."

He smiled, closed the door, and waved before walking back to comfort those standing around empty seats.

***

Charles O'Malley opened his eyes to familiar yellow water stains on a dirty aging ceiling above him. It was morning, and he lay on a bare cot. Light crept through worn curtains covering a dirty cracked window. He hoped the hangover would relent enough for him to get to the fridge for a cold beer. Life was blank. He had no job, no prospects. He had no responsibilities. He had no money. He had no plans. In fact, he barely had himself.

The physical wounds from the beating in the alley behind the Watering Hole Tavern had healed beautifully months ago. In any case, nobody could see the telltale scars for the filth on his face.

He struggled to get upright and sat on the edge of the cot, waiting for dizzy cobwebs to clear from his head before he stood up. He took a step and reached across the room to the tiny door, retrieving his coveted bottle. "The hair of the dog." He gasped as he downed it. Now the headache would subside.

Is this rock bottom? Can I fall any further? If this is the bottom, I'll stay here. All I want is another drink. Nothing else matters anymore. I'm going to lay some true justice on Lyza Lane. I'll break into her home and steal everything I can get my hands on. What I can't steal, I'll break. I'll kill her. Because of her, I lost my job. Because of her, I lost my fortune. I hate that woman. I can see her snotty little face every time I close my eyes. Up until the day we met, my life was going great.

In his dream, she smirked at him and gave him demeaning looks. Her lips curled into an evil smile, then her face faded and gold crosses appeared in front of her.

Remembrance of that night filled him. The attack had surprised him. The local authorities never found the perpetrators. He couldn't identify them, but he would never forget the blood, the pain, and the gold crosses hanging from one attacker's neck. That attacker had hit O'Malley repeatedly in the face and the chest and in the gut.

His last beer downed, a dust-covered stack of bills on the wobbly table next to him cried for attention. The overdue rent on this sorry excuse for an efficiency apartment added another puff to the black cloud over his head. He opened the refrigerator door again. Empty. He knew that. He needed to do something, anything, but he had no energy. He had no drive. Life was meaningless. Soon he would be on the street, homeless.

God, have you no mercy? O'Malley cried out to the God of his youth. He remembered his mother taking him to church and Sunday school when he was a little guy.

About the time he reached junior high, he decided he didn't need God, if He existed. He almost went to church once when a girl he wanted to date told him he needed to be born again.

He'd already accepted Christ as his Lord and Savior at a confirmation class graduation ceremony when he was twelve. If he had God, and God lived inside him, why did he need church? So he didn't go to church and either went to the ball game or slept in.

He remembered praying he'd get a job when he got out of college. The IBM job came out of the blue, and he grabbed the opportunity, crediting clean living and karma for his good fortune. He'd forgotten about the prayer from months before.

Then he lost the job as abruptly as he'd gotten it. His boss had broken the news to him the day he got back from sick leave. His doctor told him to wait another month, but Chuck decided to go in. He didn't feel that hot, but he missed work. That day, he found out there were layoffs, and he was one of them. That was it. No good-byes, no good lucks, and no salary. His small severance had been eaten up almost immediately by paying past-due bills, utilities, and credit card charges.

He had to leave his expensive condo, give up his Land Rover, and ended up there in the pig sty. He looked around at stacks of papers, the trash on the floor, and a dozen or more bottles on the tiny table under the small window. *Isn't this the life?*

Then he realized he might be sobering up. *God, if this is a bad dream, please, wake me up. If it's real, I don't want to know it.* He rolled over on the cot and closed his eyes. He squeezed them tight and drops began to fall out of the corners.

Oh, God, I can't pretend any more. I know how I got here. I know exactly what brought me here. It was my own selfishness and greed, and not only this past year, but for most of my life. I have ignored You and gone my own way. I have done everything but spit on You. Oh, God, God. O'Malley gripped the frame of the cot. *Oh, God, how can I ask forgiveness? I can only admit that I've been wrong.* He began to sob and talk out loud to himself.

"It's not like You never showed me the way. Mom always told me to give it to the Lord, whatever *it* was. I guess I never trusted You to do things the way I would. Never mind the results, I wanted what I wanted when I wanted it. I never thought enough of You to care that You had a better plan. 'A better plan'—that's what Mom always said You had."

He sat up, dropped his head into his hands, and continued sobbing. "I want things to be different, but I don't know how they can change. If You're out there and if You can hear me, I'm asking for forgiveness." He raised his head, wiped his eyes with the back of his hand, and realized he would have to change. The idea that he *could* change brightened him.

"Lord, I can change. You can change me. I know You can. Please change me from a greedy schemer to a man of integrity. I'm begging You. Have mercy on me, an ungrateful sinner. If You have enough love to forgive me, I can change to thank You for it."

A soft knock at the door interrupted his prayer. He stopped and lifted his head. *Who on earth could that be?*

He slowly stood and crept to look out the tiny peephole in the door. *Oh no, not him. What does he want?*

Framed in the oval peephole, Chuck scrutinized Clete Collins standing outside his door.

Chapter Twenty-Five

David called Lyza the next morning on her cell phone. Sitting on the patio, she had just finished breakfast. She smiled when she heard his voice.

He spoke softly. "I've talked with the other survivors, and they would like to have a group meeting on Thursday morning."

"You work fast. What time?"

"Ten o'clock at the church where I pastor in Lakewood. I hope that will work for you."

She didn't take a second to consider her motives. "Yes, I'll be there."

After the conversation, Lyza realized that she was as anxious to see David again as she was to make contact with the other survivors.

***

Thursday arrived. Lyza drove her gray Mercedes to the Lakewood Community Church. She wore a tan blouse with black and pink flowered print, tan jeans, and tan Skechers tennis shoes. Her tan leather bag was large enough to carry everything she always carried, plus her computer.

The laptop was sort of Lyza's grown-up 'binky' or security blanket. If she began to feel uncomfortable or bored, she could always get on the computer and tune out the world. As much as she'd wanted the meeting, she felt unnerved.

She turned on the freeway and tuned her radio onto XM Talk. A hysterical caller complained, "They want to spend all this money, and where do you think the government is going to get the money? More taxes. They think we're made of money. This nation is going into the dumper."

Lyza changed stations. "Prophecy says they will nuke us by spring…" Another station reported. "Traffic on the I-5 stands still at this hour due to an overturned tanker." She turned the radio off so she could think.

I wonder how the other survivors coped with the experience. Were they injured? Did they have an experience like mine? Were they lucky? How well does David know them? Has he met with them before today?

I think I read about them meeting after the crash. I guess I'll know more soon. It's strange to go to a meeting completely unprepared.

She drove up to the Victorian-style church and parked in the newly paved lot next to a dozen cars. As she walked up to the door, David came out to meet her.

"Lyza, so glad to see you." He shook her hand and gave her left shoulder a hug. "Come in. Everyone is looking forward to meeting you."

He led her into a small lounge with overstuffed chairs, a large coffee table in the middle, and smaller arm tables between the chairs.

"Please, have a seat." He motioned to the chair next to his. She smiled at the other people in the room and sat.

"Now that we're all here, let's introduce ourselves, and we'll start by telling our names and where we're from. Let's start with Cleo." He nodded to the woman sitting on the other side of him.

She smiled at Lyza. "Okay, I'm Cleo Burns, and I'm from San Diego, but I'm living in Geneva."

"I'm Sandy Lebowitz from New York." The woman had a slight nasal accent.

"Steve Burnatelli, Rome, Italy." Steve's dark wavy hair confirmed his nationality.

"John Simpson, Santa Barbara."

Lyza wondered if he was an accountant or a banker, as he was the only one dressed in a business suit.

"Gail Heintz, LA." Gail looked pure California girl, with her golden tan, bleached hair, and sunglasses sitting atop her crown.

When it was her turn, she cleared her throat. "Lyza Lane, LA."

David ended the introduction phase of the meeting by stating the obvious. "And I'm David Gabriel from Lakewood."

Lyza looked at the small room. A picture of what she supposed were the hands of Jesus, outstretched toward the viewer, was on the wall directly across from her. She could only see the hands and an ancient draping of cloth sleeves.

David surveyed the small group. "Let's ask the Lord to bless our time together before we begin." Everyone was silent, with heads bowed. Lyza peeked at David's left hand. She had checked it out before. He didn't seem to be the bachelor type to her.

"Father in Heaven, be with us today as we attempt to heal scars of the past few months. Tear down any walls we may have built that stand in the way of Your Will this afternoon. Open hearts and minds as we share our experiences. Be with us and bless our time together. In Jesus' name, Amen."

David raised his head. "I didn't experience the crash, so I'll be the facilitator. I want everyone to share. Some of you have shared your stories with the public, but others want to keep it private. So I want everyone to agree that anything said in this room today stays in this room. All right?"

Everyone nodded.

"Who would like to start? Don't be shy; we're all in this together. Okay, Sandy, go ahead."

Sandy started to tear up. "Oh, these tears. I'm not crying. I mean, it's not a bad crying. I'm so touched that we are all together in the same room. Last time we were all in the same place, we were on Swiss Air, and none of us had anything in common. None of us had anything to say to one another.

"Today we search for understanding and healing. As some of you already know, my experience was supernatural. When the plane exploded, I was immediately unconscious. I was unconscious, but I could see this bright light."

Lyza sat upright in her seat while Sandy continued, "It was the brightest, warmest, most calming light I have ever seen, and yet my eyes were closed. The light was all around me. It totally enveloped me. Immediately after the explosion, I thought I was falling, but when I became conscious of the light around me, I felt as if I was peacefully drifting to the earth below. I am a believer in Jesus Christ, and I know it was His light. I remember landing on a piece of airplane wing floating on the water. I landed softly. It didn't even knock the breath out of me. Then I blacked out, still feeling the warmth of His light."

"Thank you Sandy. I read your story in *Christianity Today,* and we appreciate hearing it in person." David nodded to Steve.

"Well, my experience is similar, with one exception. At the time, I didn't believe in Jesus Christ as the Risen Savior. I never heard the explosion. I had just put on my oxygen mask when suddenly I was alone and surrounded by light. I didn't understand the light all around me at first.

"Then I remembered things I'd learned, growing up Christian in Rome. My parents were in the military and ended up in Italy. When I recognized His light, I knew who He was. I had the most incredible faith that everything would be all right. I spent a week in the hospital, and the doctors and staff couldn't believe I was in that crash.

"By the way, it was a business trip for me and I was traveling alone."

"Thank you, Steve. How about you, John?"

John Simpson had tears in his eyes. "I still can't believe I was spared when so many died. I was so wrapped up in my life, making money, climbing the corporate ladder, doing all the right stuff. I had forgotten what life is about. My experience with the light was astonishing. He never spoke a word to me, but I knew it was Him. I spend every day now praising Him and thanking Him for His mercy.

"I, too, dumbfounded the doctors and nurses in the hospital. I remember telling one nurse that Jesus saved me. She replied, 'Then He's an idiot—why would He save you instead of the innocent babies?' I have no answer for that." His eyes teared up as he looked directly at David.

"As my sister often testified, everything happens for a reason, and Jesus knows what He is doing. I'm comforted by the fact that my sister and her baby now praise Him in Heaven while we praise Him here. Thank you for your testimony, John. Cleo?"

"Wow. I, too, struggled with why I survived. I love to tell my story because it's not really about me. It's about the graciousness of God and the boundless mercy He extends. I've been a Christian for many years, but the last several years, I haven't lived the Christian life at all. In fact, if someone had asked me six months ago if I was a Christian, I might have denied it.

"I moved to Geneva a year ago from San Diego. I was traveling back here for vacation with some of my friends. We used to travel together often. None of them survived, though they were sitting all around me. My experience with the Light was as amazing as each of you has explained. It really is indescribable, isn't it? The Light surrounded me, and I will never forget the peace that immediately took over my entire being. I was falling, but I wasn't concerned about it. All I could do was focus on that Light, the true Light, the Light of the world."

After dabbing her eye and blowing her nose, Cleo continued. "Here's the thing. There's no way that I deserved it. No way did I come close to deserving life instead of death. Why He chose me is beyond understanding, but I accept it because He is the One who decided it would be me. I refuse to argue with His decision.

"I was with my best friend, Sally, and she didn't make it. I miss her, but I don't begrudge God His choice. I know I'm not worthy. My life has changed, and I am again walking by faith and choosing Him instead of the world, but I know that doesn't make me worthy. I changed because I know it will please Him. Only He saves. He brought me back."

David smiled and nodded toward Gail.

Gail finished dabbing her eyes and blew her nose. "I'm sorry. Each story touches me and I can't help it."

Cleo handed her another tissue from the box in the middle of the coffee table. "Don't worry, tears are cleansing, right?"

Gail nodded and wiped her eyes again. "Right." She swallowed.

David leaned forward. "Gail, you don't have to share."

She straightened up. "No, no, I want to. I'm ready." She took a deep breath. "My mother and I toured Europe for the first time. We started in Zurich, took the train to Bavaria, and then drove a rental car along the Rhine to tour the castles."

She sniffed. "I can still see Mom's face when I told her I was taking her to Europe. She never traveled much in the states and this vacation fulfilled a long time dream. I saved for two years to give this vacation gift to her for her 60th birthday. She was so excited. And I have to admit that six days of traveling Europe seemed to invigorate her. I don't think I ever remember Mom being more alive. She had just opened the box of chocolates that I bought in the airport terminal when the captain announced a problem. I'll never forget her winking at me and telling me that chocolate makes everything better. Moments later everything went black. I felt myself floating in that warm light everyone mentioned earlier. I knew everything was going to be all right. I felt peace."

Gail shuddered. "The next thing I knew I was in the hospital and I couldn't find out what happened to Mom. I kept asking for her, but no one would tell me anything. My father came to see me the next day. By then I had already guessed. He told me she died instantly. I don't blame God. In fact, I'm so thankful we spent those last six days together. We had such a wonderful time. My mother and I were more like sisters than parent and child. I miss her."

Gail blew her nose again.

David smiled. "I know you do. Your mother surely enjoyed spending time with you on this special trip. You have a wonderful testimony as a loving daughter. But Gail, God loves you and you are here for a reason."

She sniffed again, then smiled. "Yes, pastor, I know He loves me. All my life Mom talked about being in Heaven with Jesus some day. I know she's in His presence and surrounded by His love. He's even better than chocolate."

David reached over and patted Gail's hand. Then he turned toward Lyza.

"Lyza, it's your turn. Share only what you want to, no more, no less. Let me remind you that nothing you say here today will leave this room." David smiled comfortingly. "No one is here to judge. We are all trying to make sense of what happened."

"Thank you, David. Forgive me for not meeting with all of you sooner. I was deep in that river in Upper Egypt—denial. Now that I'm here, and now that I've met you and heard your stories, I am so glad to be here. My story isn't different from yours.

"You may have heard of my family's corporation, L. L. Lane Unlimited. I've been working hard for the corporation ever since I can remember. Nothing seemed more important than bringing income to the corporation. After hearing your stories, I understand why everything changed for me."

Lyza's eyes glazed over as she went back to that day. Sitting there with the other survivors comforted her. She looked at each caring face. At last she felt she could tell her story.

"I was falling, falling slowly; it was like floating. My soul cried out to God. My eyes were closed, yet I, too, saw the brightest, warmest light I ever experienced. I wasn't afraid. Before the explosion, I was terrified. I blacked out. But when I felt strong arms beneath me, embracing me, I felt loved for the first time in my life.

"The most caring voice I've ever heard said, 'Lyza, you can come to me now. I want to give you life and life more abundantly.' I remember thinking to myself, how can I have a more abundant life? I have everything already. In an instant, I realized that spiritually I was poor—in fact I was destitute. Spiritually speaking, I had nothing.

"Then the warm voice spoke to me and said, 'I am the Way, the Truth, and the Life. No man comes to the Father except through me. Lyza, I am your Yeshua HaMashiach, your salvation. I was with you from the beginning. I created your inmost being. I knit you together in your mother's womb. You are fearfully and wonderfully made.'

"I was moved beyond comprehension, and I asked the Lord to forgive me for my unbelief. You see, I'm Jewish. I'm not a practicing Jew, but I am Jewish, and my grandparents were killed in the Holocaust. I've distrusted Christians all my life."

The group gasped. Cleo put her hand to her mouth. Steve and John shook their heads in sadness.

"Before the explosion, I cried out to God. I cried out to God, and Jesus showed up to save me and told me He was Lord. Then the Lord embraced me, He held me in His arms. I heard Him talking in my ear, telling me that I would live because I have work to do. I could feel His warm breath. He told me not to worry about anything, but to pray to Him about everything and to thank Him in everything, but whatever I do, I'm supposed to make my requests to Him.

"Then He told me the most incredible thing that I never would have believed or understood until that moment. He told me He would give me the peace of God, which transcends all understanding. And that He would guard my heart and my mind in Him, Christ Jesus. He said Christ Jesus, then He said 'your Yeshua.' Later, He taught me that Yeshua means *salvation* in Hebrew.

"I don't remember where He finally laid me down because I awoke more than two months later in my old room in my parents home. I have so many questions. What kind of work does He have for me to do? How can I tell my family that I believe in Jesus, Yeshua, when all my life my family's told me that Christianity is a lie? Yet when I cried out for God's help, Jesus showed up. All I can say is that I know He's real and I know He is my Redeemer."

No one spoke for a moment.

Sandy got up, walked around the coffee table to Lyza's seat and bent down to give her a hug. Then, one by one, each of them did the same thing. By the time they had each hugged her, all of them smiled through tears.

Tears in David's eyes confused her. *Why is he so sad? I'm one of them now, or am I? I'm so confused.*

"Lyza, you are the bravest woman I know." He smiled and everyone applauded. "First, I understand that you have many questions. It's important you understand that all of us here care about you. Another thing you must understand is that Jesus was Jewish; He is Jewish. None of his disciples stopped being Jewish when they accepted Him as their Messiah. We don't expect you to be any different. The Jewish people are God's chosen people; I'm sure you've heard that before. It's true. God never changed His mind about that. Please feel free to ask any questions. We want to help you."

David and the others stayed three hours talking to Lyza and answering questions for her.

Driving back home, Lyza's heart soared. She felt happiness at last. She couldn't remember if she had ever been so happy before. She rejoiced in it. She burst out singing "Amazing Grace." She knew all the words; famous singers recorded the song often.

But now when she came to the part about being found, tears of joy flowed down her cheeks into her smile.

Chapter Twenty-Six

When Leesa returned from Kramer's Island, she went to find Lyza. She knocked at her bedroom door. "Lyza, are you there?"

"Yes, Leesa, you're home!" The door burst open, and Lyza gave Leesa a big hug. "I missed you. Did you have a good time?"

Leesa had expected Lyza to be angry at her for missing the memorial she had promised to attend with her. "Oh, Lyza, Lyza, I messed up big time. I'm so sorry about not going to the memorial."

Lyza grinned. "It's all right, really. It turned out fine."

"Did you go by yourself?"

"Yes, I did, but I met some nice people, and it turned out fine, really, it did. No worries."

Leesa continued apologizing. "Are you sure? I wouldn't blame you being angry. I don't know what I was thinking."

Lyza's grin faded. "Do not apologize. It's all right, and that's the truth. Now, tell me about your week."

Leesa bubbled. "My week was wonderful. You know how much I love this project. We worked on the layout for the train tracks around the island. We also worked on the design of the train itself. I'm telling you, working on this project is like going to Disneyland every week."

Lyza picked up her hairbrush and started brushing her hair. "Everyone at the office knows how wrapped up you are in this project. How's Tim?"

Leesa wrinkled her nose. Then she recognized that Lyza was fishing for information about Tim. "Tim's fine. Why? Oh, I see what you're up to. No, there is nothing but business between me and Tim. He's a good egg and a brilliant architect."

Lyza put the brush back on the dresser. "Did you say he's a good egg? I haven't heard that expression in a long time."

"Let's just say he's helping me fulfill my dreams for Kramer's Island."

"Dreams, huh?" Lyza's cell phone rang. She looked at the caller identification and saw the call was from David Gabriel. "Oh, Leesa, I need to get this. Hi, David."

Leesa tilted her head, looking curiously at Lyza. *Hi, David? Who's David?*

***

When Lyza greeted him, David's cheerful voice responded, "Lyza, how are you doing?"

"I'm doing well, thank you, and you?"

His voiced sounded pained. "I'm not doing too well."

She was genuinely concerned. "I'm so sorry. What's wrong?"

He chuckled, then paused. "Uh, I'm in your area, and I can't find a coffeehouse. I wondered if you could help me find one and make it all better."

She shook her head. "You got me, didn't you?"

He shouted into the phone, feigning a lost signal. "Did you say I should come over and pick you up? You're breaking up, you're breaking up." He gargled into the phone. "I'll be there in ten minutes!"

The phone went dead.

She turned to Leesa. "This is hilarious. I think I have a coffee date. Sit and talk with me while I dress. Call security and tell them to admit David Gabriel."

Lyza stepped into her closet and picked a pair of designer jeans with sparkling appliqués down the sides and matching design on the back pockets. A white T with matching appliqué completed her outfit. She chose pink flip-flops with sparkly bands across the top of her little feet. Her denim whale-sized purse was the final accessory.

"Leesa, what do you think? Is this all right?" Lyza made a full turn between Leesa and the full length mirror.

Leesa tilted her head. "Lyza, you look terrific. Who is this guy?"

Lyza had no intention of going into detail, but the flush on her face spoke volumes. "Oh, just a man I met at the memorial."

The doorbell rang. Lyza raced downstairs to beat the butler to the door. She turned around and waved at Leesa, standing at the top of the stairs. "See you later."

She opened the door and stepped outside. "Hello, David. I'm glad you found your way."

"Well, I knew you were rich, but I have to admit my surprise when I drove up. The security gate opened when I told them my name, so you must have alerted someone."

She laughed. "Oh, yes. I thought it was safe to let you in." She jumped into the white minivan. "The nearest coffeeshop is five miles; we turn left at the freeway."

He closed the door for her. "Well, all right, then. We're on our way."

He went around and got in to start the ignition. "How are you doing?"

Lyza started babbling, and she knew it, but she couldn't stop. "I felt so good after the meeting. Words cannot express how beneficial spending time with the other survivors turned out to be. I mean, Cleo is such a doll, and her story touched me. And Sandy. And Gail. And John and Steve—all their stories spoke to me in different ways. And I have to tell you, I love those people.

"I talked to Sandy and Gail yesterday. They called to see how I was doing. I can't believe how quickly we became fast friends. It's so good to know they have heard my story and understand."

"I'm happy to hear you're making connections with fellow believers in Yeshua."

"It's new to me. I still have some trouble with the Jewish versus Christian perspective, but I have no doubt about who Yeshua is."

"Lyza, Christians often forget—or perhaps never realize—that Jews remained Jews after they accepted Jesus as the Messiah. All the disciples were Jewish. Even after Yeshua ascended into Heaven, Peter and John and the other disciples went up to the Temple at the time of prayer.

"Yeshua never asked them to discontinue that practice. He never told them to stop being Jews. Paul and the disciples preached the message of Yeshua after He ascended into Heaven. Did you know that most of the New Testament was written by Jews?"

"The Christian Bible was written by Jews? No, I didn't know."

He continued. "Don't put Christians in a box and Jews in another box. God wants us to be united. Christians honor the Torah, just as

Jews are commanded. The book of Deuteronomy says, 'For you are a people holy to the Lord your God. The Lord your God has chosen you out of all the peoples on the face of the Earth to be his people, his treasured possession.' Jews are still the chosen people."

They got out of the car and walked into the coffeeshop. He ordered the house coffee. She ordered a vanilla latte. They found a booth in the back corner.

"So where do Christians fit in this? I mean if we're the chosen people, why do Jews get so much grief from Christians?"

"Lyza, just like any other religion has fanatics and ignorant people, some Christians are ignorant. Right now, Christians are the best friends of the Jews. Christians support Jews and Israel. And Christians have apologized again and again for not acting to stop the Holocaust. Christians have vowed that nothing like the Holocaust will happen again on our watch."

He pulled a small Bible out of his shirt pocket. "Look, I want to show you how Christians fit in."

He opened the book to Romans, chapter 11, verse 1. "Let me read this. It's written by Paul when he was in prison in Rome. 'I ask then: Did God reject His people? By no means! I am an Israelite myself, a descendant of Abraham, from the tribe of Benjamin.' Paul wrote most of the New Testament."

"So Paul was a Jew, too?" Lyza tried to take that in. *The main writer of the New Testament was Jewish?*

David took hold of her hand. "Lyza, I want you to learn about Yeshua and what He wants for you and me, for the Jew and the Christian. Further in the book of Romans, Paul asks whether the Jewish rejection of the Messiah, Yeshua, caused them to stumble beyond recovery. He says that Christians should be grateful because their transgression caused Him to come to the Gentiles in order to make Israel envious. You see, it's about making Jews jealous; the Lord is still working to save His people."

He released her hand and found another passage. "Look here in verses 17–22: 'If some of the branches have been broken off, and you, though a wild olive shoot, have been grafted in among the others and now share in the nourishing sap from the olive root, do not boast over those branches. If you do, consider this: You do not support the root, but the root supports you. You will say then, 'Branches were broken off so that I could be grafted in.' Granted. But they were broken off because of unbelief, and you stand by faith. Do not be arrogant, but be afraid. For if God did not spare the natural branches, he will not spare you either.'

"Lyza, it's so exciting because later, in verse 23, Paul says, 'And if they do not persist in unbelief, they will be grafted in, for God is able to graft them in again.'"

She tried to understand. "David, it's a lot to take in."

"But listen, Paul goes on to say that if you were cut out of an olive tree that is wild by nature, and contrary to nature were grafted into a cultivated olive tree, how much more readily will these, the natural branches, be grafted into their own olive tree!"

David's voice picked up as he read. "In verse 26, Paul comes right out and says that all Israel will be saved!"

Lyza decided to pull no punches with David. She heard her father condemn Christians for calling Jews Christ-killers. "What about Jews being called Christ-killers? Is that what the rejection is about?"

"Christ-killers? That's ridiculous. All the practicing Jews were at the Temple for their directed prayer times when Christ was crucified and when He died. Between those prayer times, they were preparing for Shabbat. It's ignorance when people talk like that. I don't believe Jews are Christ-killers, and neither do any of the Christians I know. What's more, Yeshua said Himself that no one killed Him; He laid His life down for us willingly."

Lyza considered Yeshua with new eyes. "He did? He really did! No one could take His life. He is the King of the universe. He could have stopped it anytime. That's right. Thank you, David! Thank you, Yeshua!" She didn't understand everything, but she understood that the Christ-killer accusation was propaganda, pure and simple. She found enormous relief in her newfound knowledge.

Three hours later, they were still chatting in the coffee shop. Dusk suggested their coffee date was over, and David said he should take her home. With her mind processing all the new information she'd gained, Lyza begrudgingly agreed and was lost in thought for most of the ride home. He walked her to the door and gave her a hug that surprised her. *Are preachers supposed to hug like this?* she wondered.

"Thanks for a wonderful afternoon."

She turned to go in and stopped. "David, I'm so glad you called."

Lyza stepped into the house and softly closed the door. She stood there for a moment. Her head spun with all this new information to absorb and with how happy and peaceful she felt.

Leesa appeared at the top of the stairs where she had been standing when Lyza left. Her hands on her hips, she asked, "Lyza Lane, who was that?"

Lyza grinned. "That is David Gabriel."

"Who is David Gabriel?"

Lyza's grin turned sheepish, and she blushed. "He's… he's my friend."

Leesa started chanting as if in a teenaged frenzy. "Your *boy*friend. Lyza's got a boyfriend."

Lyza frowned. "Oh, you stop it. He's not my boyfriend. He's a friend."

Leesa pushed for answers. "I think he's your boyfriend, and I want to know all about him."

"Well, he's not my boyfriend, and the rest is for me to know and you to find out, when I'm good and ready to tell you. That's final, Leesa; now back off. I'm going to bed."

Lyza went into her suite and lay on her bed, staring at the ceiling smiling and mentally reliving the afternoon. *Is he my boyfriend? I don't know, but I do like him. He's a man of integrity. He's good-looking.* For the first time in her life, she admitted she felt a romantic interest. *David Gabriel could be the man I want to spend the rest of my life with.*

The exciting afternoon had keyed her up. She went down to the gym for a workout; she couldn't remember the last time she had done her Pilates. It felt good. Afterward, she stepped into the sauna for a few moments, then sat in the hot tub. Feeling refreshed, she showered and changed into pajamas.

She dropped by the kitchen to see what Cook had in her stock of snacks and goodies. *Mmm, mini pizzas and chocolate chip cookies.* She snacked, then took a bag of popped corn upstairs to her suite, where she chose the movie *Casablanca.* She remembered watching it with her mother while waiting for her father to come home from late nights at the office.

After finishing her popcorn, she turned the TV screen so she could keep watching from her comfy bed. She fell asleep to the distant sound of voices from *Casablanca.*

In her dream, she shook her fist at the darkening afternoon sky as a fat raindrop smacked her between the eyes. Muttering, she shook it off and trudged down a street littered with rubbish. Wearing a dirty black coat, she pushed a grocery cart filled with trash bags. Her filthy face and cracked hands yearned for soap and warm water.

Yes, Lord, I am filthy. I don't deserve a man like David.

A gust of wind blew a ragged scarf off her itching head. As raindrops splashed on the pavement, people hurried past, not seeing her. She seemed invisible.

Yeshua, please don't leave me. I'm afraid to be alone. You're my shepherd. Lead me in the paths of righteousness. Why am I having this nightmare again?

She recognized the voice that had whispered to her as she fell from the sky months ago. "My child, I have more to reveal."

Her dream continued. The air reeked like the dress she wore, and her stomach grumbled. A volunteer nodded a familiar 'Hello' as he opened the door to the rescue mission. She looked at the man straight-on.

Startled, she stopped, horrified. She knew that face. *It's impossible—it can't be—but it's… David Gabriel! No! He cannot see me like this.* She looked down at the dirty sidewalk and tried to cover her face with one ragged sleeve.

"Come in, Lyza." She couldn't resist his reassuring voice, that soothing, reassuring voice. She was mesmerized. He pushed the door further open. For the first time, she entered the building. Brilliant light burst from the room. David took her hand, leading her inside. The warm Light transformed everything in the room. Everything looked bright and clean and new. Lyza looked down, her drab clothing changed into beautiful white garments. David's clothing changed to radiant white. She touched her hair. It felt clean and restored. Her skin felt soft and moist. David glowed. The heaviness she felt seconds ago vanished. She knew this Light. It surrounded her as it did when she fell from the sky. She felt the same presence. *Yeshua is here!* Her spirit soared as David smiled toward her. Excitement for life and the future filled her heart, soul, and spirit.

She took a deep breath and her eyes flickered open. The last scenes of *Casablanca* played on the TV in front of her. Rick told the Laszlos to board the flight to Lisbon before the authorities arrived. She'd seen the movie a hundred times.

Her greatest desire at that moment was to return to her own beautiful dream. She clicked off the remote and closed her eyes.

Once, she'd dreaded the dream. Now, all she wanted was to return to it.

Author's Epilogue

One by one, and in God's perfect timing, Cook's (Beverly Grayson's) prayers are being answered. The Lane family depended on Cook for over thirty years to cook, clean, and serve them. Little do they know that she has served them in an even greater way. Her constant prayer has been salvation for every one of them. Cook's latest prayers focus on preparing Lyza and Leesa for the perfect men to come into their lives. They have a long way to go before they know what it means to share their lives, but change is on the move.

God is working in Lyza's life. She's changed from a spoiled, materialistic young woman to a woman focused on God's purpose for her. Her past ambitions for increased wealth and power faded the instant she felt the presence of Jesus, her Yeshua. Confusion about her Jewish heritage and Christianity troubled her, but her new best friend, David Gabriel, helped her understand that Jews and Christians are eternally entwined.

Now Lyza's desire is to please Yeshua and live a life that glorifies Him. Exactly how to do that is a mystery to her now, but God is not finished with her yet. Find out how she overcomes extreme obstacles in *The Legacy*.

Once Lyza's Christianity is revealed, lives will change. Find out how her father, Lawrence, resists her newfound faith. Learn the way her mother, Lana, responds (in true Lana fashion). Finally, discover the reaction of her twin sister, Leesa, to Christianity.

Their lives will never be the same.

CPSIA information can be obtained at www.ICGtesting.com
Printed in the USA
BVOW081605160113

310809BV00001B/5/P

9 781593 307820